A STRAIN NOVEL

BANE

AMELIA C. GORMLEY

ACG Publications
www.ameliacgormley.com

Bane (A Strain Novel)
Copyright © 2018 Amelia C. Gormley

Cover art: Danielle Fine
Editor: Danielle Poiesz

ISBN: 978-1-62-622619-7

First Edition
September 2015

Second Edition
April 2018

The weapon that nearly destroyed humanity may be their only salvation.

RHYS COOPER has proven immune to the virus that nearly wiped out humanity, and the Clean Zone's scientists want to know why. Summoned for testing, Rhys is about to learn why his Juggernaut partner, Sergeant Darius Murrell, and the rest of his superhuman comrades in Delta Company don't trust the remnants of the government that unleashed the epidemic.

For a decade, Zach Houtman has yearned for his lover, Nico Fernández, but fear of infection kept them apart. Separately they keep tabs on the last vestiges of the corrupt government, particularly the head of the Clean Zone's virus research division. Secretary Littlewood seeks to unlock the secrets of the Bane virus. But Nico knows how dangerous Littlewood will be if that ever happens.

Now Zach and Nico have the perfect bait to draw Littlewood out: Rhys. But Delta Company isn't about to let Rhys walk into hell alone. They'll take Littlewood down together, or not at all. Even if they succeed, however, for Zach and Nico one question remains: can infected and uninfected people ever be together safely?

For my husband and son, whose patience with the sight of the back of my head as I pay more attention to the computer than them makes it all possible.

And for Chris, Angie, Elin, and all the other people who helped me brainstorm this story and the books that have gone into this world.

1

TRANSITIONS

"What are you doing?" a low voice growled behind Rhys. He smiled to himself, abandoning the piano keys to fiddle with the buttons on his shirt.

"Taking advantage of the fact that we're in an area that's already been patrolled." He shrugged out of his shirt and turned to face Darius, leaning back against the piano in the lounge of the Denver hotel they were camped at for the night. Delta Company's operational protocol dictated that when camping in areas that hadn't been patrolled for revenants and rogue survivors, everyone slept in one barricaded room with guards posted to prevent them being cut off from one another in the event of an attack. But Colorado and most of the surrounding states had been swept long ago, before the Jugs had been exiled from the Colorado Springs Clean Zone.

Which meant that for the first time since he was nine years old, Rhys could venture away from the safety of other people without fear of being shot or eaten. Whatever his misgivings about the reason for their journey, the lack of an audience and the ability to roam freely while on the march was a luxury he could get used to.

Darius walked slowly forward until his body brushed Rhys's, reaching out to tweak a bared nipple. Rhys gasped and shuddered, his body tensing, his cock filling. The look Darius gave him was half-heat and half-amusement. "I meant the piano. I didn't know you could play."

"Oh . . . that." Rhys blushed in the dim light of the setting sun as it filtered through dust-and-cobweb-covered windows. "There was a piano at the monastery. My mom used to play the flute, so she knew how to read music, and, well, there wasn't a lot else we could do for entertainment, so she taught me and Cady to play. The music in hymnals is pretty easy. Or it was until we had to burn them."

Darius smiled, and there was something tender in it, something that only ever came out when he looked at Rhys. This hard-bitten soldier, fierce and world-weary, always had a soft regard for him. He cupped the back of Rhys's neck with one hand, his skin warm. "Wish I'd known. We had plenty of time to find you a piano at Fort Vancouver. I'll make sure we get one for you when we're done with this business in the Clean Zone and go catch up to the rest of Delta Company at Lewis-McChord."

Discomfort trod quickly on the heels of Rhys's affectionate surprise at the offer. There was no sense to Darius even suggesting such a thing. Even if Jugs could probably move pianos single-handedly, Rhys probably wouldn't get much use out of it before life or fate or what-the-fuck-ever came along and screwed things up. "You don't have time to worry about that. It doesn't matter. I've been too busy to think about playing, too."

It had been almost a year and a half since Rhys had become Delta Company's de facto supply officer. He'd needed something to occupy himself while Darius was out patrolling with his squadron, so the assignment made sense. The fact that he didn't have the abilities of a Jug meant that taking him along was asking for trouble. If he took charge of inventory and provisions, then another Jug was freed up to help their comrades sweep the formerly populated areas for revenants and pockets of survivors instead. Rhys was happy to be useful and grateful for the opportunity to pull his weight in the face of the muttered criticisms some of the other Jugs leveled against having a civvie in their midst. His contribution to their operation was now quantifiable, and he worked his ass off to make sure no one could accuse him of doing a sloppy or inaccurate job of it.

The past six months had been particularly demanding. Last fall, the squadron that had escorted a group of civilians to Colorado Springs had brought back word that the Clean Zone's Department of Pandemic Research and Prevention had summoned Rhys to have his apparent immunity to the Bane virus tested. While technically the Clean Zone didn't have the authority to command him or the Jugs to do a damned thing —and the fact that they apparently didn't realize it was more than a little troubling—Rhys had been unwilling to decline the opportunity to understand why he wasn't infected.

He should have been, a dozen times over. Since the day the revenants had attacked the monastery where Rhys, his family, and a handful of other survivors had sheltered for seven years, he'd been exposed to various strains of Bane more times than he could count. He'd been in close quarters with people dying of the Rot, the illness that manifested with the Beta strain.

He'd grappled with revenants, the feral, cannibalistic victims infected by the Gamma strain. He'd gotten rev blood all over him while trying to keep them from eating him. He'd even been bitten by one.

And he'd been exposed hundreds of times to the nonlethal Alpha strain of the virus that gave Darius and the Jugs their superhuman speed, strength, and reflexes. To no apparent effect.

He wanted to know why, especially if finding out came with the opportunity to help prevent another outbreak. When his summons had arrived, though, Delta Company had just begun preparations to leave Fort Vancouver and move their base of operations closer to Seattle. He'd had to quickly prepare their inventory for transport and make sure they had enough supplies to get them through the transition from a well-established base to someplace entirely unsettled. And in the process, he'd had to catch his replacement up on where everything stood and prepare her to oversee the transition to Lewis-McChord in his absence.

"It wouldn't have taken long," Darius argued, interrupting his musings. He swept a finger through the light film of dust on the lid of the piano at Rhys's back.

That was the other nice thing about traveling to areas that had already been patrolled. The Jugs had established way stations along the common routes to Colorado Springs and maintained them diligently during their semiannual treks to escort uninfected survivors to join the rest of the population in the Clean Zone. So their recent lodgings hadn't had the same derelict feel that being out on patrol often did. If not for his unease about their destination, this journey would almost feel like a vacation.

"I'll make sure you have a piano to play at Lewis-McChord if you want one," Darius added.

Rhys swallowed and looked away. "Assuming I get to leave Colorado Springs with you."

"Hey." Darius wiped the dust on his fatigues and hooked his finger under Rhys's chin, forcing Rhys to meet his eyes. "Ain't no way I'm letting them make you stay."

"What if they order you to?"

Darius snorted. "They exiled us, remember? Told us we weren't citizens, so they can't order us to do shit. If they want to take you from me, well . . ." Darius's lips twitched. "I'd like to see them try."

Rhys's mouth curved in an answering grin. He loved Darius's sense of humor. It was wry and understated and didn't shine through all that often, but when it did, he always made Rhys laugh. Even though he was a big, scary-looking guy who could be downright lethal.

Darius's smile faded and his face softened. His lips brushed Rhys's. "Not leaving you behind, boy."

Rhys closed his eyes as they started to sting and grasped twin handfuls of Darius's shirt, pulling him closer and giving him a deep kiss. Darius's tongue slipped between his lips, and Rhys sucked on it greedily, trying to convey his devotion and gratitude with something more effective than words, which always failed him anyway.

With a lurch, Darius had Rhys off his feet and seated atop the baby grand. That was better. More familiar than Darius's tender solicitude. This was something he knew how to respond to. He leaned back and lifted his hips while Darius worked at his buckle and fly, sweeping the fatigues down his thighs. He stripped off Rhys's boots with impatient jerks and tossed the lot of it aside before Rhys grabbed his neck and pulled him down for another ferocious kiss.

"Not letting you go," Darius muttered urgently, his mouth traveling down Rhys's throat to his chest. He paused at Rhys's nipples, tongue flicking, teeth scraping, then his mouth closed in a careful bite. Rhys yelped, his hips coming up to push his hard cock against Darius's chest, but Darius wasn't inclined to take the hint and move lower. He bit again, slowly increasing the pressure until Rhys's moans became pained and he shoved at Darius's shoulders, his body instinctively trying to escape the agony even as his libido reveled in it.

"Yes," he whimpered, caught in that eternal struggle between resisting the pain and embracing it. He could never surrender without a fight, no matter how badly he wanted it. It was as though it took his reflexes a while to get on board with what was happening.

That, and it was also just sexy as hell to fight Darius and be overpowered. He needed Darius to defeat him, to make him take it. The conclusion was foregone, but that didn't stop them from performing the steps of their well-rehearsed dance.

Darius waited for Rhys's cries to escalate to a scream and then switched nipples to repeat the process on the other one.

"Darius!" Rhys clutched his shoulders, his fingers digging in. His body was warming up to the game now, and the pain was no longer something he needed to resist. "God. Yes. Hurt me."

Darius's head came up, his lips shining with saliva and his rich brown eyes sparking fiercely in his mahogany face. "How bad you want me to hurt you, boy?"

"Bad," Rhys gasped, panting as the ache in his nipples began to fade into the background of his arousal. "I want . . ."

Rhys's voice trailed off, and he fought against his inability to ask for what he wanted. Even after two years with Darius, it was a struggle for him, shame choking off his words. For as long as he lived, he would hear voices in the back of his mind, condemning him for the desires (*perversions*) that had always come naturally. But he knew he wouldn't get what he wanted unless he said it. Except when they were playing their game of Darius overpowering Rhys's token resistance, the days when Darius would truly force him had ended when Rhys's life no longer literally depended upon it. "I want marks."

Darius growled, his hands tightening on Rhys's hips. "You sure about that? They won't fade before we get to Colorado Springs."

Rhys shuddered, but he held Darius's gaze. Darius knew that was his greatest challenge, owning up to the things he craved. When they were alone together, he could behave with utter abandon, but he struggled when someone else might think him deviant. He licked his lips, his throat tight as he said, "I need it. Need to feel it before we get there."

"Feel what?"

Rhys closed his eyes and whispered, "That I'm yours."

"Damn right you are." Darius abandoned his chest and crushed his mouth against Rhys's, driving him down flat against the piano again. He grabbed Rhys's dick and began jacking him like he meant business. He drew back and pinned Rhys with a glare. "Don't want to wait before I fuck you tonight, but tomorrow on the march, we're gonna find a nice switch for me to whip your ass come night. Leave welts for a week. Ain't no one gonna doubt you're mine."

"Yes! God, please!" Rhys thrashed, trying to thrust up into that stroking, but still pinned by Darius's torso. It was too much, so intense he didn't think he could bear it, so perfect he wanted to demand more. "Darius!"

Then Darius's weight was gone, and Rhys was cold and free, sprawled out on the piano.

"Flip over, boy."

He rolled eagerly onto his stomach before Darius had even finished pulling the lube out of his pocket. The piano pressed uncomfortably into his midriff, but he was beyond caring. At least he could bend over it without his feet dangling off the floor. Darius had been right in the prediction he'd made two years ago: once Rhys had received proper nutrition, he'd shot up in a late growth spurt and now he was one of the tallest men in Delta Company, second only to a gentle, soft-spoken man-mountain named Joe.

A swipe of oil, the sound of Darius slicking it over his cock behind him, and then his body was against Rhys's, nudging at his hole, breaching him with a stretch that always bordered on too much in the beginning. It was a pain Rhys had come to love, a pain he knew Darius would push him through until it all became searing, mind-breaking, soul-shattering pleasure.

Which it did by the time Darius was balls-deep inside him. They groaned together.

"Fuck! Darius . . ." Rhys pleaded, and Darius began to stroke. "Yes! Oh God. Right there. More!"

"I got you," Darius muttered, then grabbed Rhys's hips, hauled him back until he was bent over further, and slammed into him again.

So full. So right. Pleasure too great to endure. Beads of sweat popped out of his pores and trickled down his forehead until he wiped his face on his upper arm to keep it from dripping into his eyes. Darius's hands were slick where they gripped his hips, his fingers leaving bruises. He hammered against Rhys's flanks with the slap of damp skin on damp skin, grunting each time. Unable to wait any longer, Rhys grasped his cock, stroking quickly.

"Yeah, that's it. Shoot for me, boy. Let me feel it."

Rhys threw back his head and jerked harder, straining to reach the edge. Sometimes it was quick and easy, but other times he had to work for it, and those were the times when the resulting climax threatened to melt his spine and liquefy his brain. "Oh God. Oh, please. Please. I need it. Need to come. Darius . . ."

"Do it. Come on, do it . . ." Darius's voice had a hitch that said he was close to losing it himself, and Rhys could tell by the way Darius changed his angle and rhythm ever so slightly that he was trying to hold off. The shift helped him nail Rhys's prostate more directly, though, giving Rhys the extra push he needed to get over the top.

He yelled and dropped his head to his arm on the piano lid, while his other hand clutched his pulsing shaft, drawing out another stream with each pull. Darius shuddered and gripped him harder, groaning low in his chest before he collapsed against Rhys's back. He only paused a moment before he began pressing fervent kisses to the side of Rhys's sweaty neck.

"Jesus. Never get enough of you."

Rhys smiled against his forearm, reveling in the openness Darius shared with him and no one else, not even his closest friends in Delta Company. Two years ago he'd been a terrified virgin forced to do things he didn't think he should want in order to save his own life. And Darius had been the gruff soldier who Rhys didn't think had a sympathetic or tender bone in his body. Along the way, though, grim necessity had become passion and then something even better. Darius hadn't just kept Rhys alive. He'd taught Rhys how to live.

A familiar knot tightened in his chest, comprised of words Rhys couldn't untangle to thank Darius for giving him that. To let Darius know that, however they started and for whatever minuscule amount of time they might have together, he appreciated what they had now. The sentiments tangled around themselves, threatening to choke him until he gave up the idea of trying to give them voice.

Slowly, Rhys became aware of the prickly itch of dust clinging to his sweat-damp skin and tried to straighten, forcing Darius back.

"I need a bath," he announced, gathering his clothes and debating whether or not to try to get dressed.

Darius smirked and tucked himself away, fastening his fatigues. "Do you now? Seem to recall crossing over a stream a mile or so up the road, if you don't mind walking."

"I don't mind." The distance decided the matter of whether to dress or not. No way was he walking a mile barefoot. Reluctantly, he pulled on his pants, socks, and boots, though he decided to forgo the shirt. "I like this."

"What's that?"

"Being able to venture out whenever we want to. Go for a swim after dark."

"I do too." Darius caught him by the arm and tugged him close for a long, slow kiss that had Rhys ready for another round. "Did I mention that the place where we'll make camp outside the Clean Zone is right on a lake?"

"Sounds perfect." Rhys pulled away and paused by the door to the lobby, waiting for Darius to shoulder his assault rifle. Even now, he wouldn't go anywhere without it. The region might have been patrolled for revenants, but bears, wolves, and mountain lions might still be an issue.

On their way out, they passed Schuyler, who was standing first watch in the lobby of the hotel. Rhys averted his eyes, unwilling to meet her scornful look. She hadn't forgiven him for his role in the events that had led to her lover Kaleo's death. For that matter, Rhys hadn't forgiven himself. He ignored the bitter ache of disappointment that always accompanied his awareness of Schuyler's hatred. One of the last things Kaleo had ever said to him was that Schuyler would love Rhys once they had a chance to get to know each other. But that had been before Jacob's vendetta against Rhys had led to him blowing Kaleo's head off. It would never have happened if Rhys had been honest from the start about how far Jacob was willing to go to indulge his malice.

Now Rhys just tried to stay out of her way.

Normally, it wasn't difficult since she was usually out on patrol. They had only ever bumped into each other when he was provisioning her squad for another sweep. It was his bad luck that the squadron Schuyler commanded had been tapped to deliver this batch of uninfected survivors to the Clean Zone. He hadn't had a choice but to travel with her. The only thing that made it bearable was that he wasn't actually under her command. Darius had refused to let Rhys go to Colorado Springs alone, so his own squadron had split in two. Some had stayed to help with the transition to Lewis-McChord and the rest had gone with Darius and Rhys, accompanying Schuyler's squadron on the escort detail.

Xolani had been one of those to come along, at her own insistence. And where Xolani went, so did Titus. Joe still considered himself Rhys's bodyguard when away from base, which meant he and Toby had come as well.

In the parking lot of the hotel, they crossed the path of the other member of Schuyler's squad standing first watch. Emilina Cruzado waved and grinned, jogging over to greet them.

Rhys gave her a smile. "Hey, Emmy." Of the three civilians Jacob had abducted, she had been the only one to survive. A full-fledged Jug now—and with none of the odd effects that had turned Jacob from a tyrant into a monster—Rhys was fond of her, and he often wished she had been assigned to Darius's squadron to replace Kaleo, but Schuyler had insisted Emmy join her squad instead.

"Ay ay ay! When'd you get those muscles, *papi?*" she demanded, giving Rhys's naked chest a friendly leer and laughing when he blushed. He'd bulked up somewhat from working in the warehouses, though he didn't think anyone but Darius had noticed. Except, perhaps, Xolani, who was as smug about it as if she'd raised Rhys up from a runt by tirelessly hand-feeding him.

Darius's arm came around Rhys's waist and pulled him a little closer, making Emmy laugh harder. For all that he teased Rhys with the possibility of sharing him around—it turned them both on to think he had the right to exert his claim on Rhys to that extent—it was all talk. Darius's possessive streak was well-known. It had grown intractable once Rhys had no longer required multiple partners to try to pass on the sexually transmitted Alpha strain that they had thought would save his life, and it didn't appear to have a sense of humor where even the most harmless flirtation was concerned. Which made it ridiculously easy for members of Delta Company to get a rise from Darius.

"We're going swimming," Rhys called over his shoulder as Darius propelled him toward the road.

"Have fun!" Emmy gave him a knowing wink and waved, then continued her patrol.

It was gearing up to be another sweltering summer. The thaw had come early to the mountains, leaving the stream swollen and just barely slow enough to bathe in. The evening air was muggy, but the water was frigid, and if not for the dust clinging to his skin, Rhys wouldn't have dared it.

But Darius's body was hot against his in the water, his hands deliberate as he helped rub away the sweat and grime. When they finally mounted the bank again, he was shivering, but Darius surrounded him, squeezing warmth back into his flesh.

"Hey," Rhys murmured, turning his head to kiss Darius's jaw. "Is that shadow over there a willow tree?"

A soft chuff of laughter brushed his damp shoulder. "Yeah, it is."

"Then why wait until tomorrow?" Rhys turned more fully for a thorough kiss, his hands sliding down Darius's broad back to cup his ass. Darius groaned and set him back.

"Go get a switch."

2

HAUNTINGS

Rhys's first assessment of Colorado Springs was that it looked more like a demilitarized zone than a clean zone. Miles of trenches had been dug around the suburb that was being resettled, but the rest was desolate and empty. That shouldn't have been unusual after all the ghost towns he'd seen while traveling with Delta Company, but he'd never before seen what appeared to be an old battlefield. A couple of areas they walked past had been damaged during the skirmishes that had taken place when the Jugs and the surviving civilian population had overthrown the military government.

They paused for a moment within sight of a cluster of apartment buildings that had been demolished. The rusted-out remnants of several tanks stood nearby. Rhys watched the people he'd lived among for two years bow their heads and pay their respects to the comrades they'd lost in that long-ago battle, and then they'd turned away and continued on.

The path Darius's and Schuyler's people took through the

rubble also led them past the burned-out skeletons of some old employee-housing tenements. The sight of them made Rhys shudder. Within those massive complexes lay thousands, sometimes tens of thousands, of corpses. People who had been denied the opportunity to quarantine themselves and had wound up wasting away inside their own bodies from the Beta strain, or waiting to starve to death or be cannibalized by revenants.

Sometimes it seemed that the whole world was haunted, but if there were any places that were truly, *actually* inhabited by restless and vengeful spirits, it would be the tenements.

"Creepy, aren't they?" Xolani asked, startling Rhys. He'd been so absorbed in staring at the charred remains of the buildings that he hadn't heard her approach.

He nodded. "Looks like they had a fire when they were sealed off by the National Guard."

"Not quite," she said. He glanced sideways to see Xolani's lips tighten, the scar down her cheek growing pale. "When the military government at Cheyenne Mountain first established a quarantine for the survivors, they were put in those buildings. Predictably, though, all it had done was enclose the uninfected population with the infected, and when they decided the plague was beyond containment, they firebombed the build-ings rather than risk anyone getting out."

"What?" Rhys gasped. "But . . . how did the civilians rise up and overthrow the military government, then?"

"That was the second wave of survivors to arrive. The mili-tary government got smarter about how to quarantine them, put them in pens on an old fairground and delivered rations there. It was still a squalid setup. There was no climate control." Xolani shook her head, her mouth twisting in disgust. "People were dying of heat stroke in summer and freezing to death in winter. The latrines were badly dug, the water supply was compromised, and the rations were barely enough to survive on. But believe it or not, it was an improvement."

Rhys took a moment to study her. Xolani could be bitter about the plague under the best of circumstances, but the closer they'd journeyed to Colorado Springs, the worse she'd become. In fact, she'd been violently opposed to Rhys answering his summons in the first place.

"You don't know what it was like, Rhys." Her husky alto was rougher than usual, and he thought he saw a sheen in her eyes as she stared fixedly at the tenements. "We didn't know what they were doing to us when they gave us the nasal spray. If we had, I'd like to think we would have refused, but we'd probably have faced court-martial, so maybe not. But once we started noticing the Alpha changes, they briefed us medics. I was there when they fed us a line of bullshit about what the virus was supposed to do, and I could tell from the way the R&D brain trusts dodged my questions that corners had been cut in the testing process." She turned her bleak gaze to him. "We weren't chosen for Project Juggernaut because we were the Army's elite forces. We were chosen because if it went wrong, we were expendable. They could terminate us and try again."

She growled, a feral sound Rhys had only heard her make once before, when she'd snapped Jacob's neck.

"And then the fuckers brought us in to put down a rebellion by the few civilians who'd managed to survive the death and destruction we had caused."

"You didn't cause this," Rhys murmured, reaching out to squeeze her shoulder. "You know that."

"I don't think any of us know that, Rhys." She huffed a soft, bitter chuckle. "Not truly."

He stood there at a loss for what to say to comfort her, but after a moment, she straightened, and he watched the Xolani he knew reappear.

"C'mon, kid. Let's catch up with the others."

Rhys fell into step beside her, his longer legs easily keeping up with her brisk pace. As they walked, Xolani began speaking again, her voice as steady and brusque as ever. "Listen, Rhys, I don't know who the scientists studying the virus here are. After the overthrow, when we were exiled from the Clean Zone, there weren't many scientists left to speak of. A couple of the Pentagon R&D types had made it to Cheyenne Mountain, including McClosky himself, but they were tried and executed for their roles in bringing about the plague. I tell you, the thing that pissed me off most was that we were exiled *before* the trials, so I never got to see those fuckers die."

"What are you saying?" Rhys adjusted the straps of his rucksack, watching their surroundings. He thought he could see the first hint of the perimeter fence in the distance. "You think the researchers might not be qualified?"

"I don't know." She grimaced. "A number of scientists were among the survivors the Jugs have recovered and brought back to the Clean Zone for the last ten years. We've known that since the Clean Zone announced the formation of the DPRP about six or seven years ago, when they asked us to relay our observations of the virus in the field. That's why I wrote that report about you after we realized you hadn't been infected, despite your exposure. I knew you would be of great interest to them because if you *are* immune, rather than merely asymptomatic, it might help them understand this thing."

"But?"

"I don't trust them." Xolani stopped abruptly and faced him. "Don't believe anything they tell you. If you don't like what they're saying, if you get so much as an uncomfortable feeling about anything they're doing, come to me immediately."

Rhys blinked. "What do you think they could do to me?"

"I don't know. But knowing what I do about the Bane virus, if *I* were a scientist completely lacking in scruples and I found someone who was immune . . ." She looked away and began walking again, leaving Rhys to scramble to catch up. "The first thing I would do is imprison you to harvest your immunoglobulins and produce a crude antiserum."

"What's that?" Rhys asked, frowning.

"It's a serum containing your antibodies. It's not a vaccine; it wouldn't teach someone's immune system to make its own antibodies. So it wouldn't be a practical solution for widespread inoculation, as the passive immunity would only last a few months and then everyone would need to be injected again. Depending on how much serum we could harvest from you, you might not naturally produce enough blood to cover the whole population." She shot the words at him in a rapidfire torrent, rattling off the possibilities. "So I'd probably give you the maximum doses of drugs to accelerate your blood production, which wouldn't be good for you long term, and you'd feel like shit. In the meantime, I'd be trying to isolate the antibody and synthesize it. I doubt the DPRP has the technology or expertise to do that effectively, though. I'd also look into seeing if your immunity was genetic, and if it was, I'd harvest your sperm to begin inseminating as many people as possible."

"You really think they'd try to do all that?" Rhys swallowed hard, stopping her and asking her to face him with a hand on her bicep. "Xolani? Do you really think that's a possibility?"

"I don't know, Rhys." She sighed, tugging her silver-shot braid over her shoulder and fiddling with it. "I don't know these people. It's possible this new civilian government hasn't gone corrupt the way every other government seems to, but . . ." She shrugged. "You know that if they try, we'll fight them. We'll get you back."

"Can you do that without risking the civilian population? I mean, if you're wounded and there are civvies around . . ."

Xolani licked her lips. "Probably not. But if that's the sort of corrupt shit they pull, I'm not sure we'd care. Not after everything they've already done to us. We've dealt with being exiled. We understood the why of it, even if we don't like being denied a home with the rest of humanity." Her mouth pressed into a tight line and she folded her arms over her chest. "We'll bring them the survivors we find to help grow the population, and we'll even share information about the virus when we see it in action. But we won't put up with them making one of our own a lab rat."

"But—" Rhys looked down, shuffling his feet "—if it's the best way to prevent another outbreak, can I really refuse?"

"Aw, *Christ*, Rhys." His gaze snapped back up when she groaned loudly. She closed her eyes, a pained expression on her face. "Look. For once, just once, can you not be so fucking self-sacrificing? I know it's who you are. You'll always think of the greater good before yourself. You've been doing it since the day we found you. But think about Darius and what it would do to him to lose you. And to the rest of us. You're our brother. We need you, kid."

His eyes began to burn, and he quickly leaned forward, pressing a kiss to her scarred cheek. Xolani gawped in surprise, but Rhys turned and began walking again before his blush could incinerate him on the spot.

His cheeks had cooled by the time Xolani caught up. "You're not getting out of this that easily. Promise me you won't play the heroic martyr."

"I promise," he said, his throat tight. "I won't let them take me from you."

FENCES SURROUNDED the perimeter trench on both sides. Anyone trying to get into the Clean Zone without going up the causeway and through the checkpoint would need to scale twelve feet of razor-wire-topped fence—now electrified, since they'd gotten the power plant back online—traverse a steep gully twenty feet wide and filled with more razor wire sharpened, rusty shards of metal, and wooden stakes; and then scale another electrified fence. The measures were intended to keep out both revenants and potentially infected survivors trying to bypass the mandatory quarantine, but they made the Clean Zone look and feel like a prison camp.

Within the outer perimeter was the quarantine ring. It wasn't much different than what Xolani had described, though houses had replaced the tents, and the revival of the hydroelectric plant on the river had provided climate control. Each residence had two fences and ten yards of space between it and its neighbor. Groups that arrived together were housed together in as few units as possible, and kept separate from other groups. If any member of a group turned out to be infected and began to manifest symptoms, the entire group would be euthanized and the residences they'd inhabited would be burned to the ground and rebuilt. Or so Joe explained to Rhys.

Luckily, since almost all of the survivors had already been quarantined for up to six months by the Jugs who had recovered them, this was more a case of planning for the worst rather than a procedure that was habitually instituted.

A causeway passed through the quarantine ring and into the suburbs the survivors had claimed. A large building with an adjacent guardhouse was set up fifty yards before the gates, staffed by armed forces in hermetic suits. They greeted the Jugs and the civilians being escorted, and for all their precautions, they welcomed the Jugs like old friends.

"Hey, you made it! You're our first batch this spring!" The first one out of the guardhouse cheered before he introduced himself. "Gillett Morris, Chief of Clean Zone Perimeter Security. Glad to see you!"

"Delta Company reporting. We've got fifteen survivors for you to take off our hands," Schuyler said as Darius and Xolani hung back with Rhys. She didn't bother to look their way, but her voice held a note of disdain as she continued, "And, as requested, we've brought in the asymptomatic survivor we've been sheltering for testing."

Four hooded heads turned to stare at Rhys. The sun reflected off their masks, making them seem featureless. He suppressed a shudder.

"You're the one they sent the report about?" Morris asked, stepping closer. "Possibly immune?"

Rhys's words abandoned him, his tongue sticking to the roof of his mouth. He looked from Darius to Xolani in alarm, and Xolani strode forward, putting him a little behind her as she spoke.

"*Possibly*. The extenuating circumstances were explained in our report. We don't want anyone getting false hope about the chance of immunity when we have no idea what's going on in his cells."

Morris nodded. "The DPRP scientists will deal with that. Secretary Littlewood himself issued the order; we're just here to give the refugees their intake interviews and questionnaires. But it's damn good to see all of you again."

"Order?" Xolani's voice grew cold. "We're not Clean Zone citizens, remember? We don't answer to the DPRP. We brought Cooper here as a courtesy because we don't want to see another outbreak, but let's keep in mind that he's here *voluntarily*, okay?"

"Right. Of course." Morris actually sounded embarrassed. Rhys didn't know what had happened when the Jugs had been exiled, but he got the impression that they had been pretty much shafted by the new government. If the way he cleared his throat and shuffled his feet was any indication, this Morris guy agreed. "At any rate, I know no one wants any false hopes raised, but they're all really excited about the potential here. Wallace, go to DPRP headquarters and let them know he's arrived."

One of the suited guards left, and the others escorted them into the building. The interior was fairly spartan. A large lounge with comfortable chairs and sofas led off to a series of glassed-in cubicles. Rations and water had been laid out and the Jugs were told to make themselves at home, and then the civilians were escorted—with the exception of women with children—into separate cubicles. More people in hermetic suits arrived with clipboards and sat down across from them, presumably conducting interviews.

"I thought you guys didn't get along with the people in the Clean Zone," Rhys murmured as they settled in.

Darius shrugged. "Perimeter Security's a little different. We fought beside a lot of them during the overthrow, and they weren't much happier than we were when the new congress kicked us out. They're mostly good people, usually happy to see us."

Rhys sat on a sofa between Darius and Xolani, twisting his hands nervously in his lap, until he felt Darius lay an arm across the back of the sofa behind his shoulders.

Xolani patted his knee, speaking with the guards who remained with them. "Since when does the DPRP interview the incoming civilians?"

"Started after that business with Charlie Company," Morris said. He looked rather absurd sitting there, still in his hermetic suit, as if he were having tea with them. His voice was strange and muffled. "I'm not sure what all the DPRP techs ask them. Probably making sure there's not any chance that they've, y'know, become Jugs themselves."

The Jugs all tensed, though Rhys wasn't sure if it was because of the implication that the Jugs were infecting their charges or the reminder of what had happened with Charlie Company six years ago. The company had gone rogue and started enslaving the civilians they were supposed to be protecting and escorting to the Clean Zone. The rest of the

Jugs had been forced to take action, going to battle against people they'd considered their brothers and sisters.

"We don't mess with the survivors," Darius rumbled. The guard looked rather pointedly at the way Darius had his arm nearly around Rhys's shoulders. "What happened with Rhys here is a different story. No one in Delta Company has touched a civvie except for that situation, and the reasons why we made an exception in those circumstances were included in our report."

"Well." Morris cleared his throat again, the sound echoey in the small speaker that transmitted his voice. "That may be the case, but we can't be sure all the other companies are holding to that. It's just a precaution."

One of the other guards snorted. "Ask me, they should be worrying more about the people who have been leaving the Clean Zone."

"What?" Xolani sat up straighter. "Who's been leaving the Clean Zone?"

"Just a few here and there," Morris said dismissively. "Tucker here is just worried because one of them was a friend of his."

"Why would they leave?" Schuyler asked, sitting forward in her chair. Rhys noticed Emmy was watching her almost as closely as Darius tended to watch him.

Morris shrugged. "Not sure why. I think some of them think that since the region is now completely free of revs, they'll be okay living elsewhere. Guess it doesn't matter, so long as they don't come back."

"There's also been a lot more protest about the Genetic Diversity Mandate as the population grows," the third remaining guard said. "Not everyone likes being forced to spread their genes around, even if it's just by donation."

The guard Morris had called Tucker gave the third one a look Rhys couldn't read through the mask. "Yeah, try having a uterus and bitching about that, Alvarez."

"What?" Xolani went rigid beside Rhys. "Have they expanded the GDM to require any citizen with a uterus to gestate?"

Tucker nodded. "The claim that they wouldn't attach that requirement to the GDM went out the window pretty quickly after the mandate was signed into law. My name's in the lottery again next year for being inseminated. It'll be my third time, and my wife isn't at all pleased to have to deal with a pregnant husband again."

Every Jug in the room with a uterus looked ready to shred something, and the others hardly seemed any happier. The tension grated across Rhys's already frayed nerves, and he desperately wanted to ask what they were talking about, but one glance at Xolani's and Schuyler's faces convinced him silence was the better option.

"I did *not*," Schuyler growled, "help overthrow the Cheyenne Mountain Martial Law Committee so that the civilian government that replaced them could start forcing citizens to act as incubators!"

"Jesus. Thank God Jamie isn't here," Toby muttered behind Rhys, referring to one member of Darius's squad who had stayed behind to help with Delta Company's move. "He'd mount an assault on the Clean Zone single-handedly if he heard about this shit. All the times he's had to have an abortion when he wants a baby so bad his heart is breaking and they're forcing people here to be pregnant against their wills?"

"He'll surely hear about it when we get to Lewis-McChord and fill the rest of Delta Company in on what we've heard here." Xolani spat a curse. "How widespread are the protests?"

"Rumblings here and there," Morris answered. "You know, mostly the people are still devoted to rebuilding, though a lot of the nationalist sentiment we saw after the overthrow has faded. Not everyone's happy with the way things are being done. My wife doesn't want any more children, either, especially since we've maxed out our particular genetic pairing so any others we have will be by insemination from other donors. But no one is discussing any drastic measures." He rubbed his face mask, an almost unconscious gesture, as though he would have been scratching his cheek if the hood hadn't been in place. "The Clean Zone Congress has assured us that the expiration clause on the GDM will not be extended. Ten more years and we'll be well into the second generation reproducing, and it won't be necessary anymore."

"It's not necessary *now*! The GDM was instituted back when the population was a fraction of what it is today, but even *then* you still had more than enough people for genetic sustainability." Xolani's clenched fists came down on the arm of the sofa hard enough that Rhys heard the wood under the upholstery crack. "It was a knee-jerk reaction to an astronomical death-to-live-birth ratio. But that was a direct result of mismanagement, and lack of supplies and infrastructure, when the Martial Law Committee was still in charge."

"The suicide rate for survivors after the pandemic wasn't helping either," Toby muttered.

Xolani nodded a distracted agreement. "True. But the point is, it was a call made by politicians who didn't know jack shit about science. And now, with better living conditions and all the survivors we've recovered, there have to be, what, ten thousand adult citizens in the Clean Zone?"

"Close: 8,954 at the annual census; 12,572, total population," Tucker replied. "We've got close to a thousand babies being born each year now. People who were just children when the Clean Zone was established are starting to hit reproductive maturity, and we've got a couple hundred new refugees coming through quarantine every spring and fall." He shook his head, sounding disgusted, or so it seemed from what Rhys could tell through his suit. "The only reason the congress hasn't repealed the GDM is because no one is protesting very loudly. They feel secure. They have adequate shelter, comfort, enough to eat. No one wants to risk that."

"How old do people have to be before they go into the lottery to gestate?" Schuyler demanded.

"Sixteen," Morris answered. "My wife's eldest was four at the time of the rebellion, so she just came of age. But she got pregnant by her boyfriend before we had to deal with her going into the lottery. As long as any able-bodied citizen is carrying a pregnancy to term at least once every four years, or has had six live births—no more than three of which can be with the same genetic partner—they can stay out of the lottery."

Xolani hissed between clenched teeth, looking as furious as Rhys had ever seen her. "Fuck. There's *absolutely* no reason for these draconian measures. Is there any way I can address the Congressional Science Committee while we're here? If no one has filled them in on the realities of genetic diversification, then I will."

"Perimeter Security is under the DPRP umbrella since quarantine maintenance falls under pandemic prevention, but

I know someone on the congressional clerical staff who works for the Science Committee. I'll pass on your request." Morris gave her what looked like a grateful nod. "My wife sure would be happy not to have to carry another one—" He broke off when the door opened and two people wearing hermetic suits walked in. "Wallace, is this . . .?"

"One of the DPRP medical techs," Wallace answered. "He's supposed to take the subject to one of the quarantine units and get some intake information before testing begins."

Quarantine unit? Rhys trembled and fumbled beside Darius until he brought his hand down from the back of the sofa and laced their fingers. "Relax, boy. No one's gonna hurt you."

"Mr. Cooper?" The other suited man stepped forward, extending a gloved hand. After a moment of hesitation, Rhys stood and wiped his palms on his fatigues before shaking it.

"I'm Zach," the man said. "I'm going to be interviewing you, settling you into your quarters, and drawing some blood. Nothing scary at all. Once we get the results of your blood work, the DPRP researchers will have a better idea how to proceed."

Rhys looked rapidly between Darius and Xolani, trying to unstick his tongue from the roof of his mouth to protest, but Xolani spoke up first.

"He's not going alone," she said firmly. "And he's not staying in the quarantine ring. We'll bring him in for testing, but he makes camp with us outside the Clean Zone at the end of the day."

"The DPRP has set up quarters specifically for testing him, including putting him on the same ventilation circuit as animals known to be able to contract the Bane virus," Zach explained. "If he doesn't stay there, we won't know whether he's capable of spreading the virus in its airborne form."

"Too bad. Come on, Rhys, we're leaving." Xolani rose and gestured for him to accompany her, and Rhys followed.

Darius stood and fell into step beside him. "Let's go, people," he barked. "Schuyler, you'll stay here until you're done handing over your civvies. We'll meet you by the lake."

Titus, Toby, and Joe all rose and spread out behind them, surrounding Rhys as if afraid that they would try to take him by force.

"You can't leave, Xolani," Schuyler protested, coming to her feet. "*We* can't. Not yet. Not until you talk to the Science Committee. They're turning people into *incubators*."

"Goddamn it." Xolani hung her head, muttering to herself as Darius made an irritated sound beside Rhys. Then she turned to look at him. "She's right, Darius. Permission for me to detach and remain here while you take Rhys away from here?"

"Granted," Darius said with a short nod.

"*Please*—" Zach held up a hand in what Rhys assumed was meant to be a placating gesture. It would have worked better without the hermetic suit. "I'm sure I don't need to tell you all how important this might be, if Mr. Cooper is immune. What can I do to reassure you that he'll be all right staying in the quarters we've prepared for him?"

Rhys looked between Darius and Xolani again, distressed. He didn't want to cause any worry, and Xolani was right. He needed to consider how they would feel if they lost him. They had taken so much time and care to get him away from the monastery and bring him back to health and give him a home. He couldn't risk himself, and yet he couldn't turn his back on the possibility that he might be able to somehow help prevent any future outbreak of the plague. The United States population had been reduced to the twelve thousand people here, not including the Jugs and survivors not yet recovered. Another outbreak could ensure the complete extinction of humanity on the North American continent.

He straightened his shoulders, lifted his chin, and cleared his throat as he faced Zach head-on. "I won't go alone. I want these five Jugs who accompanied me to come as well, and *only* until you don't need me to breathe on your lab animals anymore."

"Hey, now!" Wallace stepped toward them, his gloved hand tight on the strap of the weapon slung over his shoulder, as though he thought he might need to grab it. The other guards—except Perimeter Security Chief Morris—flanked him, looking equally alert. "Jugs aren't allowed past the outer perimeter. That's the *law*."

"Stand down," Morris snapped at him. "We don't threaten Jugs. These people did us a favor bringing Cooper here. They don't answer to us, especially after the way we treated them. If Cooper wants to walk, we let him."

The Jugs gave Morris looks of varying surprise, but Rhys's attention was focused on the DPRP stooge. He turned a cool look toward Zach. "You asked what you could do to assure me I'd be safe. This is it. If the DPRP wants to test me badly enough, they'll make an exception. The quarantine ring is safe for keeping potentially infected civvies away from the population, so it should be safe for keeping Jugs away, as well."

Zach shuffled uncomfortably. "I can—" He cleared his throat and began again. "I can take this back to the department. It might require Secretary Littlewood's approval, and that could take a while."

"Then I guess you'd better get a move on, son," Darius snapped. "We're not going to wait around forever for the DPRP to get their hands off their dicks and decide. You've got seven days, then we leave. We'll be camped by the lake until then."

3

ASSESSMENT

Z ach took a breath to brace himself, then knocked on the door of the quarantine unit that had been remodeled as a testing facility for Rhys Cooper. The number of refugees coming through quarantine had dwindled in the decade since the Jugs had started their operations, so the unit was in an all-but-abandoned portion of the quarantine ring. It kept the other uninfected separate from this one survivor, since they had no way of knowing yet whether or not his exposure to the Bane virus made him contagious.

He pressed a fist against the knot that had formed just below his sternum and closed his eyes, whispering a brief prayer until he felt calm again. He needed to let God guide him to the right thing to say. This was too important to let his fears and doubts sabotage him.

Secretary Littlewood had been livid when Zach had brought word that Cooper and the Jugs were digging their heels in about where Cooper would be housed. At first, the intensity of his rage had left Zach deeply uneasy because he didn't know if his failure to persuade Cooper would undo his years of work ingratiating himself with Littlewood and the upper echelon of the DPRP. But while Littlewood had arranged for Cooper and his Juggernaut escort to be quartered together within the quarantine ring, more profound misgivings had taken root in Zach's brain.

Littlewood's fury went beyond the frustration of clinical and scientific ambitions. While his excessive irritation could actually result in an amazing breakthrough in bringing to light the secret agenda Zach suspected Littlewood of advancing, it could only benefit Zach if he was willing to risk putting Rhys Cooper in harm's way after he'd promised the young man he'd be safe.

Zach's churning thoughts were interrupted as the short, olive-skinned Jug with the scarred face and silver-shot braid answered the door. She was familiar, as were several other Jugs; he was sure he'd seen her around in the months it had taken for the military personnel barricaded inside Cheyenne Mountain to surrender. She probably wouldn't recognize him even if she saw him out of his suit, though. Ten years had passed, after all, and he hadn't interacted very closely with many of the Jugs during the standoff when he'd lived with Nico. Right now, she was looking at Zach like he was something she would snap in two if she didn't like what he had to say. She was every bit as formidable this afternoon as she had been the day before when she'd refused to let him take Cooper to his quarters.

"Hi," he said, his hands sweating inside his gloves. "I'm Zach. You might remember me from the other day? I came to make sure you are all settling in okay, and to see if Mr. Cooper is ready to begin some of his tests."

He sucked in a breath to keep himself from babbling

further. He hadn't been prepared for the resistance he'd encountered from the Jugs, or for the fact that Cooper was clearly much more than just another survivor they had custody of until they could turn him over. Zach had to proceed carefully with these people or they'd take Cooper and bolt. Well, not bolt. They'd walk out, and there wouldn't be a damn thing Zach, or the DPRP, or Perimeter Security could do about it. Short of shooting them, of course, which was an option of mutually assured destruction.

Zach blinked slowly, letting his sense of God's guidance and wisdom fill his soul before he smiled through his mask. It probably wasn't the disarming expression he'd hoped for, but the suit could be blamed for spoiling the effect. He remembered his own time in quarantine all too well and how disconcerting the copper-toned, polarized coating on the masks could be.

"Of course I remember you," she said flatly. "Rhys is napping. He was too anxious to get much sleep last night, thanks to the shit you people tried to pull. You try to separate us from him again and we're out of here, no negotiation, no second chances. Got it?"

"Yes, ma'am." Zach nodded enthusiastically, and Xolani stepped aside to allow him to enter. He couldn't begrudge her resentment. His limited association with the Jugs had been more than enough to allow him to witness firsthand how devastating congress's decision to exile them had been.

The communal living quarters spread out before him as he crossed the threshold. Beyond them was a small hall that led to the bedrooms and lavatory. Normally, two small families or up to six adults would live in one of these units. It was useless to put furniture in a house that might have to be burned down if its inhabitants turned out to be infected, so the great room was sunken, with benches built in around the edge like a conversation pit. In their spare time, some of the citizens of the Clean Zone made cushions for the benches, to help make the newly arrived survivors more comfortable while they waited out their quarantines.

Around the dining table—also built into an alcove—three men sat with cards in their hands. They had paused their play, abandoning their game to fix their attention on Zach.

Their CO—the tall, forbidding black man named Darius —sat on one of the sleeping mats that would usually fill the bedrooms but were now spread around the living room floor. He had his assault rifle laid out on the mat in front of him and a small unassembled sidearm was in his hands as he cleaned it. On the mat beside him lay Rhys Cooper, curled into a fetal ball with his head almost in Darius's lap.

For all his stature, Cooper looked *young*. Way too young.

Oh, yes. Littlewood's interest made perfect, sickening sense.

"Rhys," Xolani called softly, stepping over to him and crouching to touch his shoulder. "You got a visitor, kid."

Cooper bolted upright, blinking at Zach in semiconscious alarm and distrust. Then he drew a shuddering breath and nodded, pushing himself to his feet. He pulled his shoulders back, standing almost at attention.

"Hello. Thank you for arranging for everyone to stay with me. I guess you want to start those tests now?" The greeting was stilted, abrupt. Like a kid trying to mask his nerves by appearing mature and dignified but falling short of the mark. Or maybe someone who had lived in isolation so long that he really didn't know how to act with new people. He didn't glance around at any of his companions, either, as if he were deliberately making himself face Zach without their backing.

Zach nodded soberly. "If you don't mind. We have one of the bedrooms all set up for you. You can—"

"Thanks, but I saw that thing. The bed is barely wide enough for one person." Cooper grimaced. "I'll sleep out here, where I belong."

Darius lifted his eyes at that and finished reassembling his sidearm while glancing up at Cooper's back. It was only a split second, but in that unguarded instant before a stern, threatening look settled on his face, Zach saw everything he needed to see to understand *that* situation. Zach had seen similar looks before. He'd even been the recipient of them, once upon a time.

Much more than just another survivor, indeed.

"Um, if you would consider at least spending a few nights in that room, it would help us very much. The test animals are set up in there, well within the twenty-foot hot zone for airborne contamination. At least spend as much of the day as possible there, please?"

Cooper dropped his chin, sighing. "I'll think about it. I'd prefer to just get this over with."

Zach nodded again, holding out an arm to gesture down the hall. "After you."

Cooper didn't move. "Xolani?"

"Go on, Rhys." Her voice was gentle, though Zach thought he heard a note of reluctance. They were paranoid, and the hell of it was that Zach couldn't even blame them. "I doubt they'll want a Jug near the test animals. If I happened to be wounded or menstruating, it could fuck up their whole experiment. But we'll be right out here. If you need us, yell."

"Okay, look." There was understanding the reasons for their distrust, and then there was letting himself be the whipping boy for it. "I've been in the Clean Zone since before the overthrow. I *know*, probably better than anyone else here, that you Jugs have no reason to like or trust us. But I don't devour unsupervised children or ritually sacrifice fluffy little bunnies, and I don't mean Mr. Cooper any harm." He swallowed, glad they couldn't see his face. Technically, at least, the claim was true. "I'm just here to do some tests, okay?"

Six pairs of eyes all fixed on him, and from each set Zach thought he saw a spark of something other than mistrust. Dare he call it *respect*?

Then the grizzled one playing cards at the table with the short redhead and the giant of a man chuckled. "I think this one might actually be worth the powder and lead to shoot 'im dead."

A ripple went through the room, and everyone relaxed in its wake.

"Maybe I should introduce everyone," Cooper said, sounding less wary. "You know Xolani and Darius. That's Titus." He pointed toward the one who had made the quip and then to the man next to him. "And Toby, and the big guy is Joe."

"It's nice to meet all of you. I'm going to be around quite a bit, doing periodic tests and blood draws. I'm sure we'll all get to know one another better in time."

They each murmured a greeting, and Cooper drew a breath, then straightened his shoulders and preceded Zach down the hall.

Never had Zach been so grateful for his mask, which kept the blush threatening to incinerate him from showing. He cleared his throat and shifted, readjusting the position of his clipboard, checking the list of questions he was supposed to ask.

"I'm sorry, *how* many of the Jugs did you say you had intercourse with each day?"

He tried not to cringe at the intrusive questions. The Jugs' report on Rhys had been classified, and he hadn't even been allowed to see the questions the DPRP researchers wanted him to ask until right before he'd put on his suit. They obviously hadn't been written by anyone with an ounce of tact. The only consolation was that Cooper was blushing nearly as vividly. "Um, I'd say an average of three while we were on the march . . . Once we got to base I'd say it was more like five or six. Not including Darius."

"So you were exposed to Bane Alpha up to six times a day."

"No. Probably closer to ten."

Zach blinked. "But you just said—"

"I said I was with up to six Jugs a day. But I was usually with Darius at least two or three times, and sometimes the other Jugs would want to have sex more than once." Cooper heaved a frustrated sigh. "Look, I'm really not comfortable talking about this, especially with a stranger. After a while, it wasn't so bad, being with all of them, but I was glad when I didn't have to be with anyone but Darius anymore. I don't like to look back at the rest. Didn't Xolani cover all this in her report?"

"I, um, I think the doctors wanted to confirm or clarify some of the details to better ascertain your level of exposure."

Zach shifted again. What Rhys was describing was very far from what he would normally find arousing, but it had been way too long since he'd been with anyone, which meant his body was primed like a teenager's and any mention of sex was enough to get its attention.

He bowed his head, swallowing against the wave of melancholy that crashed over him. Even knowing why he had to be alone didn't make it any easier, sometimes. He missed Nico so intensely it ached.

"How about for now I just document your physical condition, and if we need to go over more of the questions, we'll deal with that later, once we've had a chance to become more comfortable with each other?" he proposed.

"That sounds good." Cooper gave him a small smile that held a hint of warming. It seemed that Zach was making headway through some of the mistrust.

"Perfect." Zach tried to make his own answering smile as inviting as possible. "If you wouldn't mind stepping over here to the scale . . .?"

He took Cooper's weight and height. Pulse. Blood pressure. Respirations. This part was easy. It wasn't hard at all to slip into the familiar routine. Zach would always miss his days working to aid the sick and injured survivors, but he'd never been able to bring himself to go back to it. The people he'd trusted back then had betrayed him, turned their backs when he'd chosen to be with a Jug. They'd supported exiling the Jugs, forcing the separation he and Nico had suffered the last ten years.

Working for the DPRP wasn't anywhere near the same. He didn't get that sense of truly helping people. He was just a drone, doing busywork and keeping his head down and ears open. Still, it was nice to at least be in the position of dealing hands-on with a patient again, even if he wasn't offering comfort and healing.

"Okay." He straightened his shoulders and gave Cooper another smile. "I'm going to need to do a visual examination, report on the condition you appear to be in. The doctors will do a complete physical later, but for now, would you mind taking off your shirt, Mr. Cooper?"

Cooper nodded and drew a deep breath, then reached for his buttons. He wore the same fatigues as the Jugs he accompanied, no doubt scavenged from the military installations they came across in their travels. It made it harder to remember that Cooper was a civilian, a bystander who might be the recipient of a very special, very dangerous gift from God.

"You can call me Rhys, you know," he said as he stripped off the shirt, exposing a healthy, well-muscled chest. Zach made a note that he appeared to be receiving good nutrition and had no visible maladies.

"Well, Rhys . . ." Zach's voice died when Rhys turned and he got a look at his back. "Dear God!" A chill ran through Zach, followed by a wave of rage. "Who did this to you?"

"What?" Rhys peered over his shoulder and flushed. "Oh, that. It's okay. I asked for it."

"Rhys." Zach gentled his voice and stepped forward, setting his clipboard aside as he laid a gloved hand on the young man's shoulder, just above the welts. Some of them had at one point been open enough to scab over. It wasn't Rhys's first beating, either. Beneath the stripes on his back, Zach could see a few faint, silvery scars from previous whippings.

Damn. Any thought of using Rhys to trick Littlewood

into exposing his scheme fled. He couldn't possibly subject an abuse victim to what Littlewood's keen interest in the young man might very well portend. "Look, I know abusers try to make their victims blame themselves, but no one asks for this. It's not your fault. And if you want to confide in me, I'm here. Maybe I can help get you away from him."

The crimson flush that had worked its way up Rhys's pale shoulders and neck deepened. His voice was a reluctant mumble.

"It's nice of you to be so concerned for me and all. I don't expect you to understand, but it's what Darius and I—" He turned, looking Zach directly in the face for the first time without a room separating them, perhaps getting his first good look past the coppery shimmer of the mask, and his hazel eyes grew huge. He paled and stumbled backward until he pressed up against the wall, staring at Zach in horror. "Darius! Xolani!"

Footsteps thundered down the hall, and the door crashed open. Zach found himself pulled away from Rhys and flung across the room, slamming into the opposite wall with enough force to knock the wind from his lungs and daze him. Within their enclosures, several ground squirrels and an opossum squealed and scrambled in alarm. By the time Zach cleared the fog from his head and tried to stand, Darius and Xolani were between him and Rhys, looking at him with blood in their eyes. The other Jugs clustered in the doorway, ready to lend aid.

"What's wrong, Rhys?" Xolani asked, turning her attention away from Zach to look Rhys over, checking him for injury.

"What's wrong?" There was a quaver in Rhys's voice, and

he was staring at Zach as if he were something out of a nightmare. "Look at his face. *Look* at him!"

Darius didn't move, but Xolani stepped closer. Self-preservation told Zach to stay very still as she drew near enough to get a good look at him through his mask.

She hissed. "Houtman. You *motherfucker.*"

Zach licked his lips, quivering but otherwise motionless, as all five Jugs growled nearly in unison. "H-how did you know my family name? No one has called me that in years. I don't think I've even used it, except when filling out the annual census."

"How'd you manage it?" Xolani demanded, and Zach shook his head in confusion.

"Manage what?"

"Manage to arrange for Rhys to be summoned. Do you have that much pull with the DPRP?"

He swallowed hard. "I don't know what you're talking about. Please. I haven't done anything. I'm just doing my job."

Her hand snapped up, grabbing his throat through the fabric of his suit and squeezing until Zach felt his air cut off. "You can start leveling with us or I can rip your fucking head off the way I did the last Houtman we met."

Understanding dawned. *Jacob!* he mouthed, unable to speak with her hand closing off his airway. Her grip loosened just a fraction, enough to allow him to rasp, "You knew my brother? Please, I can't—"

She released him abruptly, but she didn't back down, and Zach wasn't foolish enough to think for a second that she wouldn't tear him limb from limb in an instant if she didn't like what he had to say.

"Jacob was your brother?" Rhys asked cautiously, staying well behind Darius.

Zach nodded, wishing the suit wasn't in the way so he could rub his bruised throat. "I haven't seen him in years, though. Since before I left Indiana, before the overthrow. I couldn't stay with my father and brother, so I made my way to the Clean Zone while they headed to the Northwest." All of them eased off a fraction, though Zach by no means believed they had let down their guard. "Please. I had no idea you had met him. Or them."

Xolani's eyes narrowed. "I put all that in my report."

"I haven't read the report. It's classified. Only the highest-ranking officials of the DPRP have access to it." Zach straight-ened a little more, meeting her eyes. "I'm just a tech. They told me to draw some blood, gave me a list of questions to ask, told me to do a preliminary exam. That's all."

It was Rhys whose gaze Zach sought, and after a moment, the tension left Rhys in a visible rush. "I think he might be telling the truth."

Darius glanced back at him before glaring at Zach again. "I want the whole story."

He nodded eagerly. "Of course. But, if you don't mind, can we go out to the other room? It's a little crowded in here, and as Xolani observed earlier, you're really not supposed to be around the animals . . ."

4

EXPLANATIONS

Darius watched everyone filter into the communal great room, finding seats at cautious distances that conveniently kept Zach Houtman away from Rhys and cut him off from the door, if necessary. Getting a read on his people was easy. It was a sign of how stressed they were at being in the Clean Zone, bringing Rhys in for testing, that all—for a split second, at least—were ready to murder a man simply for his resemblance to someone else.

Of course, no Jug in this room had reason to give two shits about any Clean Zone citizen, and all of them had particular cause to hate Jacob Houtman. That slimy motherfucker had not only terrorized Rhys but he'd murdered one of their brothers. They had all felt Kaleo's absence in their squad every day of the last two years. They'd all watched Schuyler, once one of the most resilient soldiers in Delta Company, sink into bitterness and grief. Kaleo had been a light in the darkness for them all.

Rhys set himself apart as they settled in. Not only from

Zach, which was to be expected, but also from Darius. He had his hands clenched on his knees, as if to stop himself from fidgeting, and he was giving Zach a stubborn stare Darius recognized.

I'm not the terrified kid who walked away from that monastery, it said. *I can protect myself now.*

He'd seen that expression on Rhys's face a lot these past couple years as he'd grown stronger and more confident. He'd built up his body and learned to fight, yes, but more importantly, he'd learned to stand up for himself. He'd faced off against Jugs who didn't believe he belonged with them, and he'd proven his worth.

Darius's boy had become a man.

"Will you tell me what happened to my father and brother?" Zach asked, managing to look nervous despite the hermetic suit. "The last time I saw them was in Indiana. My father and I had a falling out when I helped another survivor who needed shelter." He paused, and his hooded head bowed. "Father wanted to kill him, but I wouldn't allow it. I hid the ammunition, and my father tried to lock me up and starve me until I told him where it was. I escaped and left with the other survivor, and that was the last time I saw them."

"I met them in Montana," Rhys said, and Darius could see the effort he was making to keep his voice steady. His cheeks were still slightly pink, probably from embarrassment over the way he'd panicked when he'd recognized Zach. "My family never knew that people were gathering in Colorado Springs. We'd been staying in a bunker before then, and we had run out of supplies. My father used himself as bait to lure some revenants away from me, my mom, and my sister, and we never saw him again. My mom didn't know where else to go, so when Father Maurice told us about the monastery he wanted to reach, we went with them. We were there for seven years until a revenant attack killed everyone except me and Jacob." Rhys rubbed the back of his neck. "They never mentioned you."

A hiss escaped Zach's mask, sounding like a bitter laugh. "I'm not surprised. What happened to Jacob?"

Rhys hesitated, and after a moment, Xolani spoke up, her voice hard. "We infected him with the Alpha strain. He'd been exposed to revenants, both he and Rhys, and it was the only way we could try to prevent them from getting the Rot or becoming revs themselves."

"Infected? You mean, the way *you* were infected? By— With the Jugs—" Zach spluttered into the speaker of his hood. "He— Jacob *agreed* to that?"

"Jacob was more than willing to do whatever it took to live," Rhys replied, his mouth tight. "Especially since it meant he'd become a Jug. He liked the idea of being superhuman. A lot."

Zach nodded. "He always was ambitious."

"He wasn't ambitious, he was *evil*." Rhys's face tightened, his eyes growing flinty. "He and your father tortured me for seven years. I have trouble moving two of the fingers on my left hand. Xolani thinks it's nerve damage from the way Father Maurice used to beat my palms and knuckles with his cane. They nearly starved me to death, withholding my rations every time they decided I needed punishment. We still don't know how much organ damage I suffered from that. And Jacob used to hold me down while Father Maurice hacked off all my hair."

He spat out the catalog of abuses and their lasting consequences flatly, delivering his words like blows. Zach sank into himself, hunching over as the litany continued.

"That doesn't even include forcing me to pray on my knees on a hard stone floor three times a day, or every time I was told I was damned, that the plague had been retribution against me and my 'kind.'"

By the time he was finished, Zach's shoulders were up by his ears, his arms wrapped around himself. "They punished you in my place," he murmured. "I'm sorry. Oh God, I'm so sorry."

Rhys continued as if he hadn't heard. "Once Father Maurice was dead, Jacob lost all his authority. I didn't realize until too late that someone would finally believe me if I told them how awful he could be. Three people are dead because I didn't speak up." Darius opened his mouth to protest, then shut it again. This wasn't the time. "Two of those people were my good friends, and the other one was just in the wrong place at the wrong time when Jacob decided to use other survivors to keep torturing me."

They could hear Zach whispering inside his suit, though it took Darius a moment to pick up the words.

"God forgive them. Please, God, forgive them. And help me to live my life with more wisdom than they ever showed. Help me always remember the love and mercy of Your Son, Jesus Christ, and never lose my way as they did. Amen."

The poor bastard was praying. Honestly fucking praying.

"I'm so very, very sorry," Zach said again when he'd finally lifted his head. "My first impulse is to try to defend myself, to reassure you that I'm not like them. But that's self-serving, and I don't think it's what you need to hear from me right now." His breath hissed through the mask again as he inhaled and exhaled deeply. "I saw my father becoming more reactionary and fundamentalist in the years before the pandemic, but I didn't know how to stop it. Maybe if I'd succeeded, you wouldn't have gone through that." He sighed. "I take it from what Xolani said that you killed Jacob?"

"We did." Rhys's tight smile was grim.

Zach nodded. "I . . . understand. You did what you needed to do to protect yourselves and others."

Emotions played on Rhys's face as he struggled to find something to say. It was a difficulty shared by all of them. Houtman had torn a hole in their company, not only by taking Kaleo from them but by reminding them—as Charlie Company had done years before—how dangerous they were, how easily the Alpha strain could be misused.

"I don't blame you for what Jacob did," Rhys finally managed. His tone was rough, as though he had to force the words out. "I'm sorry for the way I reacted earlier. Seeing you . . . it was like seeing a nightmare come back to life."

Darius grimaced at the literal truth of that statement. The nightmares had started after Rhys had been forced to kill his friend Gabriel, whom Houtman had infected with the Rot. It took a year before the dreams had finally become rare, intermittent occurrences. He had a feeling they'd be dealing with a few more such occurrences in the nights to come.

"I understand." Zach stood slowly, as if afraid they might set on him if he made any sudden movements. "All right. Getting this back on track . . . I still need to get the blood samples I was told to collect, but then I'll get out of your hair for the rest of the day. As I said before, please give some thought to staying in the room with the animals for a few days or nights, long enough for us to be sure they've had plenty of exposure to you."

"All right." Rhys rose and crossed to the small eating nook, rolling up his sleeve. "Can I ask why there aren't, I don't know, doctors or scientists coming to talk to me?"

"Honestly?" The hunch of Zach's shoulders indicated embarrassment. "They thought it was too dangerous. We have so few researchers and physicians. Most of them died in the pandemic. Until we know whether or not you're shedding virus, they feel it best to minimize the number of people who have contact with you."

Rhys's mouth twisted. "What, so you're the guy who drew the short straw?"

Zach shook his head, wrapping a tourniquet around Rhys's bicep. "I volunteered."

"Why?"

"Because this is important." He fell silent as he carefully slid the needle into Rhys's vein and began filling a handful of vials. "I couldn't let fear hold me back from helping."

Darius ducked his head to cover his smile. The man sounded like Rhys, always the first to volunteer to put himself on the line. If Zach was telling the truth about having no other agenda, Rhys might very well have met a kindred spirit.

That thought ached more than it had any business doing. Rhys *should* have friends among the uninfected population. He was with Delta Company because they didn't know if he was safe around the civvies. But if it turned out he *was*, having a home here in the Clean Zone would make a hell of a lot more sense than packing it up and moving with the Jugs every few years, living in dusty, falling-down places that had been abandoned for over a decade. It was what the Jugs had to do until they exterminated all the revs and rounded up the uninfected civvies, but that didn't need to be Rhys's life.

"Thank you again," Zach said after he'd put a pressure bandage on Rhys's arm and tucked the vials away in a carefully locked and insulated case. "I'll be working in a lab we set up in the quarantine unit next door. There'll be a guard posted outside your enclosure to act as a runner, so if you need anything, or if you want to send word to the rest of your companions, notify them and it'll be handled. You also have free passage along the causeway to the intake facility, as long as you stay away from the other refugees and don't try to pass the checkpoint into the Clean Zone."

As he spoke, he made his way toward the door, then paused, his gloved hand gripping the lever. "Rhys, I just want to apologize again. For my father and brother. I hope . . . I hope as we work together that maybe I can help heal some of those wounds."

"Thank you." Rhys looked down at his bandaged arm, his eyes glassy, and Darius rose to go to him. He stroked the back of his boy's neck, and Rhys shuddered at the touch. He was rigid under Darius's hand, muscles twitching and jumping beneath taut skin. It felt like touching him had in the early days, when Rhys hadn't wanted it—or at least hadn't *wanted* to want it.

Darius started to let his hand fall away, but then Rhys's came up and covered his, holding it in place. They both watched Zach hesitate, as if he felt like he ought to say more, then he turned and slipped out the door.

"I can't really hate him, can I?" Rhys muttered when the door had closed. Xolani, Titus, Joe, and Toby all busied themselves with other things, giving them the illusion of privacy. Rhys leaned into Darius's touch. He wrapped an arm around Darius's thighs and hid his face in Darius's midriff.

He stroked Rhys's sandy hair, which fell between his shoulders. He'd taken to pulling it back at his nape the way Darius did. The choice not to cut it was one of the many small *fuck you*'s he sent to the ghosts of Jacob and his father.

"You can hate whoever you want, boy. You think you have reason not to trust him, we'll all back you, no questions asked."

"I don't. Not really." Rhys sighed. "And if I do, I'll be doing the same thing to him that Schuyler has been doing to me, blaming me for Kaleo's death."

"Maybe you need to stop blaming yourself before you expect her to." Darius squatted to face him eye to eye. "Don't think I didn't hear what you said to him about that. I ain't gonna tell you it's not your fault, 'cause you already know that. It's gettin' to be way past time you started believing it, though."

Rhys stared at him a moment, and then leaned in, clasping Darius's face with both hands and kissing him hard. Darius let him take the lead. Sometimes it felt like his ribs would crack with the size of the emotion Rhys stirred up in his chest. He wouldn't call it *love* any more than he could say he loved oxygen or water. Rhys was *necessary*. Essential. *Love* was too trite a word to apply to it.

Rhys pushed Darius to the floor, ripping at his belt with one hand while delving in his pocket for the lube with the other. With the rest of the squad only feet away, it was like it had been two years ago when Rhys had first traveled with them, though Rhys had never been so uninhibited then. In a flurry of frantic movements, Rhys shucked his own pants, slicked up Darius's cock, and mounted him. He wailed softly as he sank down on Darius, his whole body tense and trembling as he forced himself to take it faster than his muscles could adjust. Darius just groaned and lay still, except for his hands, which he used to stroke the quivering muscles of Rhys's thighs.

"Darius, I—" His voice broke, his breath hitching, as he lifted himself and slid down again.

"It's okay, boy. You take what you need. Do it. Let me see you."

Rhys did. He rode Darius hard and fast, rising and falling, sweat rolling down his temples and the pale chest bared by his open shirt. Darius pushed it off his shoulders, wanting to see all of Rhys's lean, tightly toned beauty. If he was once infatuated with the skinny, fragile innocent Rhys had been, Darius damn near worshipped the strong, tall man he'd become. His hands touched every inch of skin he could, knowing Rhys was all his.

Rhys reached down, grasping his own dick and jacking himself, his moans getting louder with every stroke. He was tight around Darius's prick, tight and so damn hot that Darius had to grit his teeth to keep from grabbing Rhys's hips and hammering up into him. But he wouldn't do anything to change what Rhys was doing. It was glorious to see him so open and unashamed.

Rhys cried out sharply, and scalding, slick streams splattered Darius's belly where Rhys had pushed his shirt up out of the way. When it was over, Rhys fell forward, pressing himself flat against Darius, smearing the mess between them as he lay there, panting and shaking.

"Feel better?" Darius asked, smiling.

There was a pause, and Darius could imagine the blush heating Rhys's cheeks, even if he couldn't see it. "Sorry. I—"

"Don't be sorry. I'll always give you what you need, the way you always give it to me."

Rhys's mouth tightened. "Always." But he didn't say anything else or explain the grimace. He was silent a long moment, and then, "I'm going to have to stay in that damn room by myself, aren't I?"

Darius sighed heavily, caressing his sweaty back. "You don't have to do anything you don't want to do. You don't want to be here, say the word and we'll go. But if you're serious about doing this, if you mean it when you say you want to help them understand the plague and find a way to stop it if you can, then . . ." He drew a deep breath and blew it out in a rush. "Yeah, you're gonna need to do things their way for a while. Otherwise, we might as well go home."

"I sleep alone all the time when you're out on patrol. Weeks. Sometimes even months. Why is this different?"

"It just is." Darius rolled them abruptly, sliding out of Rhys's ass as they went, then pinned Rhys to the floor. "But before you go, I'm not done with you, boy. Turn over."

Rhys scrambled to his hands and knees eagerly, and Darius didn't hesitate to sink into that shining pink hole gaping at him. His cock was still stiff, his balls drawn up and ready to boil over, to breed his boy so deep and hard Rhys would be able to taste it.

His hips slammed into Rhys's flanks with a sweat-damp smack, as he admired Rhys's back and the crisscrossing stripes of Darius's handiwork with the switch. The worst scab had cracked open, crimson beads forming along its seam, and Darius bent forward to capture them on his tongue, leaving a rusty streak on Rhys's fair skin. The metallic taste of blood awoke something in Darius, a primal thing that came to life in sex and combat. It was only too happy to hurt Rhys, to make him cry and beg and bleed. It had taken a while, but Darius had finally gotten comfortable letting go once he understood that Rhys wanted it.

Like he wanted it now.

Darius let that instinct run free. He gripped Rhys's hips and pounded into him, driving him forward with each thrust. When Rhys collapsed, pushed so far forward he couldn't keep his knees under him, Darius pulled out, hauled him back up, and shoved in again.

"Oh, no, you don't. Not going anywhere," he snarled, fucking Rhys harder.

They migrated a few inches each time they repeated the process, until Rhys's chest lay along one of the bench seats at the edge of the room and there was nowhere else for him to go. That was when he began begging, and it was sweet music to Darius's ears.

"God . . . Oh fuck, Darius! Too much. Too much. Can't take anymore. Need you to come. Need you. Please!"

The thing in him howled for satisfaction, and Darius gave into it, driving into Rhys one last time and pumping thick, hot pulses of seed deep into his guts. Claiming him. Making Rhys his all over again, like he'd done in that monastery two years ago and hundreds of times since.

Rhys knelt with his chest on the bench, panting desperate breaths, when the frenzy within Darius curled up for a nap and tenderness returned. He pressed close and kissed those heaving shoulders, the perspiration-beaded spine, the knob at the back of his neck. He withdrew carefully, knowing Rhys would be sensitive, and pivoted, seating himself bare-assed on the floor and pulling Rhys into his lap. Rhys flicked a self-conscious glance across the room, where the rest of their companions were casually ignoring them, but he was obviously too fucked-out to tense up.

"You okay?" Darius whispered, nuzzling Rhys's temple. He smelled like sweat and cum and blood, and it was enough to stir another tight spasm of lust in Darius's balls, but Darius pushed it down.

"Yeah." Rhys opened his eyes to give Darius a dreamy smile, high on something more than sex, something Darius didn't understand even though he'd seen it many times before. It looked gorgeous on Rhys. Then he closed his eyes again and hid his face in Darius's neck.

"Don't fall asleep yet, boy," Darius chuckled. "You should shower and make sure your back's not bleeding before you go into that room."

"Mmm, wanna shower with me? *Hot water*," he cajoled in a singsong tone. "When's the next time we're going to get a chance to do that?"

Darius pretended to consider for a moment, then surged to his feet with Rhys in his arms. Rhys might have grown taller than Darius, and he might have put on enough muscle to make Xolani gloat, but Darius was still a Jug.

"Don't mind if I do," he said and carried Rhys down the hall.

5

SUSPICIONS

"Well, it's been three weeks, and Gilligan, Mary Ann, Ginger, and the Professor over there still don't have any traces of Bane in their blood," Zach announced once he shut the door of the bedroom/exam room behind Rhys, nodding at the test animals in their cages. "And even better news: neither do you."

"Really?" Rhys felt his heart lurch, lost somewhere between elation and dread. Now he wished he'd asked to stay out in the common room with Darius. "What does that mean?"

"First things first. The others are at the intake center right now, I know, but does Darius have any open wounds that you know of?"

Rhys shook his head. "No, none of them do. We've been sitting here cooling our heels for weeks. What could they possibly be doing to injure themselves?"

"Good point." Zach stripped off his gloves, then lifted his hands to the fastenings at the neck of his suit. With a twist and a hiss, the seal was broken, and he pulled the hood from his head.

Zach was more handsome than his brother, who Rhys could grudgingly admit had been a good-looking man. Zach's eyes had a kind, eager sparkle, though, something that Jacob's never had in all the years Rhys had lived with him. Zach's rich brown hair was dark with sweat and clung to his temples, and he took a long, deep breath once the hood was gone.

"Mercy, you don't know how long I've been wanting to do that."

"I can imagine." Rhys surprised himself by smiling. He would have thought his first unobscured view of Zach would bring back all the instinctive panic and distrust he'd felt when he'd first seen Jacob's likeness looking back at him. But three weeks had been enough time to convince him of Zach's sincerity. Rhys was even beginning to develop a hesitant respect for the quiet but heartfelt faith he made no attempt to hide, which was an entirely different animal from the terrifying dogma Father Maurice and Jacob had bludgeoned Rhys with. Wryly, Rhys stuck out his hand. "Hi, I'm Rhys. Good to meet you."

Zach grinned, revealing a dimple in his right cheek, and shook Rhys's hand without hesitation, their bare palms connecting. "I'm Zach, and I'm beyond happy to finally get to shake your hand properly."

Rhys hadn't realized what a burden it had been, living over two years thinking that even the most casual, passing encounter with him might kill another person. He was damn near giddy with relief. "So, tell me what this means. What next?"

Zach hitched one hip on the edge of the table where the

animals' cages sat. "Well, I've sent my report on to the DPRP lab, but I don't have the results yet. I'm waiting for instructions on how to proceed, though I know what the initial plan was if it got to this point."

"Lab?" Rhys frowned. "They have a lab in the Clean Zone?"

Zach shook his head. "No, it's off-site. As I understand it, they resurrected an old military research facility somewhere west of here, in anticipation of the day that they might get close enough to a vaccine to need to work with the live virus. Thanks to you, that day has come a lot sooner than anticipated."

A knot began to twist in Rhys's gut. "How?"

"Well, I have to wait for confirmation from the lab to say anything definite, but from what I can see with the equipment I have next door—and our scientists made sure I knew what to look for when I was handling the samples, so that I could report accurately and not risk corrupting the data—you have antibodies against Bane, but none of the strains of Bane itself. Which, given the fact that you've been verifiably exposed to all three strains multiple times—" Rhys had to laugh at Zach's wording. Yeah, he was pretty sure being drenched with rev blood, fucked by dozens of Jugs, and having even been bitten by a rev would count as *verifiably exposed*. "—leaves no doubt that you're the real thing. You're immune."

"So, what now?" Rhys hopped up onto the hospital bed he'd exiled himself to the first week of their stay here, swinging his legs nervously.

"Now comes a slightly more dangerous phase of testing, assuming I get the go-ahead, because we'll be dealing with the Bane virus itself. We need to get a blood sample from one of the Jugs, expose your blood directly to Bane, and watch your immune response go to work." Zach hummed thoughtfully, flipping through his papers. "After we study that, we need to take a sample from an unexposed person, infect it with Bane, and then add an antiserum made from your immunoglobulins to see if we can cobble together a sort of crude postexposure prophylaxis. We can determine if it's possible to counteract Bane exposure that way, and if so, figure out what the window of opportunity is. Then, if it happens that we get survivors who are just recently exposed, like you were when the Jugs found you, we might be able to save their lives without, um, resorting to the measures they had to take with you."

Rhys squirmed uncomfortably, and not just at the reminder of what he'd submitted to in order to survive—unnecessarily, as it now turned out. He didn't even want to begin picking apart how he felt about *that*. Better to focus on the fact that this was starting to sound dangerously similar to what Xolani had predicted.

"They're not going to . . . expect me to produce enough antiserum to protect the whole population, right?"

"No, of course not." Zach frowned, as if that thought had never even occurred to him. "That would be absurd. Even if they gave you sufficient stimulating agents to make you stroke out, you couldn't manufacture enough blood to accomplish that. Not on a long-term basis, at least."

Rhys ducked his head, wishing he was reassured. He didn't doubt that Zach meant what he'd said, but he still had Xolani's worries echoing in his ears, in addition to the fact that no one from the DPRP had yet come to introduce themselves to him, leaving everything in Zach's hands. Zach had assured them several times that he'd been rigorously trained to handle these preliminary rounds of testing during the months between Rhys being summoned and his arrival. He'd even spent several afternoons with Xolani, discussing the methodology he'd been taught and what the DPRP researchers were looking for. But the continued silence from the DPRP felt . . . shady. Like they were lying in wait to spring something unpleasant on him.

"So," he asked, casting around for a change of subject as Zach took his vital signs, "is this the work you did before the plague?"

"No." Zach smiled sadly. "I was my father's campaign adviser."

"Father Maurice was a politician?"

"He . . . lost his way. He used to be a much better man than the one you knew. Or maybe I only saw him through the lens of a child's idolization. I don't know anymore. But I learned to love God from him." He fell silent, listening to Rhys's pulse before he removed the blood pressure cuff and spoke again. "I planned to go into ministry myself, but then he got the idea to run for office, to stop calling people to God through his ministry and start trying to force them by law to live by his own morals." Zach bowed his head. "I felt I had a duty to obey, so I abandoned my plans to attend seminary to help him."

"Then how did you become a med tech?" Rhys asked while Zach jotted down his vitals, then laid out his supplies to do another blood draw.

"When I got out of quarantine, the Clean Zone was desperately short on medical personnel. I volunteered to assist one of the few doctors we had as best I could, and I realized I had a passion for helping the sick and injured."

Rhys winced and gritted his teeth as Zach slid the needle

into his vein. "It's a long way from doing field triage to doing the DPRP's busywork."

Zach kept his eyes fixed on the vials filling with blood, avoiding Rhys's gaze. "Is there a better way to help people than trying to stop the disease that destroyed humanity?"

"No, I guess not," Rhys murmured and fell silent as Zach turned away to store the vials in his case. Now he was absolutely certain that Zach had been honest with him about everything up to that point. Because now he knew what Zach looked like when he lied.

Unlike his younger brother, he wasn't very good at it.

⚠ ⚠ ⚠

"I'll kill him," Xolani muttered, pacing the common room.

"No." Rhys shook his head quickly, eager to remove any suspicion from Zach. He'd spent the whole afternoon trying to figure out how to bring up the subject while making sure such a thing didn't happen. "He isn't trying to hurt me. I'm sure of that."

Darius cupped the back of Rhys's neck, grounding him. "But you think he's lying about the work he's doing for the DPRP?"

"Definitely."

"I don't like this," Toby said, perched on the edge of the dining table, his legs swinging with restless energy. "Sure, we have liberty to mingle with the guards and go outside the perimeter, but we're still sitting in a cage. We've had Schuyler and her squad cooling their heels down by the lake for weeks now. I don't know about you people, but I'm about to climb the fuckin' walls. We did what they wanted us to do. We brought Cooper and confirmed that he was immune—which, by the way, Little Brother? Fuckin' awesome, congratulations —now let's get the hell out of here."

"Xolani?" Darius's fingers squeezed the muscles along his cervical spine lightly, the only concession to his own tension that Rhys could detect. "Got an ETA on addressing the Science Committee?"

"Well, logistics are the big holdup. When I met with the scheduling secretary earlier today, he was wearing a hermetic suit *and* standing on the other side of a glass wall at the intake center, with only microphones to carry our voices." She made a disgusted sound, taking a break from pacing to cross her arms over her chest. "At this rate, they're going to have to build a special containment facility from the ground up before they allow me in the same building with anyone from congress."

Darius grunted unhappily, and Rhys closed his eyes. There was no way they could ask Xolani to abandon her attempt to have the GDM repealed.

Titus drummed his fingers on the tabletop. "Well, we have Cooper saying Houtman 2.0 doesn't mean to hurt him. Okay, so sure, he's hiding something. Who isn't? Taking off seems a little premature if we've still got business here."

"I don't like what we've been hearing from the guards about these missing citizens." They all turned to Joe, who had kept his usual characteristic silence until that point. Rhys smiled fondly. That was the thing about Joe: he spoke so rarely that when he bothered to do so, everyone shut up and listened. "Don't buy that people are spending months in quar-antine, building up their homes inside the Clean Zone, and then running off once they've finally made a life for themselves."

"I'm more concerned that the guards don't recall them leaving," Toby added, leaning forward. "Anyone who steps outside the perimeter either has to have a permit or they have to go through quarantine again. Which means the guards keep stringent records of who's leaving and whether they're allowed to return. So it doesn't sound like the people who disappeared were documented."

"I don't like this." Xolani began to pace again. "I swear, something isn't right here. The Genetic Diversity Mandate is one thing—inseminating unwilling people? *Honestly*?—but the level of management of everyone's comings and goings is every bit as fucking sinister. What's with these intake interviews and questionnaires? What are they screening the civvies we bring to them for?"

"You don't buy that they're trying to make sure no one who has been exposed to Alpha gets in?" Darius asked.

"Oh, please." She flapped her hand dismissively. "Forget the ethical questions surrounding whether we should be spreading the Alpha strain. 1st Juggernaut Battalion's *aging*. We've had casualties. If any of our companies are screwing their civvies, they're damn well keeping the Jugs they're making."

"Think they keep the questionnaires and interview records at the intake center?" Toby gripped Joe's shoulder. "Whatever is going on, I don't believe Perimeter Security has anything to do with it. They're stand-up people. If we asked to see the records, said we were curious about, I don't know, how survivors are getting along in other parts of the country or what recovery protocols the other companies are using, or whatever excuse we want to use, maybe they'd let us read the charts."

"They said they only started the intake processing after we took down Charlie Company. That was . . . what, six years ago?" Joe frowned thoughtfully. "Couple hundred survivors a year, we're looking at about maybe twelve hundred records."

Toby shrugged. "Better than sitting around with nothing to do but play cards with the guards."

"All right, we'll do that for now," Darius said with a nod, the firm one that said he'd listened to all the input and come to a decision. "Titus, tomorrow I want you and Toby on the records. Xolani and Joe, you and I are going to take Rhys to join Schuyler and her people out by the lake. There's no reason they need to quarter him here in the quarantine ring any longer now that they know he's not shedding virus. Then, once this business with the GDM is done, we're leaving, no matter what testing they think they still need to do."

6

TRACES

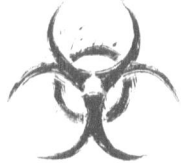

"What are you doing out here?"

That hard, inflectionless voice made Rhys's shoulders tighten, and he swallowed hard before he turned away from staring across the lake. Schuyler's arms were folded across her chest, her face set in the same bitter lines she always wore whenever she and Rhys came face-to-face.

"Nothing," he murmured. "Just looking for somewhere quiet to think."

Her jaw flexed. "With as much fuss as Darius and Xolani are making, you'd think armed commandos were going to come charging out of the Clean Zone to kidnap you. I really don't want to listen to the worry and moaning if that happens, so how about you do them all a favor and keep your ass in camp?"

Rhys's jaw dropped as he grappled to find the words to protest the petty complaint—he was close enough to camp that he could see his bedroll from the lakeshore—but she spun on her heel to stalk away before he could manage to come up with an argument.

"I miss him too, you know!" he shouted after her instead.

Schuyler went rigid. She turned slowly back around, her face flushed and her eyes promising violence. "Don't you *dare*—"

"Don't I dare what? Kaleo was my friend. He didn't have to be, but he was nice to me when I was scared and didn't really have anyone, and I miss him. And yeah, I should have told someone a lot sooner just what a monster Jacob could turn out to be, and maybe if I had, Kaleo would still be alive, but I was *afraid*, all right?" He balled his shaking hands into fists at his sides. "I was surrounded by a bunch of strangers who didn't really seem to care what I wanted or how I felt. The guy who'd made my life hell for seven years was telling them I was a troublemaker and then promising to kill me if I got in his way. As far as I was concerned, whenever it came down to his word against mine, *he* always won." He scowled at her, his eyes burning as the memory of his loneliness and quiet despair washed over him. "Was I supposed to take the chance that no one would believe me?"

One white corner of her mouth lifted in a bitter sneer. "So you were covering your own ass. Maybe someone should have filled you in that that's not how we do things in Delta Company."

"Oh, come off it!" For once, anger flushed away the guilt that inevitably accompanied thoughts of Jacob and Kaleo. "How was I supposed to know he could be a danger to one of *you*? You were *Jugs*. If I'd ever thought he could hurt anyone but me, I would have said something."

She shook her head. "Well, that's a nice story to make yourself feel better about it all, now that he's gone, isn't it?"

She turned to walk away again, and Rhys closed his eyes, futility and grief hanging heavy in his chest. But his mouth apparently hadn't gotten the message that it was useless, and he called after her, "So what story do you tell yourself to feel better about the fact that Kaleo shouldn't have been there with us in the first place? You're the one who refused to let him patrol with your squad. Yeah, he told me all about that. How your sense of authority couldn't handle his teasing, so you wouldn't have him under your command."

"One more word, Cooper," she hissed, her entire body quivering and her fists clenched as she kept her back to him. "Just one more."

He planted his feet before he could take a flinching step back. His days of being pushed around and blamed for things that weren't his fault had ended when Father Maurice and Jacob had died, and it was time he proved it.

"I'm not afraid of you. If you're grasping for someone to blame, take a look at yourself. Look at Xolani for insisting on saving me and Jacob. Look at Darius for giving it the okay." His throat tightened, and he swallowed against the knot there. "Kaleo was my friend, and I miss him. And it's not my fault he's dead."

He turned back to the lake, his body braced, waiting for her attack, but it never came. When he glanced behind him, Schuyler was gone. He slumped, leaning against a tree trunk to stare out across the reservoir for another moment before following her back to camp. Once there, he stood on the outskirts, watching as, on the far side of the clearing, Emmy spoke with Schuyler. Emmy stood closer than Rhys could remember Schuyler ever letting someone get, her mouth almost brushing Schuyler's bowed head. Whatever she said was inaudible, but then she squeezed Schuyler's shoulder and guided her away from camp. Schuyler didn't look back, but Emmy did. Her eyes found Rhys's, and she gave him a kind smile, then disappeared with Schuyler into the trees.

Something rustled in the brush behind him, and Rhys half turned, trying to smile when he saw Darius standing there. "Hi. Did I wander too far?"

Darius shook his head. "Nah." He took Rhys's hand and tugged, leading him into the clearing. "Gather up our bedrolls and packs while I have a word with Xolani. I'll be right there."

Xolani was practicing with her knives on the far side of camp when Darius leaned down to murmur something in her ear. Her eyebrows came up in surprise, but she nodded, then turned back to throwing knives into the bull's-eye of a roughly carved target in the bark of a tree.

"Come on." Darius shouldered his pack and gave Rhys's elbow a gentle tug, and he fell into step with Darius. He didn't turn back, even as the sun began to descend, the shadows growing taller as Darius led him along hilly, disused roads around the outskirts of the city.

Something about the heavy quality of Darius's silence got to him, leaving him with the need to fill it. "So I guess you heard what I said to Schuyler."

"Yup." Darius turned his head just enough to give a quick nod.

"You were the one who said I should forgive myself for Kaleo dying."

"Yeah, I did."

"But I was out of line, turning it back on her like that."

Darius looked sideways at him, then shrugged. "Schuyler's a damn fine soldier, but Kaleo dying was one hit too many. And maybe you weren't far off target."

"No. It wasn't her fault. I was grasping—"

"That's not what I'm sayin'. It wasn't anyone's fault except Houtman's. But you can be damn sure she's already wondered if Kaleo would still be alive if she'd kept him with her."

"I'm sorry." Rhys let his head fall back, drawing in several deep breaths. "Not that you're the person I should be saying that to. I should go back to apologize."

Darius's stride didn't so much as slow down or falter. "That's not what we're out here for. Keep walking."

With no choice but to follow or try to find his way back as twilight drew nearer, Rhys did as he was told.

"Where are we going?" he finally asked, as Darius's route took them south of the Clean Zone, closer to where the original survivor settlements outside Cheyenne Mountain had been.

"Nowhere but here, least for tonight." By now, the sun was behind the mountains to the west, the sky a dusky blue-gray and getting darker all the time. "We won't get where we're going until tomorrow afternoon."

He gave Darius a quizzical half-smile as Darius eased Rhys's pack off his shoulders before shrugging off his own. "So our destination is top secret? You could tell me, but then you'd have to kill me?"

Darius grinned and grabbed a handful of Rhys's ass, pulling him closer for a kiss full of tongue and teeth. "You'll find out when we get there. Just lay out our bedrolls, boy, while I get a fire going."

△△△

No amount of pestering could convince Darius to tell Rhys where they were going. Nor did sexual favors, which Rhys was only too happy to attempt. Afterward, when he lay draped over Darius's chest, aching in all sorts of pleasant ways and trying to remember how to breathe steadily, he tried another tack.

"Can I at least know *why* we're going off by ourselves?"

Darius made a grumbling sound, and his entire torso shifted beneath Rhys's as he shrugged. "Guess I figured you might like some time away from camp. Never got to see much of the world, did you?"

Rhys bit his lip against the rush of questions trying to bubble up as he lifted his head to stare. Was Darius trying to be *romantic*?

That . . . was a very uncomfortable thought.

"Got something to say?" Darius's expression was neutral as he caught Rhys's gaze. It was a studiously blank look that Rhys knew well, the sort Darius gave the people he commanded when he was waiting for them to figure something out on their own, or at least ask the right questions.

Rhys turned away so Darius wouldn't see him frown. It felt like Darius was waiting for something from him, expecting Rhys to say . . . He didn't even know what. Two years they'd been together and it had never been about overused words or easy sentimentality. Emotion, yes. God, yes, there was emotion to spare, but none of it would ever fit under the neat little labels people used to categorize their attachments to one another.

Rhys made himself smile and lifted his head. "I guess I can

handle being alone with you for a couple days," he teased, trying to shake off the feeling that his nonanswer might disappoint Darius. He nipped Darius's pec, instead, and made him twitch. "No one around to hear when you make me scream."

"You'll be doing plenty of that, boy," Darius growled, flipping them so that he had Rhys pinned beneath him. Rhys squirmed and shifted until his thighs bracketed Darius's hips, their stiffening cocks lining up alongside one another. He gripped Darius's shoulders and whimpered as a firm bite on his neck threatened to raise a bruise. "I'll see to it."

⚐ ⚐ ⚐

THE SIGN at the entrance to the park identified the place as Seven Falls. Or, more accurately, SciDoc Seven Falls. Darius grunted when he saw it, and Rhys gave him a questioning look.

"I was a kid when they started selling off the state and national parks to corporate 'sponsors.' The ones they hadn't already sold for oil and mineral rights, that is," he explained, gesturing for Rhys to precede him along the overgrown road leading into the park. "Pissed my daddy right off. Said it would mean the few places we could afford to visit would get more expensive. He was right. By the time I was out of school, we couldn't go to a lake, or camping, or anywhere to get away from home for a few days. Not that my daddy shut his shop down often, anyway."

Rhys found himself smiling, the way he always did when Darius shared bits of his life before the plague. He fell back a step to walk alongside Darius. "So what is this place?"

Darius shrugged. "Just what it says. Seven Falls. It's kinda pretty. Thought you might like to see it."

They emerged from the treelined drive, and Rhys looked up at the cliff face revealed in the clearing. A series of waterfalls tumbled down, one after the other, split by outcroppings of rock, until the water ran away into a river below a man-made vantage point.

Nature was aggressively working to reclaim what SciDoc and the rest of humanity had done to the landscape. Signs that had once flashed advertisements were being consumed by undergrowth, and pavement was being eaten by weeds tirelessly forcing their way up between cracks formed by the summer and winter extremes. The stairs that had been built alongside the falls were crumbling.

It was pretty, or it would have been if the hand of man wasn't still so obvious everywhere. "I think it'll look better once nature has a few more years to go at it," Rhys said with a wry smirk.

Darius huffed a soft laugh. "Guess that's true."

"Is this what you brought me to see?"

"Nah." Darius stared up at the falls. His jaw was set in the way that meant he was uncomfortable but too stalwart to squirm. "I mean, I guess I brought you to look around, not at this really, but just—something to get away. Take a break from everything for a few days. Like a vacation."

"Oh. Thank you." The silence between them felt laden with something Rhys wasn't sure he wanted to identify. More and more, this sort of tension crept up between them, like there were things that needed to be said that neither of them had words for. At least not words they were comfortable speaking.

Rhys turned back to watch the falls, trying for a more neutral topic. "I can't remember where we went for vacation before the plague—if we did. I remember my mom always being busy with grading papers and tests. What did my dad do?" He paused a beat. "Shit. I can't remember." He stopped in his tracks and gave Darius a searching gaze. "I can't remember what my dad did."

Darius's eyes were gentle. Understanding. Full of that unguarded look Rhys had been getting from him with increasing frequency. "It was a long time ago. You were just a kid when it all went to hell."

"Went to hell" was a good way to put it. That had been the reality of life immediately after the plague. Everything worth having had been looted, revenants were everywhere, and if the revs or the Rot didn't kill you, other survivors might, just to keep you from poaching their supplies or possibly infecting them.

"I was old enough that I should remember more than that," Rhys grumbled. He tried to remember what his dad had looked like, that moment when he'd told Rhys's mother and him to take Cady and run, but his face was a blur. Darius caught Rhys by the arm and tugged him closer.

"Some of us have pasts worth hangin' on to." He cupped the back of Rhys's neck, squeezing. "Makes it easier to face each day, remembering how things used to be. The rest of us block it out, shut it down. 'Cause we could lose ourselves in it."

"Which one are you?" He thought he knew, given how rarely Darius spoke of his past, but something compelled him to ask anyway.

Darius sighed. "My life wasn't bad, and it wasn't so great

that I can't stand to think about it now. But it's past, and I never found that a good place to live. Until lately, I got through the days by doin' what needed to be done to keep my people alive."

"Until lately?" Drawn by the need to examine the weight of those two words, the question slipped out before Rhys could filter it. Life under the tender mercies of Father Maurice and Jacob had taught him better than that. When you found a fragile bit of peace, you trod carefully around it. You didn't poke at it. You didn't goad Fate into taking it away from you. You accepted that things were okay for now and tried to enjoy it before they got bad again.

Darius lifted his eyes to look up at the falls again, pulling away from Rhys to stuff his hands in his pockets. The expression on his face was . . . unlike anything Rhys had ever expected to see, even in their most tender moments. Wistfulness. Happiness. Even, maybe, vulnerability? Rhys stared, transfixed.

"Now I get through the days thinking about my boy. How to keep him safe. How to make him happy." It was a long moment before Darius glanced over at Rhys again, and the look in his eyes was so raw and intent that Rhys wanted to hide from it. "How to give him a life."

"Darius—" How could he even begin to respond to that? It didn't feel like he could get enough air to speak.

"I want you to promise me something." The naked expression on Darius's face shut down like a portcullis falling. Even his posture changed, and he moved away from Rhys the slightest bit, stiffening. Becoming like the stern, uncompromising man who had first rescued him from that rev attack two years ago. "I want you to consider—*really* consider—staying here. With the civvies."

"No. I won't. I don't belong here." *I belong with you* were the words Rhys wanted to speak, to give Darius something back for what he'd shared, but they were locked on his tongue. That miserable sense of failure was churning in his gut the way it had the night before. Darius was offering him something, and he couldn't offer anything back.

"You could, if you tried. You're not a danger to anyone." Darius swallowed hard and looked away. "In a few years, we'll be moving on from Lewis-McChord. And a couple years after that, we'll be moving on again. Fact is, Rhys, I'll probably be an old man before the Jugs can settle down anywhere we could call home. That's the way it has to be for us. But it doesn't have to be that way for you. You could have a *home*."

Rhys's throat felt too tight and thick to speak for a moment, but then he shook his head. "I don't need to be here for that."

Darius's shoulders slumped. "Never having a place to settle down? What kind of life is that?"

"Fort Vancouver wasn't home because it was a *place*."

"Just promise me you'll give it some thought."

Rhys shook his head once, firmly. "I can't. I'd be lying if I made that promise. I'm with you, and that's the way it is."

Darius chuckled, a wry, resigned sound. "Stubborn little shit. One of these days I'll win an argument with you."

Rhys smiled and shrugged. "You don't want to win this one."

"No. Guess I don't." There was a small pause, heavy, as if Darius was tempted to say more. His gaze—and his shoulders—dropped. Just for a split second. In that almost imperceptible instant, he seemed burdened, uncertain. But then he turned and looked around, and the straight, proud, sure man Rhys was used to was back. "Come on. Let's head north around the old city. We'll go see the Garden of the Gods. Maybe the corporations didn't do as much damage there."

7

MARKS

Darius took his time leading Rhys to the scenic points surrounding Colorado Springs. He wasn't sure why the impromptu walkabout seemed like a good idea. He'd just wanted Rhys away from camp, away from Schuyler and the Clean Zone and the DPRP's tests and prodding. Except for the trip to Colorado Springs, he and Rhys hadn't left Fort Vancouver together since hunting down Jacob Houtman. And they had never been anywhere together when Darius wasn't leading his squadron.

Being alone, *truly* alone, with Rhys was different. Darius's attention was fixed on his boy, undivided by the requirements of a patrol or manhunt. He wasn't being called away to confer with Luis. Rhys wasn't spending most of his days in the warehouses. The truth was, though they'd been together for two years, they'd spent more time apart than they had with each other.

Was Rhys as content with that life as he seemed to be? His assurances that he wanted to stay always seemed to be missing something. He spoke of being where he belonged, but he never spoke of being happy or wanting to be there. Was his life with Darius and Delta Company simply such an improvement from the way he'd lived before, under Houtman and his father, that he'd rather settle than rock the boat?

Fuck. Darius wanted more for Rhys than that. He wanted to *be* more for Rhys than that, but even if he couldn't, he wanted Rhys to have what would make him happy.

On their own, they talked in a way they didn't usually, sharing details they'd never gotten around to discussing about their pasts and their families. Even when they were at Fort Vancouver, they hadn't talked like this. When Darius was on base, being together was urgent. Darius was often gone for weeks or months on patrol, and he only came back for a few days to deliver civilians to the quarantine or reprovision his squad before heading out again. What time he and Rhys managed to steal always passed in a frenzy to touch and taste and fuck as much as possible.

They still fucked now, but they could take their time with it. They could be slow and easy, and there was no one for miles to hear their cries and shouts and groans. Darius could stop them in the middle of the day to back Rhys against a tree and kneel at his feet, leisurely sucking Rhys's dick while the afternoon moved on without them.

And he could rise afterward and gently press Rhys to his knees to return the favor, staring down into those hazel eyes while Rhys licked his balls and pulled them into his mouth. Rhys's eyes crinkled at the corners before they drifted shut, the expression on his face sublime as he brought Darius to the brink and then sucked him over the edge.

Other times, he would shove Rhys, chest-first, against a

stone outcropping, strip his pants down in a few rough movements, and slam into him in little more time than it took to dig the lube out of his pocket. And when that happened, the sounds Rhys made would echo off rock walls and send clusters of birds flapping out of the trees, squawking indignantly.

They spent three days at the Garden of the Gods, taking in the beauty of the towering rock formations and ignoring the crumbling remnants of human intrusion. It took three days because Darius couldn't bring himself to make them move along.

"Won't we need to return to camp soon?" Rhys asked as Darius removed a hot towel from around Rhys's face and dropped it in the pot of simmering water near the campfire. His head was tipped back as he reclined against a boulder. His lips were still puffy, and his breath carried the scent of Darius's spunk in the early-morning chill.

Darius shook his head. "I told Xolani that if the Science Committee scheduled her address, to go ahead and give it and then take everyone and head to Seattle. We can catch up. We're in no rush."

Rhys frowned but kept his head still as Darius began to brush foam around his cheeks and jaw. "What about the DPRP tests?"

"I meant what I said before. Once Xolani says her piece, we're leaving. You gave them all the help they should need. It's time to go. Be still, now."

An intense awareness arced between them whenever he shaved Rhys. It was enough to make Darius's pulse race a little faster, though his hand was steady. He lifted the meticulously honed straight razor to Rhys's face and began to draw it through the stubble there. The thump of Rhys's heart was visible beneath the lean muscles of his naked chest, and his breath came quick and shallow. The closer Darius came to Rhys's throat, to the thin skin covering the vulnerable arteries, the more powerful the building charge became. It had been there from the very first time Darius had shaved Rhys, and it had never faded.

He held Rhys's life in his hands. He always had, since they'd first met. He'd held it in his hands when he'd fucked Rhys, trying to infect him with the Alpha strain to counteract his exposure to Beta or Gamma. He'd held it in his hands when he'd made Rhys accept the sexual attentions of the rest of the men in his squad to maximize his chance of exposure.

He'd definitely held it in his hands the morning he woke to find himself with a knife at Rhys's throat as Rhys screamed himself awake from a nightmare. He'd cut Rhys then. Not intentionally, but Rhys's response hadn't been fear at how close he'd come to death. It had been arousal. He'd kissed Darius that morning, inhaling him as if Darius were the air he needed to live.

That was the day Darius realized just how intimate Rhys's connection to his own mortality was. He'd been living on borrowed time since he was a kid, and in those seconds when his life hung in the balance, he finally let go of everything he'd been holding back whenever Darius touched him. He'd given in, given *everything*.

Rhys no longer relied on Darius for his survival the way he had then, when he'd been terrorized and half-starved and so damned fragile Darius had been afraid of breaking him. But there was still something heady in the moments like this, when the blood rushed beneath the dangerous edge of Darius's blade. Rhys was hard, the swell of his dick inching the zipper of his fatigues down, which he hadn't bothered to button when Darius told him to sit for his shave. His eyes were closed, his lashes fluttering, and a soft moan vibrated his larynx against Darius's knuckles.

Even after two years of security and stability, Rhys sometimes needed to feel close to death. He needed the prospect of his own mortality to be something he could embrace rather than fear.

"Want me to bleed you?" Darius asked, forcing the words out through a throat that felt too thick. He could already taste the copper tang, the carnal instinct that Rhys brought out in him roaring to life. He was hungry for it, hungry enough that he might have pulled back and tried to rein it in, but the need in Rhys's eyes made him set it loose, instead. It was that hungry, feral thing in Darius that Rhys craved now.

"You know I do," he whispered.

Of course he did. They didn't do this often—truthfully, Darius was afraid of how far they might go if they made a frequent habit of it—but it was always the same. When the last of the stubble was gone, his blade slipped, made just the tiniest nick, more symbolic than anything. But then that sweet, primal iron flavor was on Darius's tongue, and Rhys was rutting against him. His fingers clawed at Darius's shoulders and back when their mouths found each other, sharing the faint taste.

Darius was so intent on getting to Rhys's cock that he didn't notice that Rhys had taken up the straight razor he had set aside. At least not until Rhys pushed him back ever so slightly. His hazel eyes were feverish, his pupils huge. His chest and cheeks were flushed, sweat trickling down his temples, and his eyes weren't on Darius's, but on the skin of his throat.

"What do you think you're doing, boy?" Darius rasped between pants.

"Your blood's no danger to me." His gaze drifted up to meet Darius's. "I mean, I guess that was always the case before, but now we know—"

Darius closed his hand over Rhys's, which trembled in his grasp. He drew the razor closer to his own skin and pressed it against the muscle just below his collarbone, twitching at the chill of the steel. Then he went still, waiting.

A small flick of Rhys's hand, and he felt the blade catch on his flesh. Almost painless, but he winced anyway. They both stared at the welling spot of blood as Rhys fumbled to set the razor aside again without taking his eyes from it. He licked his lips and leaned forward, and Darius shuddered to feel the sting of Rhys's tongue pressing on the tiny wound.

That was all. Just that one taste, and then Rhys was scrambling for Darius's mouth, straddling Darius's lap to get their flies open and grasp their cocks together. Darius rocked, but Rhys was in the driver's seat, humping, thrusting, generating friction as their cocks slid against each other in his grip. Rhys opened wide to Darius's tongue and met it with his own, his teeth firm against Darius's lips, the noises rising from his throat hungry. His other hand twisted in Darius's unbound hair, and they ground together urgently until, one after the other, they pumped seemingly endless streams of cum between their bellies.

Afterward, Rhys wrapped himself around Darius and clung to him unusually tight, like he was shaken and needed shelter and safety to pull himself back together. Darius was happy to provide it, to wait kneeling on the hard ground until

Rhys finally drew back and looked at him with wide, stunned eyes.

"I don't know why I just did that," he said, clearing his throat and blinking, as if coming out of a trance.

Darius huffed an affectionate laugh, refusing to let go. "I do." Rhys's brow furrowed as he waited for Darius to explain. "Since we got that summons for you from the Clean Zone in the fall, you've been tryin' to tell me not to treat you like you're weaker. Nothin' to do with you not being a Jug, just weaker in general, you know?" He traced his fingers down Rhys's spine, mapping each bumpy ridge. "You've been determined to make your own decisions. You won't let me shield you, won't let me decide what's best for you. You're not that scared kid we found in the monastery. And sure, I can hurt you and cut you, because you allow that. You want it. But you can cut me too. If you wanted to."

He searched Rhys's eyes, wondering if Rhys understood that he wasn't talking about the razor anymore. For months, the ground between them had been shifting, becoming more level. Rhys frowned, but he relaxed into Darius again, laying his head on Darius's shoulder. "I *don't* want to. I never have."

"No." Darius shifted to take the burden off his knees, sitting on his ass and holding Rhys in his lap. "But maybe it's important to know that you *can*."

🔺 🔺 🔺

RHYS WAS quiet the rest of the day as they left the Garden of the Gods behind and began picking their way through the ruined and uninhabited portions of Colorado Springs. It would take a couple more days to get back to camp, if they kept up their leisurely pace, and Darius tried not to be disappointed that their time alone together was ending.

That night, Rhys sat on their bedrolls as Darius lay behind him, staring into the fire, his knees drawn up to his chest. It was a long while before he spoke. "If I asked you to mark me, the way Joe is marked, would you?"

Darius frowned. Rhys had practically turned green the first time he'd seen the scars on Joe's skin. Before the plague, Joe's husband had carved words into his flesh—slurs and insults that appealed to Joe's well-known humiliation kink. Toby had never added to those, but he'd left his own marks, as well. Typically burns.

"I've left marks on you." Darius dragged his fingers down Rhys's back, where under his shirt, the faintest scattering of silvery lines remained from times when whipping Rhys had left welts that had split the skin.

"Barely." Rhys turned to look over his shoulder. "Would you?"

"Are you asking me to?"

"I don't know. I just wondered if it's something you'd consider."

"Guess that depends on if you'd really want it. And why."

"It scares me." The shiver that ran down Rhys's spine under Darius's fingers testified to the truth of his words. "Makes me ashamed. Advertising it—the things we do—like Toby and Joe. It shouldn't, I know. Everyone knows. Your squad has seen it, and I've stopped minding about that, but the rest of Delta Company . . . Since it's been just you and me, we've kept it all private. I've been comfortable with that."

"Then why ask?"

"I don't know. I can't stop thinking about it." With a

disgruntled sound, Rhys turned and lay down beside Darius, facing him. "Maybe it's like you said earlier, about wanting to prove I'm not weaker. No one would think Joe wasn't as strong as Toby. I may be taller than you now, but I'll never be as strong. I'll never be a Jug."

The tension in his voice made Darius sit up, looking down at Rhys. "That's a problem?" he asked, frowning.

"No. Yes. Hell, Darius, I don't know." Rhys rolled away, but Darius grabbed his shoulder and rolled him back.

"Spit it out, boy. What's going on?"

Rhys pressed his lips together, plucking at the blankets of their bedroll. "I— I guess I— I think I always held out for it, you know? That maybe one day the Alpha strain would just . . . take hold. Then I'd really be one of you. I wouldn't just be your 'pet civvie.'"

Did Rhys hear how much bitterness bled into his voice on those last words? It made Darius's jaw clench, not in anger at Rhys but at the rare but persistent remarks, both subtle and overt, that had left Rhys feeling that way.

"Anything you had to prove, Rhys, you've proved."

His shoulder was tense beneath Darius's stroking hand, rigid. "Have I?" Rhys's eyes sought out Darius's in the firelight. "Because it sure feels like a lot of people are waiting for me to slip up and demonstrate that I'm not one of you."

Darius watched him a long moment as Rhys's hands twitched restlessly. "This is still about Schuyler, ain't it?"

"Not *just* about her." His eyes darted around, unwilling to meet Darius's again.

"Maybe you're the one who feels you don't fit."

"Says the man who tried to convince me to leave and go live with a bunch of strangers."

Ouch. He had that coming. Still . . . "I want you to have a future."

Rhys shook his head as if dismissing the idea. "I just want today not to be awful. That's all I need. And when I'm with you, it's not."

The words, spoken so simply and with such complete candor, made Darius's chest tighten. His boy set the bar for happiness so low. A little kindness. A little affection. Some pleasure and maybe some pain, so long as Rhys got to choose it himself. It wasn't right, and Darius shouldn't let him settle the way he was. He should make Rhys demand more for himself, but Darius was selfish enough that he couldn't, no matter how much he knew he should.

He planted his hands on either side of Rhys, caging him in.

"And I won't ever let it be, if I can help it," Darius promised instead, punctuating the vow with a short, hard kiss. "You ever come to me and say you want my marks on you because it's what *you* want, I'll give you anything you ask for. But not if it's to make a point to anyone else. We ever do that, it's gonna mean something just between you and me."

8

SCHEMES

Contrary to Darius's hopes, everyone they'd traveled to Colorado Springs with was still at the lakeside camp when they returned from their walkabout. Xolani was fuming because her address to the Congressional Science Committee had been put off due to scheduling conflicts.

"I don't understand," Rhys said as the sun sank, staring into the fire from where he sat next to Xolani. Titus and Toby were curled on their bedrolls across camp, while Joe and Darius had disappeared into the woods to patrol the perimeter. The light of the fire Schuyler's squadron was clustered around flickered some ways down the reservoir, tiny in the distance. "Why did they postpone it?"

Xolani made a disgusted sound, tossing twigs into the fire. "I think all this running around and logistical crap is a delaying tactic. They have no intention of hearing me. They just want to keep us around because they know that when we leave, you go with us."

"*Why*? Why won't they even consider rescinding the GDM if they've got a viable population?"

The gaze she turned on him was one of affectionate pity, and it filled Rhys's heart with worry. Xolani never looked down on him, never made him feel intolerably naive. She might tell him outright that he was being a dumbass, but she didn't condescend.

"Rhys," she said gently, and there was something bleak in her demeanor. "Have you noticed anything about the Clean Zone population, at least what little you've seen of it? About the survivors we rescue and how they're . . . different than we are?"

"Um, no?"

One corner of her mouth lifted, but she didn't seem amused. "They almost all look like you."

"Like me?"

"They're *white*, Rhys. And the Jugs are mostly people of color—Black, Latino, Asian, Middle Eastern, indigenous . . . Now, that's because we're military, and that was one of the few career paths open to us that had any hope of advancement. It kept us out of tenement serfdom. It offered some of us an opportunity to, say, go to med school." She smiled tightly, then turned her face away from him, and the next twig she threw into the flames was launched with a particularly violent motion. "But the brown people who weren't military? They were in cheap, overcrowded housing. They were the people who didn't have the money for supplies to isolate themselves while the first wave of the plague ripped through the population. They were the people who were shot on sight for being out of quarantine and for looting when they tried to scavenge for supplies. The people who survived the plague, besides the Jugs, are mostly wealthy white people."

Rhys frowned and wrapped his arms around his knees. He thought about all the survivors he'd seen come through quarantine in his two years with the Jugs and realized she was right. The difference was so marked it was amazing he hadn't noticed before. "Okay. But I'm not sure I understand what that has to do with the GDM."

"Think about it," she said briskly. "You have a white population who doesn't really dare go anywhere outside their settlement, while out in the world are these groups of mostly brown people doing things that they don't know about. And the white people *rely* on the brown people to exterminate the revs and bring in more survivors, which puts them in a position of weakness. Those brown people are armed, trained, and *not answerable to them*." She made a horrified, aghast face, then sneered. "What's worse, some of them have a major grudge about being exiled. Sooner or later, they're going to come together and form their own settlement. That has to be pretty intimidating. And traditionally, when white people decide that they're afraid of brown people, it doesn't go well for the brown people."

"But you're Jugs. You can defend yourselves."

Xolani shrugged. "Definitely. And if they go on the offensive against us, we'll shut that shit down fast. We're more capable of defending ourselves than our ancestors were, and a fuck of a lot less trusting. But that also makes us more threatening."

Rhys blinked. "What do they think you'll do?"

"Does it matter? What happened with Charlie Company aside, they don't have to have a defined threat." She shook her head, picking up another twig to snap. "They *exiled* us. And now, all they need to stir up panic is to intimate that there is *something dangerous* in the fact that we're out there and we're stronger than them. That we can't be trusted. And our weakness is that our numbers are limited."

Rhys nodded. He'd been there the day Xolani had informed Emmy that she would have to abort the baby she had been carrying when she'd been infected. Childbirth involved blood, she'd explained, and so any infant a Jug delivered would be infected with the Rot as it was being born. "So you think that's the reason for the GDM? They're trying to explode the Clean Zone's population, balance the Jugs' strength with numbers?"

"Possibly. Let's be charitable and assume it's purely defensive. Maybe they think if they grow their population fast enough, they'll have sufficient forces if we attack." Xolani's scarred cheek flexed. "In that case, my attempts to have the GDM repealed could look like a subtle strategic maneuver. It might seem like I'm trying to discourage them from achieving tactical parity. Which would then make them wonder what we have to gain by such a ploy, what we're up to out there where they can't keep an eye on us." She sighed heavily, her shoulders slumping. "Then we become even more threatening. Now, if they took the long-term view, all they would need to do is wait a couple generations for us to die out. But who knows what we could get up to in the meantime? The best defense is a good offense."

Rhys swallowed. "But they couldn't seriously mean to attack you?"

"I don't know what they intend. And honestly, I don't know what *we* would do if they did go on the offensive." She gave him a bleak look. "A lot of us resent the fuck out of them for the way they treated us after the overthrow, but we don't want to fight them. We *can't*. It's too risky. They're the only ones who can reproduce." She snorted bitterly. "*They're* the fucking hope of humanity."

He wanted to ask more questions, but Xolani cut him off with an impatient gesture. "This is too fucking frustrating to talk about. Go to bed, kid. Zach said he'd be here early to check if you and Darius were back, so you need to be all fresh and ready to be poked and prodded again in the morning."

▲ ▲ ▲

RHYS ALMOST FORGOT about what he and Darius had done when they were alone together out on their walkabout until Zach made a distressed sound when he took off his shirt.

"Oh God. *Rhys.*" Zach's voice cracked, and when Rhys spun around, he had tears in his eyes. He was whispering under his breath, and it took Rhys a moment to make out the almost-inaudible prayer. "What do I do? Lord, I don't know what to do."

"Stop that!" Rhys jerked away and yanked his shirt back on, suddenly feeling exposed. They had stepped away from camp to talk and do the exam, but Zach's reaction still made him self-conscious. Grappling for some dignity, Rhys looked around at the trees. Propped against one was a bicycle Zach said he rode to get around the Clean Zone when he was doing interviews and exams for the DPRP.

"I can't do it," Zach murmured, his voice heavy with grief. Then louder, as though making a declaration. "God help me, I can't do it."

"Can't do *what*?"

Zach wiped his eyes and sat on the ground, hunched over in defeat. "Can't ask of you what I was planning to ask."

"Zach, I don't expect you to understand, but I *like* it when Darius does this. I ask him to do it. Literally." Rhys clenched his fists when Zach shook his head in denial. "I do! You don't get it. This is *my choice*. I want it, and I'm not going to let you make me feel wrong for that, not when I've just gotten to the point where I don't hear your dad telling me what a pervert I am every time I let myself *be myself*."

The hope in Zach's eyes was strange. Almost like it wasn't about Rhys at all. "Really?" His voice was still dubious. "I just don't understand. After what you say my father did to you . . ."

"This is different."

"Why?"

Rhys threw up his hands, pacing across the clearing. "I don't know. It just is. Does it matter?" He planted his hands on his hips and spun to face Zach. "I'm telling you I want this, that I'm okay with it. More than okay. I *choose* to do this. You don't need to understand my reasons, even if I could explain them."

"I'm sorry." Zach put his head down on his drawn-up knees, and Rhys suspected he was praying again. "It's just . . . I was going to ask for your help with something, but I don't want to see you victimized. Not after what my father did to you, and especially not if Darius is—"

"He's *not*," Rhys growled. "And maybe you should tell me what you were going to ask and let me make my own choice about it rather than just assuming I'm a victim."

Zach didn't look up at first. Whatever it was he was praying about, he was praying hard. But finally, he lifted his head. "Secretary Littlewood is a monster. And I was going to ask for your help stopping him."

"Tell me . . ." Rhys dropped down to the earth and sat directly in front of Zach, locking eyes with him. "Everything."

Zach swallowed hard and nodded. His lashes were spiky, and his expression conflicted. "I . . . knew someone. After the first wave of the pandemic. Before the overthrow. He had been a pros—a *sex worker* before everything fell apart. And one time, he was hired to seduce Secretary Littlewood. Only, it turned out that Littlewood wasn't what he appeared to be." Zach shuddered. "The man I knew said he was a predator of the most dangerous sort, and the only thing keeping him from being deadly was that he had too much to lose if he was caught."

Zach took a deep breath, tracing patterns with his finger in the reddish dirt. "Before the overthrow, there was a series of violent rapes of young men here in the Clean Zone. There was even one fatality. That one stays with me. He was brutalized so badly internally that we had to either euthanize him or watch him die a slow, painful death." He looked off into the distance, his eyes haunted. "We never found out who did it, but the doctor I worked with suspected it was someone living inside Cheyenne Mountain, because the attacks stopped when the Jugs laid siege to the underground facility. But when the military government surrendered and my . . . Nico saw the people who came out, he realized Littlewood had made it here. He was sure Littlewood was the rapist."

"Did he start attacking people again?"

"Not right away. I think it's like Nico said: he has too much to lose. His role in green-lighting Project Juggernaut was advisory rather than executive, so he escaped facing charges there, but he was trying to set up a political career in the new civilian government and he had to keep his nose clean." Zach licked his lips and fell silent a moment before plunging on. "But eventually, the Clean Zone Congress established the DPRP and he ended up spearheading the department. He activated the off-site lab and handpicked the research staff. And young men started disappearing."

"Disappearing? You mean the people Perimeter Security have been talking about?"

"Some of them. There are— It's difficult to explain. There seem to be two groups of people going missing. One is comprised of men and women of varying ages. The other is comprised of boys in their mid- to late teens, maybe early twenties." Zach frowned, fidgeting. "And it all seems to be part of the same trend, except that if you look at the missing people as a single group, you'll see it's disproportionately made up of young men of a certain type."

Rhys rubbed the back of his neck, looking around. Now he wished he hadn't asked for privacy while he and Zach talked and did the usual examination. He was just some guy who'd spent his entire life in almost complete isolation. Surely the Jugs would be better qualified to give Zach help or advice or whatever he was seeking.

"The Clean Zone must have some sort of police force, right? What do they have to say about it?"

Zach looked bleak. "That people get restless or rebellious. Adolescent boys, in particular. They say that what we're seeing is probably no more than kids deciding life in the Clean Zone was too confined and restrictive, striking out for adventure. No one is taking it seriously, and I can't figure out if it's a cover-up or just naïveté."

"Are you sure it's *not* just . . . restlessness?"

"I knew one of the boys to go missing more recently," Zach whispered, bowing his head. "Adrian. He was in my Bible study. Just sixteen years old. He'd spent his life in a colony in the South, where some of the elders were abusive. I imagine it was much the same sort of situation you lived in with my father and brother." His eyes shimmered when he looked up. "He was so *glad* to be here, Rhys. *Grateful.* He finally felt safe and like he'd found people who wouldn't mistreat him. He had a girlfriend. He was getting schooling for the first time in his life, and he was so eager to learn and make a life for himself. He wouldn't have run off; I know it."

Zach fell silent, and Rhys stared down at his hands in his lap.

"The same sort of situation you lived in with my father and brother."

What if things had happened differently two years ago when the Jugs found him in that monastery? What if the revenants hadn't attacked? What if he hadn't been exposed to the Beta and Gamma strains of the virus, condemned to death? What if, instead of trying to make him a Jug, Darius's squadron had just quarantined him like the rest of the civvies and shipped him off when the time came?

The boy Zach was talking about, Adrian, could have been Rhys. He would have felt the same way, coming here to the Clean Zone as a civilian refugee. So damned grateful to be out of that situation that life in the Clean Zone would have seemed like paradise, even with all its obvious faults. He wouldn't have wanted to leave, either.

He sighed. "What is it you were going to ask me to do for you?"

"You have to understand, Rhys. I have no proof of any of this. None. Just Nico's word about what Littlewood is. But I *absolutely* believe Nico, and there is no one within the Clean Zone, except maybe Gillett Morris, whom I would trust to help me with this. And I can't ask Gillett because I don't know if any of his Perimeter Security people are complicit." Zach licked his lips, his hands twisting together. "Before I got to know you, before you became my friend, I had a plan. Sort of. It's not one I'm proud of. I don't know if I could have gone through with it. You see, Littlewood has taken an *interest* in you. And from the feeling I get in my gut the times I've been present while he's spoken about what the DPRP needs from you, I don't think that interest is just about your exposure to Bane."

"You think he's . . . targeting me?"

Zach nodded slowly. "Or rather, he would, except he didn't count on the Jugs being so protective of you. He was furious when they refused to leave you unguarded, which was another big tip-off."

The thought of what someone like Littlewood might intend for him was enough to make Rhys shudder. "What was your plan?"

"I had thought I would stay silent, let Littlewood try to make you disappear, and let the Jugs deal with him." He gave Rhys a shamefaced half-smile. "Your Jugs would have beaten the tar out of Littlewood's people, found out where they got their orders and taken Littlewood down. Or, if Littlewood's people had succeeded in grabbing you, the Jugs would have tracked you down, with the same end result."

"But you changed your mind."

Zach shrugged. "I can't bring myself to use another person

that way, much less someone I've come to consider a friend." Heat spread across Rhys's cheeks, which Zach thankfully chose not to notice. "Besides, taking Littlewood out would only solve part of the problem. The young men I suspect are Littlewood's prey aren't the only people going missing from the Clean Zone. And the rest of those people—I think—are being taken by the DPRP, just not for Littlewood's personal amusement."

"*What?*"

"Seven years ago, about a year before the Jugs went to Texas and put a stop to what Charlie Company was doing down there, the DPRP sent a request to each of the squadrons, carried back by the Jugs who were delivering groups of refugees, just like they did with your summons." Zach rose and began pacing. "Technically, the Clean Zone has no authority over the Jugs, but they asked anyway. They wanted the Jugs to start reporting on their observations about the transmissibility of various strains of Bane. Including Alpha."

Rhys frowned. "I don't understand. Before the Jugs took down Charlie Company, no one knew Alpha was transmissible, period."

"*Exactly*. It was a strange request. Why would the DPRP have any interest in whether or not Alpha could be transmitted? Well, the official explanation was simply 'research,' to try to understand the virus and help manufacture a vaccine." Zach paused his pacing to reach out and pluck bare a branch of scrub pine hanging nearby. "But that didn't sit right with Nico, especially after we discovered Alpha could be sexually transmitted. So he asked me to take a job working within the DPRP. Which I did, but I've found out as much as I can."

Rhys mulled that over for a moment. "What is it you think they're up to?"

"Littlewood is only in the Clean Zone part-time. He travels back and forth to the off-site research facility. I think that is where these people who have been disappearing are being taken."

"You mean Littlewood's preferred victims or the other missing people?"

"Both."

"What for?" Rhys asked.

"Lack of scrutiny and oversight, I imagine." Zach shuffled back to sit on the ground near Rhys. "Away from the Clean Zone, no one who isn't complicit already would have any idea what he's doing with the young men he's been taking."

"And the other people?"

"I'm not sure." Zach shook his head, a look of frustration furrowing his brow. "I suspect they're culling the people who they think may have had sexual relations with Jugs, people who might be Alpha-infected, or at least Alpha-exposed. That's part of the intake exam process, trying to get the new arrivals to slip and admit to having feelings for or relationships with the Jugs who brought them in. I know because I've interviewed many of them. I helped with the intake process when they came to the Clean Zone. I *wrote* their records. And when I went back and looked at the records of the young men who have gone missing, they had been altered to indicate that the men may have been exposed to Alpha, as well."

Now it was Rhys's turn to swallow against the lump of fear in this throat. "He's trying to make it look like they're part of whatever the DPRP is researching." Zach nodded, and Rhys inhaled deeply, bracing himself for what he suspected was coming. "You still haven't said what it is you wanted me to do."

Zach closed his eyes briefly, as though he were praying again. "I wanted you to play bait. You're his type."

"And what type is that?"

Zach's jaw flexed. "The way Nico described it to me? Littlewood doesn't want a partner. He wants a *victim*. And whatever you may or may not willingly do with Darius, you're sweet, and shy, and just—" He shrugged, clearly running out of words to get his point across. It didn't matter. Rhys knew what Zach was saying. He may have acquired more height and muscle mass over the past two years, but he was still, as Toby put it, a baby-faced ingenue.

"Why not just have me take this to Darius, ask the Jugs to put a stop to Littlewood's operations?"

"Because—" Zach drew a deep breath and released it slowly "—we need to see what his operations actually *are*, what the DPRP is up to, and we can't do that if we've laid waste to the place. We need to get someone inside, see what they're working on and who else in the Clean Zone—particularly within the government—knows what Littlewood's true agenda is. How far does it go?"

"So you want me to let myself be taken." There was something wrong with the calm with which he could face that notion. He felt numb. Resigned. It was the way he'd felt when he'd begun slipping his already-insufficient rations to his pregnant, then nursing, sister. The way he'd felt that day at the monastery when the revenants were breaking down the gate and Father Maurice told Rhys to use himself to lure them away so the rest of them could escape. Like it was inevitable that it should come to this.

Shouldn't it bother him more?

Zach nodded reluctantly. "You're heavily guarded, so he can't get his hands on you, not unless I have your cooperation in getting you away from the Jugs."

Rhys snorted. "Oh God. I'm trying to envision Darius's reaction when I tell him about this." Zach gave him a pained look. "What?"

Zach gnawed on his bottom lip. "There's a way to do this without involving the Jugs. Nico could come after you by himself."

"That's not going to happen." Rhys shook his head firmly. "I can't hide something like this from Darius. I won't. Why would you even want me to?"

"I guess I still keep hoping that someday the Jugs and the Clean Zone population can learn to trust each other and live together. Back before the overthrow, the Jugs were going to make their homes here with us. But the uninfected didn't want them. They were too afraid. And now the Jugs are resentful." Zach looked away, blinking rapidly, but not before Rhys saw the naked yearning on his face. "And there are a lot of ways this situation could make that worse. If the Jugs decide the DPRP's research is a sham, they're going to stop submitting their field reports and cooperating with research efforts. And I worry what popular opinion would be if you did agree to act as bait and the Jugs followed and attacked the research facility."

"If Littlewood and the DPRP are doing what you say they're doing, they need to be stopped," Rhys argued. "The Jugs won't give a damn what public opinion about them is."

"I know, but if it happens, they'll never be welcome to make a home here!" Zach squeezed his eyes shut, his hands balled into fists. "With the potential for an antiserum from your immunity—and others, if we find there are more people like you—the reasons the Clean Zone feared the Jugs enough to exile them don't need to be a problem anymore. If we have postexposure prophylaxis—" He cut himself off with a brusque shake of his head. "No. Never mind. Ignore that. I'm being selfish. This isn't about me or what I wish for."

He looked so crestfallen that, even though Rhys knew he couldn't keep Darius out of this, he felt he had to offer Zach *something*. But that inclination warred against the certainty that Zach was still holding back. The way he'd cut himself off before he could discuss whatever it was he personally hoped to gain threw Rhys right back into the dilemma of not knowing how much he could trust Zach.

"Okay, look. I can't promise not to tell Darius, but I'll consider it once I know what is going on."

Zach was silent a long moment, no doubt arguing with himself. Or praying. But finally, he drew a sharp breath and blurted, "We—Nico and I—think Littlewood wants the Alpha strain for himself."

Whatever he'd been expecting Zach to say, it wasn't that. The impact of his words hit Rhys like a fist to the gut.

"*Fuck.*"

9

RESOLVE

"They're keeping records on more than the new arrivals," Toby said when Rhys finished describing his discussion with Zach. "They've gone back and done retroactive interviews with everyone in the Clean Zone."

Darius was beginning to wish he'd heeded Toby's suggestion about getting away from Colorado Springs back when they'd been climbing the walls in the quarantine unit. Especially since it was pretty clear from the way Rhys was behaving that he was holding some things back.

Titus nodded. "There are thousands of files at the intake center, not hundreds. They have a few computers, but they don't dare keep anything on them in case the plant goes off-line. They want their research somewhere that they can get to it whether there's power or not."

"Well, at least someone learned something from the plague." Xolani scowled. "Even when there was still battery power, no one could break the security on the data solids scavenged from the Pentagon. The lack of records meant anyone researching Bane had to start from square one." She drummed her fingers on her thigh. "Do any of the files have information about the blood tests Zach said he collected samples for?"

Toby and Titus both shook their heads. "All that's there are the interview transcripts and forms the survivors filled out. Medical data is kept elsewhere."

Darius rubbed his jaw and then nodded irritably. "Fine. Xolani, if you still think it's worth trying to address the Science Committee, you can detach and remain here with Titus. But tomorrow morning I'm giving Schuyler and her people orders to gather provisions for the trip to Lewis-McChord." He grimaced. "I know we're all concerned about the missing people, especially if what Zach told Rhys about Littlewood is true, but when it comes down to it, that's not our detail."

"*What?*" Rhys's voice climbed high with surprise. "We're leaving?"

"We're not Clean Zone citizens. *They didn't want us*, remember? He can't get his hands on Alpha unless he's willing to try to grab one of us, and that's too damn risky for him or he'd have already done it. So yeah, we're leaving." He scowled into the fire. "I'm not particularly comfortable bringing more survivors here to live under the GDM or be used in . . . whatever it is the government and the DPRP are up to, so there are other things we can do. Once we get to Lewis-McChord, we'll confer with Luis about dispatching messengers to the other companies about finding someplace new to take the survivors we find, forming another settlement."

"Whoa!" Xolani held up her hands. "Darius, if the Clean Zone population already feels like we're a threat, establishing a settlement is going to look like a declaration of open hostility.

You're not doing things the way we want, so we're going to stop supporting you. The ramifications are huge."

He arched an eyebrow at her, keeping his hands flat on his thighs to prevent clenching them into fists. *Using Rhys as bait . . .* It was taking everything he had right now not to hunt down Zach Houtman and pound the shit out of the motherfucker. "So you think we should keep handing survivors over to them?"

Xolani looked like she wanted to argue about that, but she just grimaced and gave a jerky shake of her head. "No. *Fuck.*"

"Fine." Darius pointed at Toby and Titus. "Keep digging in those records until we're ready to go. We want to know everything they're up to if we're going to present this to the other companies. Xolani, keep talking like you're trying to get through to the Science Committee. Don't advertise that we're prepping to leave. But we're fucking out of here as soon as we're ready to travel."

They all nodded and got to their feet, except for Rhys, who stayed firmly planted on a log next to the fire.

"No." They turned in unison to face him, and he raised his voice. "*No.* I'm not going. I'm going to do what Zach asked. I'm going to play bait."

"The hell you are," Darius growled, reaching down to pull him up by his arm. Rhys jerked away.

"No. And don't you *dare* try to haul me away like some piece of baggage!" He narrowed his eyes at Darius's grasping hand.

Appalled by the way he'd just attempted to manhandle Rhys, after he'd sworn to himself that he'd never again force *anything* on Rhys, Darius dropped it.

"People are being hurt, or killed," Rhys went on. "If Zach

is right about what Littlewood is doing to these boys who are missing . . ." Something tragic crossed Rhys's face, and he swallowed hard. "We have to stop that. And what if Littlewood *does* find a way to get ahold of Alpha? It would be Jacob all over again. Worse, maybe. I'm not going to walk away."

Joe, who had been sitting silently behind Rhys, laid a hand on Rhys's shoulder with a look of approval. Damn. And there was Toby, stroking his chin thoughtfully.

"What was Zach's extraction plan, once Littlewood took the bait? Did he even have one?" Xolani challenged.

Rhys broke off his staring contest with Darius to turn his attention to her. "I'm supposed to observe what is happening inside the research facility, see if I can get into their records, find out what they're doing and who is involved. As far as getting me out, he said he has someone who could help me, someone named Nico."

Toby frowned thoughtfully. "Who is that guy supposed to be? Why would Zach think he could help you?"

Rhys shrugged. "He didn't explain much, just that this Nico had known Littlewood before the plague." He took a deep breath and released it carefully. "Xolani . . . I *know* what you said about playing the martyr, and I'm not. At least, I don't *want* to. But I keep thinking about what you also said the other day, about the GDM and that people in the Clean Zone might be preparing to go on the offensive against the Jugs. What if . . . what if it's not just *Littlewood* who wants the Alpha strain? What if congress is sanctioning his operations?"

She groaned, falling back on her bedroll. "Oh hell."

Titus grunted. "You trust 'im?"

"Zach?" Rhys pondered that one for a moment. "I . . . trust his intentions," he said slowly. "I believe he's a good guy who wants to help people. But without knowing who he's working with, who he's getting his information from . . ." He sighed, seeking Darius's eyes. "I'm doing this, one way or the other. Whatever is happening here has to stop. But I'd feel a lot better knowing you've got your eyes on Zach and Nico. To keep them honest."

Darius wanted to snarl at all of them for listening to Rhys. They were honestly considering letting Rhys do this. They followed Darius's orders when it came to how to conduct patrols; it was a way of keeping operations orderly. But this was something else entirely. None of them had any official rank over the others now. If Rhys's arguments swayed Xolani and Joe, the two people aside from Darius who were most invested in keeping Rhys safe, Darius was going to have to go along with this fucking plan.

Toby hummed. "I know you don't want to hear it, Big D, but Little Brother's right. He can handle this. We need to let him do it and have his back."

Darius shook his head in adamant denial, but Rhys's voice stopped him before he could speak.

"Would you let Toby do it? Or Gina? Or Jamie? Or *any other* member of Delta Company?" He looked up at Darius with a challenge in his eyes. "Did you mean it when you said I'm one of you?"

He unfurled his fists to realize his hands were shaking. He wanted to hit anyone who wanted to force him to accept this. God help him, even Rhys.

Darius saw the resolve in their eyes and swore, storming off into the trees.

It was hours before he'd cooled down enough to return to camp. Rhys was already in his bedroll, facing the fire. It was nearly Darius's watch shift, so he took up position on the edge of their camp, refusing to look at anyone who was still awake and studying him, trying to gauge his mood.

"Darius?"

He turned at Rhys's murmur. "Why ain't you asleep, boy?"

Rhys scoffed. "With all this unresolved?"

"It's resolved. Just because I don't like it, don't mean you're not right." He sighed and approached the spot where Rhys lay. "Just want to keep you safe." He reached down to stroke the tousled hair back from Rhys's face.

"I know you do." Rhys's hazel eyes glowed up at him, golden in the firelight. "Did you mean what you said, about a new Clean Zone?"

Darius shrugged. "Maybe. Xolani's right. Could be a whole mess of trouble we don't want." He sighed, his thumb brushing Rhys's palm. "Overthrowing the military government was one thing. They weren't elected, they had no real right to be in authority, and honestly? *We* wanted revenge for what they had done to us. But it's different now."

"Why?"

"They were elected. Corrupt or not, we have no grounds to interfere with that. And if they decide to start a fight . . ." Darius suppressed a shudder. "Putting us up against civilians is a recipe for disaster. Someone will fire a gun at us, we'd be wounded, and then these thousands of people and everything they've built here are dead. All the work we've done for the last ten years would be gone."

Rhys gulped. "I think Zach was afraid of that, too. Can

you promise me we'll never be the first to attack the civilians? No matter what?"

"'Course we won't. Why would you think that?"

"Just making sure. Zach *really* wants the civilians and Jugs to live together in peace."

"Can't blame him. Doubt it'll ever happen, though. Best we can hope for is to just keep to ourselves."

"Maybe . . . maybe if you set up a new Clean Zone, it won't have to be that way." Rhys's eyes shone with a hopeful innocence that made Darius's chest ache. "The survivors you rescue, they trust you, right? Not like the people who were already here right after the plague?"

"Maybe." Darius stood, brushing off his fatigues. "I'll have Schuyler detach some of her people to backtrack along the routes used by the other companies, leaving notices at the way stations to divert with the survivors they bring. We'll tell them to converge in . . . ." He rubbed his forehead, considering the cities they had cleared in the last decade of patrols. "Portland. Or maybe outside the city, down the valley around where we found you. Good farmland, lots of wildlife and surviving live-stock, not too cold in the winters."

Rhys blinked slowly. "You've been thinking about this for a while. I thought it was something you just came up with tonight, but it isn't, is it?"

"Been considering it since we learned about the GDM. What we'd do if Xolani's address didn't work out. I thought a lot of our people would have trouble with bringing the civvies here if they were going to have to live under laws like that. Hadn't decided anything until tonight, though." He rubbed his chin. "Think Portland should work just fine. We'll meet up with them there, give the survivors the opportunity to decide if they want to join the population at Colorado Springs, or set up a new settlement. It's the best I can do until I talk to Luis and we approach the rest of the Jug companies. It'll have to be enough."

🔺 🔺 🔺

"A NEW SETTLEMENT, huh? You're serious about this?" Xolani appeared out of the trees, coming in from the edge of the old reservoir, while Darius took up his watch position on the outskirts of camp.

"If you got a better idea, I'm dyin' to hear it. 'Cause right now I'm not sure about a damn thing. Seems the best of a lot of bad options."

She shook her head, her mouth pressed in a grim line. "I'm fucked if I do. You weren't wrong in what you told Rhys. We can't play kingmaker with the Clean Zone leadership."

Darius snorted. "So we just build a new city—hell, guess it would be a new nation, wouldn't it?—when the old one doesn't work out."

Xolani shrugged. "Sure, why not? And sooner or later they'll all go to war against one another and start developing weapons of mass destruction, and then it'll be just like old times, albeit on a smaller scale. Ah, nostalgia!"

Darius stared at her before a reluctant grin tugged at his mouth. "Sometimes your sense of humor is just fuckin' wrong." After a moment, though, the amusement faded and he shook his head, sighing. "You were right. We're getting old. Way too old to be dealing with this shit."

"That hot young thing curled up on your bedroll over there doesn't seem to think so."

"Think we'd be trying as hard as we do if it weren't for him?"

"I don't know." She looked up through the canopy at the moon. "We were getting pretty damn jaded. Or maybe we were just tired."

"Is that what he has to look forward to?" Darius snapped a thin branch off the limb above his head and began peeling the bark from it. "We're in our second decade of dealing with all this, never havin' a place to really rest, always knowin' there's somewhere we have to move on to, still work ahead of us that we might not get done before we die." He forced himself to speak the thought that had been haunting him since he'd learned of Rhys's test results. "He's not contagious. Not a danger to anyone. I keep thinkin' maybe he'd be better off—"

"*He* isn't asleep yet, and *he* can hear you just fine," Rhys called out, drawing grumbles from the Jugs trying to sleep around him. "And *he* says, 'Don't even fucking think it.'"

Xolani dissolved into laughter, pressing a hand to her mouth to try to silence the chortles, and after a moment, Darius gave in too.

"Well, there you have it," Xolani snickered, clapping him on the shoulder. "Now quit brooding. I swear you're getting positively mopey in your old age."

10

SNARES

"You *have* to go." Rhys gave Darius a gently sympathetic smile as he spoke. The plan was never going to work if Darius kept hovering over him. "I'll be okay."

Darius looked as though he wanted to start tearing trees and boulders apart with his bare hands. It had been a week since Zach had asked for Rhys's help. Since then, they had been laying the groundwork to provide an opening that would allow Littlewood's people to snatch Rhys. He'd told Zach to drop the word in the right ears that the Jugs would be at the intake center today. Darius had been insistent—and everyone else had agreed—that they would give Littlewood one shot at Rhys. No more. If he didn't take it, Rhys would bid Zach good-bye and head to Seattle to join the rest of Delta Company.

Darius gave a growly sigh. "I know." He leaned in close to Rhys, his breath brushing Rhys's face. "Be safe, boy. Don't take any unnecessary risks. I'll be right behind you."

"Right." Rhys grabbed the front of Darius's shirt and

jerked him down into a hard kiss. He didn't want to leave any more than Darius wanted him to go, but they had no choice. Not if they wanted to stop Secretary Littlewood.

Darius kissed him back as if he were suffocating and Rhys was air. Then he crushed Rhys to his chest for a moment before stalking away, leaving Rhys yearning to call him back.

Xolani snorted as she followed Darius, muttering as she went, "Big, bad hard-ass getting all dotty over a civvie. Never thought I'd see the day."

"Fuck off," Darius snapped, and then they were out of earshot.

Titus and Toby had left a couple of hours earlier to play cards with the Perimeter Security guards, and now Darius and Xolani were supposedly going to make another bid to address the Congressional Science Committee. That left Joe, who was placidly fishing at the edge of the reservoir as he ostensibly kept an eye on Rhys. Eventually, he would wander farther down the shore, hopefully far enough away that he wouldn't seem like a threat to anyone going after Rhys.

"I don't like this," Rhys complained, propping up a nearby tree. "What if they decide you're too much of a liability, no matter how far away you are? What if they try to hurt you?"

Joe shrugged. "We agreed it would look suspicious if we left you completely alone. One of us had to stay for show. So which of us would you rather take that risk? You want it to be Darius? Xolani?"

"*No.* I don't want it to be any of you."

"That's just too bad." How had he never before noticed just how annoying Joe's mellow complacency could be? "You're taking a risk none of us wants to see you take, either. Don't think that just because we support you we actually like it. But we respect that it's your choice. Think maybe you should do the same for me?"

"Shit." Rhys let his head thunk back against the tree trunk. "Sorry."

Joe didn't even bother to shrug this time. "Walk it off. Head that way along the lakeshore. I'll move along in the other direction soon. Stay in sight of the water if you can, so I can keep an eye out for you. If not, remember to leave marks so we know where they grabbed you."

"Right. Okay." He wiped his sweaty palms on his fatigues. "Thanks, Joe. For everything."

"Be safe, Little Brother. See you soon."

It was astonishing how easily the Jugs made promises like that. Every single one of them had said something to that effect, especially Darius. Were they saying it to reassure Rhys that he wasn't being as foolhardy as he felt? Or did they really believe it?

Either way, there was no guarantee they could deliver on it. His parents had promised that everything would get back to normal soon, but when they came out of the bunker, the entire world was dead. His dad had promised to rendezvous with them. His mom had promised Rhys she'd be fine when the lumps on her breast became more inflamed and painful.

They were just comforting words. Rhys had said much the same to Cady seven years later, before he'd tried to lead a pack of revs away from her and her baby. He'd known he couldn't deliver on those, either, though he'd fully expected to be the one to die.

That plan hadn't worked out any better than he anticipated this one working.

Promises meant nothing. Plans meant nothing. They were

just words attempting to pacify the people left behind. Rhys didn't need anyone to tell him all the ways this scheme could go wrong. He could find himself in the hands of an evil man, either for testing or for something much worse, and if the Jugs couldn't track him and find a way into the research facility, it would all be for nothing.

The thought made his farewell to Darius seem particularly unsatisfactory. Should he have said more, in case they couldn't get him out? Thanked Darius for making the last two years the only good years Rhys had known since he was nine years old and the world had changed forever? He tried to remember what his dad had said to his mom, but they'd had their heads together, whispering desperately to each other. And then his dad had sprinted away, shouting at them to run and not look back.

"What are you doing out here? Where is everyone?"

Rhys's heart slammed against his ribs as he whirled to face Schuyler, who was glowering at him from just a few yards away. "Jesus!" He pressed a hand to his chest, which ached with the shot of adrenaline. "What are *you* doing here? I thought you and your people all left."

"I sent my squad on and came back because I wasn't willing to let this issue with the GDM rest. I wanted to discuss it with Xolani some more. But then I get here to find camp empty and you sneaking around on the other side of the lake from Joe, looking like you're up to something."

"Wow. You caught me. I managed to shake them all off so I could take a walk and do absolutely nothing, but you've foiled my master plan." Rhys grimaced, trying not to look conspicuously around for any sign of approaching kidnappers. "Look. I get it. You don't like me. You don't trust me. You blame me for Kaleo's death. *Fine.* I'm used to being hated whether or not I actually did anything to deserve it. But it's a little hard to stay out of your way when you're following me, so why don't you do what you came to do? Go talk to Xolani —who's at the intake center—and leave me alone."

She gave him a derisive look. "So you're the victim now. Typical."

"Jesus Christ! What is your problem with me?"

"You're a *civvie.* That's my problem."

"Yeah, I know I'm a *civvie.* Not for lack of trying, but there you have it."

Schuyler's eyes widened. "Oh my God. Is *that* what you've been after?"

"I have absolutely no idea what you're asking, but if I say yes, will it make you go away faster?"

"How much longer are you going to keep this up?" She crossed the space between them, glaring up at him. "How long until you decide you've gotten what you're going to get out of us and leave?"

Fuck. He braced his hands on his hips and focused on giving the impression that he was *not* fighting the urge to glance anxiously around.

"I'd ask what you're talking about, but right now I don't actually care. Just *go away!*"

"I won't let you do it," she snarled, poking him in the chest with a fingertip. Which, coming from a Jug, felt more like a punch. "I won't let you use Darius and Xolani and Joe and everyone else I care about the way your kind always use us. Go join the rest of the civvies in the Clean Zone and leave *us* alone."

"Okay." Anything to shut her up and make her leave.

Never mind that he didn't mean a word of it. Never mind that even the suggestion of leaving Darius made his chest hurt for reasons that had nothing to do with the way she'd poked him.

"Just like that?" Schuyler sneered, as if his agreement confirmed all her worst suspicions about him.

"Sure." Rhys's eyes burned, and damn it, he wasn't going to give her that. Not after what she'd accused him of. Darius could see his tears, but she wasn't allowed. He turned his back, keeping his voice flat. "Whatever will make you leave me the fuck alone. Just go."

Sensing her there behind him was like waiting for a physical blow. His shoulders twitched in anticipation of the moment her rage would turn violent. This wasn't about him—he wasn't even sure it was about Kaleo anymore—and he didn't have time to deal with it.

Silence settled around him, leaving him braced for an attack that never came. When he turned, Schuyler was gone. Which was a good thing, right? He couldn't have her hanging around while he was playing the sitting duck. So why was it fucking bothering him that he might never get to set things right with her if this scheme to use him as bait went badly? Defending himself to someone who had already decided to hate him *didn't work*. He'd learned that years ago with Father Maurice and Jacob. Some foolish, futile part of him was tempted to tear off into the trees after her and try anyway.

"Forget about it," he whispered, leaning against a tree and scrubbing his hands down his face. Between nerves and Darius's rather rigorous, and multiple, leave-takings throughout the night, he was far too short on sleep to focus on anything else. "Just forget it."

He almost dozed, standing there with his hands blocking

out the light. At least it seemed as though he'd zoned out, because the next thing he knew, there was a weird concussive pounding in the air around him, thumping in his chest like a bass drum. It was so low it was almost inaudible, something he felt in his bones and eardrums more than heard. He stared in disbelief as a large, repulsion-lift lightcar sank down to hover above the water at the edge of the reservoir.

It took Rhys a moment to recognize it for what it was. They weren't common vehicles, and he'd hardly ever seen one outside of vids when he was a child. It created ripples on the surface of the lake. Not the violent splashing an air turbine engine would generate, but neat concentric circles, like sound waves made visible.

Make it look good.

Rhys didn't have to feign the fear that started his heart racing and sent his feet pounding against the reddish soil and into the trees. Darting a look back over his shoulder, he saw a hatch drop open like a giant, dark maw spewing several armed and suited troops as they hopped out. He faced forward and put all his concentration into leading them on a chase without actually getting away.

At least until he crashed into Schuyler. She caught him easily, though she was knocked off-balance. Her Jug strength saved her from being slammed to the ground.

"Come on!" She jerked hard on his arm. "Shit! Who the fuck is that? Since when does the Clean Zone have skim-craft?"

"No!" Rhys tried to rip his forearm free of her grasp, twisting violently enough that he thought he'd lost some skin. "They're here for me. You need to go!"

"Are you fucking kidding me? Darius would—"

"*Darius knows!*" he hissed, shoving her away. "I *have* to let them take me. Go find Joe. He'll explain."

He saw the frantic movement of her eyes as she worked her way through that, saw her struggle with whether or not to trust him.

"*I don't have time for this!*" He looked frantically behind him as he heard the sound of the kidnappers calling to one another, getting closer. "Try to track my course, leave a trail Darius can follow. We didn't count on them not transporting me by ground. *Please.* Just go!"

Schuyler took two steps deeper into the woods, then stopped and met his eyes, her chin lifting. "Even a Jug can't chase a lightcar from the ground. If Darius can't track you, you'll need someone on the inside to help you get out."

"They'll kill you—" he started to argue, but then it was too late. The voices were practically on top of them. "We have to make it look good."

Schuyler grinned savagely. "With pleasure."

The first armed and suited figure to emerge from the trees caught her feet square in his chest as she launched herself at him horizontally. She moved with dizzying speed and crushed him to the ground as she tore his weapon from his hands and then bent down to rip his mask off. Another person entered the clearing to find himself staring down the barrel of Schuyler's newly acquired assault rifle while the man on the ground wheezed desperately, "Don't shoot! Don't shoot!"

The instant of hesitation on the part of the new arrival was enough for Schuyler to flip her rifle and smash the butt against his mask, dislodging it. He reeled backward, howling in pain and fear, and Rhys saw a smear of blood on the semitransparent, copper-toned face shield.

Schuyler spun to face two more guns trained on her, and then something cold and metallic pressed against Rhys's skull behind his ear. A woman's voice barked, "Drop it!"

He had to hand it to Schuyler, she put on a good show of being torn between the need to keep fighting and the urge to save him. It was all the more astonishing for the fact that she actually did a convincing job of looking as though she cared if he died. He'd half expected her to tell them to shoot him.

Slowly, Schuyler lowered her weapon to the ground, keeping her hands spread wide, her eyes still burning with a barely banked battle rage. He'd seen a similar fury in Darius, Xolani, and even Kaleo once. Bloodlust. Heightened adrenal responses. Once a Jug was caught up in the heat of a fight—or sometimes sex—it took them a while to come back down. Until then, it was uncertain whether they could make themselves stop.

"Please don't hurt her," Rhys pleaded, a convincing quaver seeping into his voice without any effort on his part. "We'll come along quietly."

"Damn right you will," said the woman holding the gun on Rhys. He felt her make a gesture, and the man on the ground—the one whose mask Schuyler had torn off and whose gun she had stolen—sat up and grabbed something off a clip on his belt.

An electric sizzle crackled in the air, and then Schuyler was on the ground, convulsing with two golden darts stuck to her neck.

"Schuyler!" Rhys almost forgot he was supposed to be cooperating, until the gun drilled against his skull behind his ear, where the bone was barely protected by flesh.

"She'll live for now," the woman detaining him said

through her mask. "Bring her with us!" she called to her comrades, jerking Rhys into motion. "We don't want her reporting back to anyone, and the docs at the lab will be shitting themselves to get their hands on a Jug."

△△△

DARIUS SWORE as he and Xolani paced outside the intake center. Her attempt to petition yet again for an audience with the Science Committee had gone nowhere. Now they were spinning their wheels over the ramifications of the Clean Zone government actively seeking the Alpha strain and reaffirming to themselves that they were doing the right thing in letting Rhys act as bait. Each point they discussed felt like a band of steel around his chest, confirming that he had no choice but to risk Rhys. He rubbed his sternum, his helplessness battering his ribs and lungs and temples. "*Fuck.*"

"I'm s—" Xolani broke off, pressing a hand to her own chest while she shook her head as if trying to clear her ears. Then her eyes widened, and she stared at him. "Someone's using grav-repulsion turbines nearby. Who the hell has a lightcar these days?"

The squeezing, drumming feeling in his chest disappeared in favor of what felt like a direct kick to the gut. He saw the realization dawn on Xolani's face.

"Fuck!" He took off at a dead sprint, knowing Xolani would only be a pace behind him. As they rounded the building to head down the familiar road toward the reservoir, he heard Titus and Toby burst out the front doors of the intake center and shouted to them, "They're taking him by air!"

🔺 🔺 🔺

JOE WAS GONE. From the footprints Toby was able to locate, it looked like Joe was chasing after Rhys by ground, trying to track the flying craft as far as he could. There was no way he'd be able to keep up with it for long, but maybe he'd have a sense of its trajectory.

In the clearing where they'd made their camp, they found Zach Houtman. Darius grabbed him by the throat, driving him against a tree. "I'm going to rip your fucking head off," he snarled. "Where are they going with Rhys?"

"I don't know! But I want to help!" Zach protested, gripping Darius's wrist in a futile effort to pull it off his windpipe. "Please!"

"Why didn't you tell us they'd take him by air?" Darius snarled.

"I didn't know!" He met Darius's glare steadily, despite the red creeping over his face as Darius's hand tightened on his larynx. Darius dropped him with a mutter of disgust, and Zach sprawled on the ground for a moment, coughing. "I had no idea how they'd been getting people out of the Clean Zone."

Xolani's mouth tightened. "We just lost any hope we had of tracking them."

Zach shook his head. "No. Nico has been searching for the research facility for years. He'll have an idea where we can look for him."

Darius grabbed him by the shirt front and jerked him forward. "Walk," he growled in Zach's face. "Whoever the fuck this Nico is, I want to talk to him. Now."

"He was keeping an eye on Rhys from the woods. After

that he was going to approach you, tell you where they were headed."

"Why hasn't he introduced himself before?" Xolani demanded. Darius watched her fall in step to box Zach in on one side while he closed off the other himself. Toby fell in behind, while Titus took point.

Zach bowed his head. "I'll let him explain that. He had his reasons."

"This is bullshit," Toby snapped behind him. "Fucking cloak-and-dagger *bullshit*. Instead of coming to us yourselves, you use Rhys to persuade us. How are we supposed to trust you?"

"We didn't know if you'd help us. Honestly, I've been working in the DPRP for so long now, I'm not even sure who I trust anymore. I've been keeping an eye on Secretary Littlewood since the overthrow, watching him build up the DPRP from a powerless committee to one of the most influential departments in the government." Zach paused for a moment before gesturing for them to go east around the southern shore of the reservoir. "People are terrified of another outbreak, and he's been able to use that terror to generate a sense of fervent nationalism. As long as the population believed the DPRP would keep them safe, they would go along with anything he proposed."

Xolani rolled her eyes. "That's all very enlightening, but why Rhys?"

"Because Littlewood is a psychotic predator. He's a sadist, a rapist, and a murderer. I've seen what he does to people. I helped put a teenaged boy out of his misery because whatever Littlewood raped him with perforated his colon so badly he was going to die of sepsis." Zach's lips curled in disgust.

Another red-hot shot of rage pulsed through Darius at the thought of Rhys in the hands of someone like that, but Zach's next words were even more chilling. "*That's* the kind of man who wants to become a Jug."

For some reason, his words gripped Darius in a way that the thought never had. Before, it had sounded almost antiseptic to hear Rhys report that Littlewood wanted the Alpha strain. It was entirely different to consider someone like that *being* a Jug.

"He's that bad?" Xolani's expression mirrored Darius's own horror, and she voiced what they were all thinking as they stutter-stepped to a halt, the revulsion in her tone a verbal expression of the ice clawing at Darius's chest.

"If Nico is right about him being the rapist, then yes. And I have no reason to doubt Nico." Zach's eyes were bleak. "You know information on Alpha transmission was part of the DPRP's request for field reports from the Jugs. And since we found out that Alpha *was* transmissible, he's been working to get his hands on it."

"It's not possible," Toby argued. "The tech for that level of viral engineering doesn't exist anymore."

"It does if you get your hands on one of the virologists who originally worked on Bane, and gain access to the lab facility where it was developed."

"Oh shit," Xolani whispered. "*How?*"

"Her name is Dr. Thanh. She was a researcher with Pentagon BioWeaps R&D and General McClosky's right hand when developing Bane. It was *her* brainchild."

Darius stared for a moment longer, then shook himself out of his paralysis and gestured for them to continue in the direction Zach had indicated. "How do you know this?"

"I didn't until the DPRP started collecting data on the whole population. They expanded the interviews they were doing on the new arrivals and started collecting data on everyone who had arrived since the overthrow. Somehow, in the first few years after the pandemic, she had managed to make it through quarantine and into the population unnoticed. She was using an assumed name. I think the Jugs found her in Nevada." Zach sighed. "She'd been here about five or six years when I interviewed her, took her blood sample. Then a few months later, she vanished. She was the first one to disappear, in fact, and it happened right after the DPRP got their off-site research facility operational. She had a husband and two children in the Clean Zone. She'd built a life for herself. There was no reason for her to have left of her own free will."

"How do you know it's Dr. Thanh?" Xolani asked.

"I'd been making copies of all my interview records before turning them over to the DPRP, so I looked up her file, saw that the name she had given me in her interview was slightly different from the one she'd used when they put her down in the intake logs, back before Perimeter Security began collecting more thorough information. Like she couldn't remember the exact identity she'd used back then. I realized something was off— Keep going left along this trail here." Darius adjusted their course at a fork in the faint trail through the trees, and Zach continued his explanation. "I managed to speak to her husband, and he told me she'd always been very secretive, even paranoid, about her life before she came to the Clean Zone. But she had developed a bit of a drinking problem and let things slip when she was drunk. Including her *real* name and the fact that she blamed herself for what happened."

Darius kept putting one foot in front of the other, shoving aside his fear for Rhys in order to focus on the task at hand and to process what he was hearing. "I'm still not understanding how you figure Littlewood wants to be a Jug." He glanced sidewise at Zach again. "It makes more sense to assume Littlewood wants to engineer a vaccine than it does to think he wants to get his hands on Alpha."

"Did you miss the part where I said he's a sadistic rapist? Of course he wants to become a Jug. Imagine the damage he could do, the harm he could inflict."

"You got proof of that?"

Zach scanned the trees around them as if looking for someone. "Not the sort that would hold up in court. All I have is a first-person report from a man who had the misfortune to spend a night in Littlewood's clutches before the pandemic. And that man wouldn't be allowed to testify in a Clean Zone courtroom."

"Why not?" Toby asked.

"Again, I'll let him explain that."

Xolani paused. "Even assuming it's true, I'm having a hard time seeing how one guy—even the head of the DPRP—can use the resources of the department for such a singularly personal agenda without anyone knowing."

"Exactly. Which is why I need someone to get a look at the records being kept inside the research facility. We need to know how high up this goes. You of all people know how much mistrust there is within the Clean Zone for the Jugs. Are they trying to even out the power imbalance? I don't know." Zach made a frustrated sound. "And I don't know what is happening at the off-site facility, or what is happening to the people who have been abducted. Maybe the legitimate research into finding a vaccine is being used to cloak the alternate agenda. Or maybe people are so afraid of another outbreak that they're willing to do anything if they think it'll prevent that. Stop."

Darius froze at Zach's demand, and without a word, the five of them closed together, forming a loose, outward-facing circle. They scanned the perimeter, waiting for something to approach.

"Give it a few minutes," Zach said. "Nico and I have been passing each other word through Gillett Morris at the intake center. He knows we're here."

They all froze, their hands dropping to their sidearms.

Zach continued as if they weren't all ready to shoot whoever came walking out of those trees. "I knew Rhys had captured Littlewood's interest, and I knew a large part of that was predatory rather than scientific. The more I was let in on the testing the DPRP scientists wanted to do on him, the more I realized they weren't interested in Rhys's immunity. They were interested in your attempts to infect him with Alpha, in his ongoing exposure." He blew out a long breath. "That's when I knew Nico's instincts about what Littlewood was up to were right. I put it together—how the intake interview questions all focused on trying to find survivors who'd slept with the Jugs they'd been recovered by. They didn't just want Bane, they wanted *Bane Alpha*. Why else would they possibly want that, except in the hopes of replicating it?"

Toby made a derisive sound. "I'm still not sure I buy it. I hate these Clean Zone fuckwads as much as anyone, but can they really be crazy enough to try to harness the Alpha strain? If anything, it sounds like they want a sample of the virus to test a vaccine they have in development."

"That's because you don't know Littlewood," someone called from the trees, and a man stepped into the clearing. Darius blinked as he heard the rest of his people mutter in amazement. "I do."

"Who the fuck are you?" The guy scratched at some vague memory in Darius's mind, but he couldn't place the face.

"I've seen you before," Xolani said, at the same time as Toby burst out, "*I know you*!" They all turned to stare at him. "You were a friend of Kaleo's. Sierra Company, right?"

The guy nodded. "Yes. Nico Fernández. I left Sierra Company after we went to Texas."

"*Left?*" Xolani said with a dubious frown.

"Well, I let them believe I had died in the fighting."

"What the *fuck* is going on here?" Darius demanded.

"We need to go after your Rhys, I know, but we've got bigger problems." He pointed to tracks in the red-gold dirt at the base of the scrub pines. There were deep gouges and the underbrush was trampled, as though there had been a struggle. "They have Schuyler. She was with Rhys when he was taken. And that's much, much worse than if they just had Rhys. Because now, they really *do* have access to Alpha."

After a moment, Darius lowered his gun and shrugged his rucksack off his shoulders, his eyes never venturing from Nico.

"Start from the beginning."

11

REUNION

Z ach ached from trying to match the Jugs' pace all day as they came as close as they could to double-timing. Even on the bicycle he'd been using since his days of riding from the Clean Zone to the Jug enclave outside the quarantine ring, before the overthrow, it had been a challenge to keep up.

Darius and his people would have left Zach behind if not for Nico, who had threatened to leave them to find Rhys by their own devices if Zach didn't come along.

"Thanks for that," Zach said now, approaching Nico's watch post from the campfire. The sun had set over the red rocks and scrub brush, leaving a chill in the air reminiscent of the first months they had known each other, when spring had finally started after that fateful blizzard.

"Just try to keep a distance from all of us, okay?" Nico gave him a muted smile. There was a tension in his posture that said if Zach took another step closer, Nico would retreat. That tension had been there since Nico had left Sierra Company and returned to live outside Colorado Springs.

"You've spent the last six years working to stop Littlewood. I'm not going to let them leave you behind when it's finally time to act."

"I appreciate the thought, but what can I truly do to help?" Zach shook his head, sighing. "Maybe they're right and I should stay behind."

"No!" Nico's refusal was so sharp that Zach felt a suspicious frown drawing down the corners of his mouth.

"What aren't you telling me?"

"Nothing." Nico sighed. "It's just . . . now that they have Rhys, they're going to figure out pretty quickly that you messed with his test results. And they're going to know why, realize that you're onto them. Maybe they'll even realize we're coming after them. I don't want you somewhere they can get to you when that happens, especially with no one to have your back."

Zach hung his head. "I hadn't thought of that." Silence fell until he looked up again, smiling fondly. "You know I'd rather be outside the Clean Zone with you, anyway."

"Zach—"

"How long can we keep doing this, Nico?" His eyes burned, and he refused to hide it. "It's been six years since you returned. How long do I have to keep pretending that it isn't killing me not to be able to be with you the way we're meant to be together?"

Nico's chin came up. "You tell me. Are you willing to accept the Alpha strain?"

"You ask that like I didn't *beg* you to infect me years ago when you came back," Zach said angrily. "Don't forget *you're* the one who decided it was more important for me to be able to return to the Clean Zone and infiltrate the DPRP."

"Maybe I knew you didn't mean it, that you weren't thinking rationally at the time." Nico's reply was rough and bitter. "Except for that one incident, you've always been adamantly opposed to accepting the Alpha strain. Have you changed your mind?"

He wanted to say yes, but he *couldn't.* "No," Zach whispered reluctantly.

"Well, there you have it." Nico's smile looked forced and bleak. "One close call was enough. I won't risk your life."

He wasn't being melodramatic, either. Nico's struggle was written on his face and in his body every time Zach left the Clean Zone to meet with him, always from a careful distance of at least twenty feet. It brought a surge of shame to Zach's heart, to know that this man, whom God had made such a sensual creature, a man built for pleasure and touch, had been without human contact for six years. Maybe even longer. He'd never asked what Nico had done those four years he'd been away with Sierra Company, and Nico had never volunteered.

"I'm sorry," Zach whispered. "I wish . . . I wish I could, but I know in my heart and soul that it would be wrong for me to accept the Alpha strain. I *know*, without any shadow of any doubt, that it's not God's will for me to become a Jug. Maybe He knows I'm too weak, too fallible. Maybe He knows if I succumbed to that temptation, I'd fall prey to the corruption that could so easily come of having access to that sort of power."

Nico shook his head firmly. "Not you, Zach. If any of us could withstand it, it's you."

"Then why do I go cold every time I consider accepting? You think I haven't wanted to?" Zach plucked some twigs out of a cluster of brush and threw them away in disgust. "Every time I see you, every time I think of how much I want you, how much I love you, how lonely you must be, I want to give in. But then something inside my chest freezes. And I know —*I know*—that it's God telling me, 'This is not for you.'"

"I'm aware of your reasons. We've talked about them plenty," Nico sneered. "But I don't share your faith, and I'm inclined to call that 'cold' feeling just plain old being afraid. So, does your God expect you to spend the rest of your life celibate, *Saint Zacharias*? Or will you settle down and start a family in the Clean Zone when you can't stand to be alone anymore?"

"You know I wouldn't do that. As far as I'm concerned, I've been married to you for twelve years. Do you think I could be with anyone else, knowing you're out there all alone?" Zach slumped in weary resignation. They'd had this argument at least twice a year since Nico had come back to Colorado Springs. "And it's not like you to mock my beliefs, Nico."

"No, it isn't. I'm sorry." Nico sighed. "Maybe . . . maybe when all this is done, when Littlewood isn't a threat anymore, I'll go back to the Jugs. If we can't be together, then maybe we should just not see each other anymore."

"Damn it, Nico! No! You're *not* running away again! We can be together. Just like we were before the overthrow. I was safe then, and as long as we're careful, I can be safe now." He took an unintentional step forward, and it felt like a knife in the heart when Nico quickly stepped back. "Let me make love to you like we used to."

Nico swallowed, and the yearning on his face was so powerful it nearly buckled Zach's knees. But he shook his head. "I can't. When that building fell down around me and I was bleeding, I heard you yelling for me, coming toward me, and I wanted to *die, cariño*. I mean that literally. I was going to go jump into Royal Gorge if you got sick. I won't risk it again. Unless you promise that you'll accept the Alpha strain if there's an accident, I *can't*."

Zach closed his eyes, wanting with everything inside him to agree. He couldn't, though. That icy feeling in his chest grew, holding him back. That was how Zach knew Nico was wrong. It was the opposite of the warm feeling Zach got when he knew he was doing what God wanted him to do, a gentle warning that he was contemplating the wrong choice.

He shook his head, and the ice dissipated, replaced with the glow of the Lord's approval. Whatever plan God had for him in all this, becoming a Jug wasn't part of it.

If only every other part of him were as convinced. "I'm sorry, Nico. I can't make that promise."

Nico looked so anguished that Zach wanted to weep. What did Nico's own internal struggle feel like? Did he ever feel the same surety when he knew he was making the right choice? Nico didn't believe in God, but that didn't mean God didn't still guide him, subtly urging him this way or that, if only he would listen to those quiet impulses.

He didn't look very peaceful right now as he took another step backward, and another after that, eventually turning his back on Zach. He looked like everything within him was screaming that maintaining the distance between them was wrong. Which tracked with all Zach's impulses, as well. As surely as Zach knew the Lord didn't want him to accept the Alpha strain, he also knew that he and Nico being apart wasn't right, either. But the only alternative was to convince Nico to risk Zach's safety, and Nico would never do that.

Was it a test of faith? Maybe Nico was supposed to put his trust in God to keep Zach healthy if they were together.

Right. Zach's chances of convincing Nico of that had rounded *bad* and were careening toward *abysmal.*

"Go get some sleep, Zach," Nico said over his shoulder, refusing to meet his eyes again. His voice was rough and raspy. "We've got a long march ahead of us."

Aching and conflicted, Zach went.

⋀ ⋀ ⋀

THE CHANCES of Darius sleeping before his second-watch shift hovered in the realm of nonexistent, especially after Nico had recounted just how depraved Littlewood's sexual proclivities were.

"He wants the perfect victim," Nico had said. *"Someone gentle and sweet who will show every bit of suffering. Not someone who wants it, and not someone who will be stoic or defiant."*

He knew he shouldn't worry about Rhys in that regard. He was nothing if not stoic and—albeit quietly—defiant. The boy had elevated passive resistance to an art form. It had taken Darius a while to realize that Rhys was no one's victim and that he wouldn't tolerate being treated like one. That should keep him safe from Littlewood, and yet . . .

He couldn't deny that, on the surface, Rhys was *exactly* Littlewood's type. He looked like the sort of wide-eyed, easily wounded innocent who would suffer beautifully. And Rhys, for all his resilience, had never dealt with someone like Littlewood. Even Jacob Houtman and his father had practiced a different brand of cruelty. Their abuse hadn't been sexual, and

Rhys was wired to enjoy erotic suffering of the consensual, or at least semiconsensual, sort.

What if Littlewood's sadism broke through Rhys's defenses, confusing the part of him that mingled sex and pain? It would leave him vulnerable to agony that had nothing to do with pleasure, especially since it had taken Rhys two years to finally begin to feel safe and accept his own masochistic bent.

Darius's tormented musings meant he got to be the unintentional audience to Zach and Nico's pathos-ridden argument. When Zach had settled on his bedroll next to the fire, Darius gave up the pretense of trying to sleep and rose, coming up behind Nico where he stood looking out over the Colorado desert.

"Want to tell me why you knew all this was going on and you didn't tell us? Why did you let your company think you were dead?"

Nico scoffed. "I wanted to tell someone when we got the request for field reports from the DPRP. I knew the fact that they specifically requested information on the transmissibility of Alpha couldn't mean anything good. But what would you have done if I had? How would you have stopped Littlewood? Don't you see?" Nico hurled another stone at the ground. "He was embedded deep inside the Clean Zone then. I couldn't risk pitting a company of Jugs against the civilian population."

"We could have stopped delivering survivors into his hands, demanded he be turned over to us unless congress wanted us to set up another Clean Zone."

Nico bowed his head. "I know that now. Back then it didn't occur to me. And when all the shit with Charlie Company happened, it felt like a very bad time to stir up any more mistrust between the Jugs and the Clean Zone population."

"So you faked your death to go back to spy on Littlewood?"

"I didn't feel I had a choice. I was the only person alive who knew who he was and what he was capable of. And I had Zach inside the Clean Zone to gather information for me, to figure out what Littlewood's angle was."

"And now you think you know."

"Not exactly. I just can't see any outcome to Littlewood getting his hands on Alpha that ends well for anyone except Littlewood."

"If you're gonna gossip, men, maybe wake someone else up to keep watch." They both jumped at the sound of Xolani's voice as she came up behind them, and she snorted.

"Second I'm worried about anyone attacking from inside the perimeter, I'll get on that," Darius shot back.

Xolani crossed her arms over her chest. "Tell me something before we go storming in and raze that research facility to the ground. Do you think there's a chance, *any chance*, that he really does have his DPRP scientists working on a vaccine?"

"I don't know. Maybe?" Nico looked bewildered. "I mean, let's say congress does know what he's up to, that they sanctioned his efforts to replicate the Alpha strain, maybe to create an army to take on the Jugs. The dangers of the virus still hold true, right? Their own troops would be as hazardous to the population as the Jugs are. So they'd still want a vaccine for everyone else, right?"

"Good point," Xolani acknowledged. "I can also see Littlewood wanting it for his own purposes if he's as awful as you say he is."

Nico frowned and then nodded slowly. "If he's after the power of being a Jug, the untouchability, he's not going to want anyone else to be one too. He's going to want to keep it to himself."

"Why approach us now?" Xolani asked as she seated herself on a rock, and Darius could see her brain spinning, trying to process it all. She looked cold, despite the heat, and he couldn't blame her. "You've been sitting on this while Jugs come and go from delivering civvies to the Clean Zone for *six years*. If you didn't want to pit Jugs against uninfected people before, why set Rhys up to be captured now, knowing there was no way in hell we wouldn't take action?"

"Rhys's immunity means it's no longer unthinkable, letting Jugs fight uninfected people," Nico replied honestly.

"You're talking about a possible antiserum?" Xolani's brows rose, and she nodded slowly. "Good point. Anyone we go up against won't be in danger of taking the virus back to Colorado Springs if there's an antiserum."

"Exactly," Nico said with a tight smile. "Also, I was finally able to track down the lab." He looked satisfied with himself over that, a fact that had Darius clenching his fists to avoid clocking the guy. "I've been combing all the little secret military installations in the southwestern desert for years, trying to find any that show signs of activity, and I located where they've hidden their personnel transport skim-craft and hacked into the nav computer."

"Motherfucker," Darius snarled. "You knew he'd be taken by air and you didn't have Zach warn us?"

"I don't think I ever mentioned to Zach how I got the coordinates. We only actually talk once or twice a year. Other than that, we pass messages to each other by way of Gillett

Morris. And while we trust him, we still have to keep them brief and coded." Nico gave them an apologetic look. "I was trying to figure out what to do about the research facility— since I didn't have any backup here—when Zach learned about Rhys. Once I knew Delta Company was coming, with an immune subject you had a personal connection to, I could finally make my move."

Darius gritted his teeth before he said softly, "So you got what you wanted. Now, if anything happens to Rhys, I'll kill both you and Zach. Personally."

Nico sobered at that, meeting Darius's glower for a long, silent moment before he nodded once. "Fair enough. Just make sure we take out Littlewood first."

12

AGENDAS

The kidnappers took Schuyler away the moment they disembarked from the personnel transport, and they led Rhys to a small room. A cell, really. It had a bunk and toilet, but not much else.

He tried the door and found it locked, which wasn't a surprise. What was a surprise was how quickly someone entered his room. At the first rattle of the door, Rhys had tensed, afraid it might be Littlewood. If even a fraction of what Zach had told him about the man was true, he was someone Rhys never wanted to meet. But now, he'd agreed to put himself in Littlewood's clutches and he was so terrified his mouth had forgotten how to make spit.

But it wasn't Littlewood who appeared at Rhys's door. It was a woman with dark-gray hair and a lined, tired face, accompanied by an elderly white man whose gaunt features looked haunted.

"Mr. Cooper?" the woman asked tentatively, as though

uncertain how Rhys would react. "I'm Dr. Thanh, and this is Logan. Are you all right? They didn't injure you, did they?"

"Would you care?" He put his back to the wall, folding his arms across his chest.

The woman gave him a weary smile. "Believe it or not, yes, I would. I came here the exact way you did, Mr. Cooper. I don't want to be here, either. I have a husband and children back in the Clean Zone to whom I'd like to return. So you have my sympathy."

"But not enough to stop you from kidnapping me."

"I didn't order that." Thanh shook her head adamantly, frowning. "I wouldn't have, if I were in charge of the DPRP. Secretary Littlewood's way of doing things is not something many of us agree with."

"Yet you work for him anyway."

"*Under duress.*" She grimaced. "I've been pressed into service, just like you. I don't have a choice."

"And what about him?" Rhys jerked his head in Logan's direction, unwilling to let them think he was softening toward them.

"I'm—" Logan cleared his throat, his voice rough and rusty, as if he didn't speak often. "I'm here because I want to help end Bane."

"Fine." Rhys let his arms drop, his eyes moving between them. "What do you want from me?"

Thanh gave something that might have been a smile, though it looked like it took effort. "We need to conduct a physical examination—"

"No."

"Excuse me?"

There was no way he was undressing in front of these

people. "Zach examined me back in the Clean Zone. I'm sure you have the files. I'm in perfect health, and I'm done being poked and prodded by you people."

Thanh's mouth tightened. "Is this the level of cooperation we can expect from you?"

"Considering how I came here, I'd say any cooperation at all is way more than you have any business expecting," Rhys snapped. "Now what do you want from me? More blood for your tests?" He pushed up his sleeve and thrust his arm out. "Fine. Take it. But I'm done stripping down for your stooges."

"No!" She stumbled back a step, her eyes widening with alarm. Logan didn't quite jump back, but he flinched.

Thanh cleared her throat. "We're not suited, Mr. Cooper. We can't take your blood."

"But I'm not infected." For the first time since they'd walked in, Rhys forgot to play his role of indignant captive and blinked at them in confusion. "I'm immune. That's why I'm here, right?"

Thanh and Logan exchanged a long look, the sort of look Darius and Xolani sometimes shared, the one where they had whole conversations and planned out strategies in a single glance.

"I don't know how much the med tech you worked with back in the Clean Zone was authorized to tell you," Thanh said after a moment. "But you're here because you carry Bane Alpha. That's why your presence is so important. This could be the break we've been waiting for."

"What?" Forget playing his part. Now he just wanted to know what the fuck was going on. It wasn't fair the way a part of him still lit up with hope at the idea that he might have the

Alpha strain. He had to squash that hope. Quickly. "I'm not a Jug. I think I'd know if I were."

"You're asymptomatic, of course," she replied. "But the tests they sent us from the Clean Zone clearly indicate the presence of Bane Alpha in your blood."

Rhys swallowed against the knot forming in his throat. Was it possible Zach would have made such a discovery and not told him? Was the story about Littlewood being a monster and the abductions and all that a lie, just bait to get Rhys to agree to be taken?

But why bother? Why not just take him?

Because of the Jugs, of course. Rhys closed his eyes, feeling the betrayal like a punch to the sternum. Zach had needed Rhys's cooperation to get him away from the people who would protect him. And Rhys had given him that. Hell, he'd even made sure Darius and Xolani and everyone else would let him be taken.

He forced himself to speak past the tumult of emotion threatening to choke him. "Why is that such a big deal?"

Thanh's eyes positively gleamed. "Because all attempts to deactivate the Beta and Gamma strains so that we can use them to make a vaccine have failed. Once the virus mutates to Beta, it becomes too unstable. Alpha, however, is a very stable virus." She began speaking faster, the way Xolani sometimes did when she was excited by some theory and her brain was working too fast for her mouth to keep up. Like she couldn't contain it all and she had to get it out now. "If we can keep it from mutating, we can eventually find a way to render it inert and engineer a vaccine that will also protect against Beta and Gamma."

Rhys wasn't sure what he thought about her enthusiasm. It

was almost creepy, like she wasn't seeing *him* when she looked at him, but instead all she saw was the virus in his blood. But then, if she was here unwillingly, the prospect of being a step closer to returning to her family probably accounted for a lot of that eagerness.

"Why not just kidnap a Jug, then?" he asked. "Or better yet, ask one to help you out. They want everyone to be safe. They would have volunteered."

Thanh's eyes slid over to Logan, who grimaced. "We're the people who did this to them. To the world," he explained. "They have no reason to trust us. And trying to take one by force, well . . . that would be foolhardy, wouldn't it?"

"You've got one now." Rhys lifted his chin. "What's going to happen to her?"

"She'll be fine," Thanh answered decisively. "But considering the circumstances that led to her being here, it wouldn't be prudent to try to take any samples or conduct any tests. Especially not when she can weaponize even her own blood against us. When she fought Littlewood's people to defend you, she went straight for their masks. You're the much safer option. It would really be best for all of us if we had your cooperation."

He studied the carpeted floor for a long moment, considering. "What do you need from me?" he asked again.

"We need a semen sample." Dr. Thanh didn't even blink when Rhys's head came up and he stared at her in astonishment. "We need access to the Alpha strain without danger of it mutating."

Oh Jesus. Two years among the Jugs, and after all he'd done since he'd been with them, and he could still blush like this? "Now I see why you need me to cooperate."

She nodded soberly. "There are ways to obtain a sample without your consent, of course, but I don't want to be a party to that. Secretary Littlewood, however, might order it, and I'd really rather avoid that situation."

"Fine," he muttered in disgust. "Are you sure it won't mutate? Xolani said she wasn't sure what would happen if it was exposed to air. That's why the Jugs had to—" he cleared his throat "—infect me directly."

"Given the uncontrolled environment out in the field, that was a good call on her part." Thanh fell silent, looking thoughtful. "However, we're confident that there are no environmental factors here in the lab that will trigger mutations, and we'll be in protective gear while working with the sample, just in case." She offered him another attempt at a smile and started to turn away. "You'll find everything you need in the trunk at the foot of the bed."

"Wait. I want some things in return," Rhys said.

Thanh paused mid-motion, her brows coming up in surprise, though he couldn't quite tell if Logan had any reaction or not. Rhys couldn't even be sure what the man's role here was.

"I want to have access to see Schuyler whenever I need to," he continued. "If she's not safe, I'm not giving you shit. And I want to be able to talk to other people around here, see if what they have to say is the same as the story you're feeding me."

Finally, a reaction from Logan. He looked amused. "What do you think you're going to accomplish even if you don't like what you hear, Mr. Cooper?" His voice had a firm, no-nonsense note of authority he sometimes heard from Darius and Luis. If Rhys had to guess, he'd say Logan was a man used to being in charge. Right now, though, he sounded just a little too smug and complacent, like he thought Rhys was being silly.

"You may have transported me by air, but that doesn't mean the Jugs won't come looking for me. Especially considering you also have one of their own. It might take them a while to find me, but they *are* coming." Rhys smiled tightly. "That means you've only got so much time to either complete your research or impress me with the reasons why I should talk them out of tearing this whole facility down when they find it."

SCHUYLER HAD OBVIOUSLY BEEN TASED or gassed into unconsciousness again by the time they let Rhys see her. Looking around the cell where she was being kept, it was obvious why: the walls were pockmarked by her kicks and blows, and her knuckles were bloody.

Rhys sat with her until she awoke. She moaned and rubbed her head, then blinked up at him.

"Huh. Wouldn't have thought they'd let you in."

"I think I'm the only one they believe is safe to be near you." He rose from where he knelt next to her bunk and crossed to the sink, wetting a cloth to clean her knuckles. Schuyler was too disoriented still to do more than grunt a token protest. Rhys worked in silence as she gathered her thoughts, then murmured, "Please don't give them an excuse to kill you."

"Maybe you should tell me why we're here in the first place."

She wasn't asking about whatever the people here had told

him. She was asking him why Rhys had intended to allow himself to be taken.

"I'm not sure I can." He looked conspicuously up at the edges of the ceiling, hoping that she would catch on to his intimation that they might be under surveillance.

Schuyler hesitated a moment, clearly choosing her words carefully. "Wonder if it has anything to do with all those people the guards mentioned had gone missing from the Clean Zone."

"Probably." Rhys gave her the slightest nod he could manage. He knew she'd caught on when she nodded back.

"Did anyone tell you anything?" she asked.

"They seem to think I'm infected with the Alpha strain, though I don't have any symptoms." He didn't have to feign his confusion over that. "But Zach told me I'm immune."

Schuyler grimaced. "Gee. A civvie lied. Who woulda thought?"

"Okay, what is it with you and civvies?" Rhys shoved himself away from her bunk and tossed the damp cloth back at the basin. "I always thought it was me you hated, because of Kaleo, but you really just hate me for being one of them."

"No, I hate you because of Kaleo, too." From her flat tone, Rhys decided he could give up on any hope that the understanding that he was here trying to help people might have softened her opinion of him. "But you're right. You're a civvie. I don't trust you."

"But *why?*"

She snorted a bitter laugh. "I'm sure you know how they exiled us, right?" Rhys nodded once. "Did anyone ever tell you what we did for them before that?"

"No." Rhys frowned. "Well, I mean, you got them out

from under the military government. I know that."

"Oh, we did a lot more than that." Schuyler rolled off her cot and began crossing the cell in violent strides. "We built their damn Clean Zone for them, practically from the ground up. *We* dug their perimeter trenches. *We* tore down buildings so they could have farmland inside the Clean Zone. *We* rebuilt their housing when they had to burn down the residences with infected bodies in them. We were the only ones who could safely venture away from the Clean Zone, so *we* scavenged and hauled in clothing and construction and medical supplies from all over three or four states." The look she turned on him was raw, and for the first time Rhys thought he saw the grief that fueled all her rage. "And the *only* fucking thing we asked for was to make a home there, try to rebuild our lives after the Army fucked us all over. They let us do all that for them, knowing they would drive us out in the end."

Rhys's eyes burned at the betrayal that clung to the underbelly of her anger, the pain that she couldn't quite manage to get rid of, even ten years later.

"That's why you think I'm using Darius?" he asked softly.

"Aren't you?" She leaned against the wall, beside one of the craters her fist had made, and leveled him with a glare. "You've been with us two years, Rhys, and I'm damned if I know of any other reason why you might be, except that you need a protector and he's the biggest, baddest badass among us."

"Oh, *fuck you*," he sneered. "You barely knew me before Kaleo died, and afterward, your mind was made up."

"You think it's just me?" She arched an eyebrow. "Darius fucking *dotes* on you, and there's not one of us, maybe not even Xolani, who has any clue whether he's anything more than convenient for you."

"No one thinks that." He wished he could say that with more conviction.

"You'd be surprised." Her posture softened slightly, and she ran a hand through her unruly curls. "Look, not many people would blame you. You had it rough before you came to us. You want to feel safe. They get that. But sooner or later, when something or someone else offers more security than Darius, what happens to him?" She looked down at the floor, nudging a loose piece of plaster around with her toe. "We're family. He's a good man. We don't want to see him hurt."

Rhys tried to answer, but his throat was too tight. Was that honestly how it looked when he was with Darius? Did *Darius* think that? "I've got to go," he muttered, rising and brushing plaster dust off his fatigues.

She caught his arm as he passed. "Come back and talk to me again when you know more about what's happening here. About when they might let us go." Her eyes met his so directly that there was no mistaking that she meant for her words to be interpreted differently. *Let me know when it's time for us to try to make our move and bust out of here.*

"I will," he promised and rapped on the door for the guard to let him out.

🔺🔺🔺

THERE WAS a man waiting outside his cell. Rhys didn't need to be told it was Secretary Littlewood. Not only did he lack the presence that indicated a military background that most of the guards had, but Rhys's skin began to crawl almost immediately upon seeing him. Some gut-deep, animal instinct told him that this man was dangerous.

"Mr. Cooper." His smile was warm and welcoming, as if he was genuinely delighted to be meeting him. He suspected that people usually found the guy *charming*. Not what Rhys had been expecting at all. "I'm Stephen Littlewood, Secretary of the Department of Pandemic Research and Prevention. I'm told you've agreed to help us find a way to eradicate Bane."

Sweet and innocent. His mind replayed Zach's words. *He wants someone sweet and innocent.*

Rhys tried to find his most trusting, unsuspicious smile. Since he wasn't sure it would be enough, he bowed his head and hoped he conveyed shyness, instead. "Well, sir, I'm not sure I have much of a choice."

"Ah, yes." Littlewood actually opened the door of Rhys's cell for him and gestured him inside. "I regret the circumstances under which we brought you here. Our people in the Clean Zone suspected the Juggernaut troops you were traveling with wouldn't be willing to let you leave their company if we asked you to come voluntarily. After that business in Texas, it didn't seem unreasonable to suspect that you were being held against your will and that was why they wouldn't leave you unsupervised."

"So you were *rescuing* me?" It took all Rhys's self-discipline not to gawk at the man in astonishment. Littlewood delivered the lie as though he expected Rhys to believe it just because he'd said it, as if it were unthinkable that his version of events could be perceived as anything other than absolute gospel.

It reminded Rhys of the way Jacob used to lie: with complete confidence that if he repeated the tale *his way* enough times, he could convince even the people who knew whatever he was saying was false that it was the truth. Rhys tried not to shudder at the uncomfortable memory.

He was still trying to figure out how to react to that knowledge when Littlewood's hand settled on his upper arm, and he had to steel himself not to flinch away.

"You're an attractive young man, Mr. Cooper. I can see why those brutes in Delta Company would be reluctant to let you go." Rhys met his eyes then, hoping he looked more confused than appalled. Was this a *seduction*?

"Thank you," he whispered, unable to control his shudder this time.

"You'll have to tell me what all they did to you sometime," Littlewood said warmly, stroking his hand along Rhys's arm. "If you would like to, of course. I'd be glad to be your confidant."

"He wants a victim," Zach had said. Rhys's stomach twisted. Was the secretary *getting off* on imagining what the Jugs might have done to him?

No. He was getting off on imagining that they had *forced* it all upon Rhys. That he had been brutalized.

"Reading the reports, imagining what they must have put you through . . ." Littlewood's voice had gone a little husky. "It's been a long time since I've felt so *moved*. I knew I had to find a way to help you. I want you to trust me, Rhys."

So it will hurt that much more when you turn cruel. Rhys bit his lip against the urge to blurt out the words. Littlewood wanted to win his confidence so that he could relish Rhys's feelings of betrayal and confusion when he showed his true colors. That was why he was bothering with the whole seduction routine.

God, Zach, I'm sorry. I don't know if I can do this.

Wait . . . Why was he still worrying about Zach's agenda? Assuming Zach had ever told him the truth about anything?

That begged the question of whether or not all these reactions Rhys was having to Littlewood were valid at all. Were they simply a result of what Zach had claimed? Was there any truth to anything Zach had said, or had he lied about everything?

Rhys's skin crawled where Littlewood's hand rested on his biceps. He couldn't quite manage to convince himself it was only Zach's assertions responsible for that reaction. His instincts were screaming a full-throated alert.

"I, um, I appreciate that." He lowered his lashes, because there was no way he could hide his instinctive revulsion if he made eye contact with Littlewood.

"Have dinner with me tonight," Littlewood said graciously. "It's your first night here. It would be miserable to eat alone, I would think."

He flicked a glance at the door. "I thought I was supposed to be locked in."

"I don't see any need for that. You've volunteered to help. You won't run away, will you?"

"Even if I wanted to, where would I go?" That much wasn't a lie. It was nearly summer in the Nevada desert. Without shelter or supplies, he'd be dead within days. Unless Darius came to rescue him—or Rhys and Schuyler found a way to provision themselves and break out—he was stuck here, where the massive solar array they'd flown over en route kept the climate regulated.

"Excellent." Littlewood beamed and finally removed the hand from Rhys's arm. It took everything Rhys had not to rub away the sensation of being touched there. "I'll send someone to bring you to my quarters at suppertime."

Rhys managed to wait until he'd left the room before he rushed to the toilet basin to vomit.

13

CHASE

The Jugs of Delta Company pushed their pace as hard as they could manage without leaving Zach behind. Nico watched him struggle to keep up on his bike all day, getting wearier by the minute but never saying a word. Finally, Nico fell into step beside him and put a hand on the small of Zach's back to help propel him forward without making him pedal so hard.

"Thanks," Zach panted, giving Nico a nod.

Nico returned it and fought very hard to forget about the fact that this was the first time he'd willingly laid a hand on Zach in ten years. He'd kept his distance when they had checked in with each other periodically, discussing what they had learned about Littlewood's operations from a safe distance. After six years, it had almost begun to feel normal.

At least until last night, when Zach had finally stopped ignoring the issue.

"You think Joe is going to stop and wait for us, or try to

trace the skimmer until it lands?" Xolani asked Toby, who snorted and shook his head.

"Knowing how Joe is about Cooper, he's probably not going to stop until he has to. I suspect provisions will become a problem. That's when we'll catch up to him."

Darius, who was leading the group and looking as though he wanted to press them to go faster, spoke over his shoulder. "Toby, when we find Joe, I want the two of you to break off and head north to Seattle. Get Bailey, Gina, Jamie, and anyone else who wants to come along and bring them back with you. We don't know how fortified this research facility is, and I don't want to have any issues tearing it apart to find Rhys."

"Let me take Titus, instead," Toby argued. "We'll head out next time we come across a road that seems to be heading north. That way we're off to Seattle that much sooner, and Joe can be there when you recover Cooper, which you know he'll want."

"Fine." Nico didn't know Darius, but he suspected the man didn't normally speak to his people in that short tone. But then, if what Zach had said about him and Cooper was true, he supposed he couldn't blame Darius for being ready to tear people's heads off.

The rest of the day passed in grim silence, broken only by farewells as Toby and Titus broke off to head north. They stopped long enough to eat and then went right back to double-timing it across Colorado and into Utah.

Zach didn't dismount his bicycle so much as collapse off it at the end of the day. While the rest of them briskly built a fire and laid out bedrolls, he sat on the ground where his shaking legs had dropped him, his chin tucked to his chest.

"You're going to have to leave me behind," he said when

Nico dug his rations out of Zach's pack for him. "I can't keep up, and you can't slow down."

"Sure we can. Cooper isn't going anywhere."

Nico didn't consider his cavalier words until his breath was driven from his lungs as Darius slammed him against the wall of the old supermarket they were camping next to.

"Easy for you to say," Darius snarled. "What's happening to him while he's *in* there?"

"Nothing!" Zach tried to wedge himself between them, though he might as well have been trying to move a boulder.

"It's okay, Zach," Nico murmured, meeting Darius's eyes squarely. "I'm sorry. I shouldn't have been so blithe. I know what Littlewood is capable of, believe me."

Darius jabbed a finger into Zach's chest. "*You* talked him into going in there, with a guy that *you*"—the finger turned on Nico—"say is a twisted motherfucker who needs to be put down. If any of y'all can't keep up, I will leave your ass in the desert, but I'm gettin' my boy *out*."

"Damn right we are." Xolani planted her hand in the middle of Darius's chest and pushed him away from Nico. "But we need these two assholes. So let's eat something and bed down so we can be on the road when the sun comes up."

Darius still looked like he wanted to fight, but he stepped away and turned his back on Nico and Zach. Nico swallowed his irritated words. If Littlewood ever got his hands on Zach, he doubted his reactions would be any better.

Darius sat next to Xolani in front of the fire, his head slunk down like he was trying to duck his own thoughts. "What's happening to him, Rasa?" he murmured, and at first Nico wondered who he was addressing. But he turned his head to look at Xolani, and she answered.

"We can't think about that." She shoved a wrapped piece of jerky at him. "This was Rhys's choice. When he gets out of there, whatever he's been through, we've got to be sure we don't take that away from him. If he's strong enough to handle it, we've got to be strong enough to let him."

Zach cleared his throat. "They think he's infected with Alpha." Darius and Xolani jerked around to look at him, and Zach stood a little straighter. "I falsified the reports I was sending in."

"Why?" Xolani demanded.

"The guy who was attacking men in the Clean Zone before the overthrow—the one we believe was Littlewood—he couldn't perform . . . sexually." Zach gave them each an uncertain look. "He would get increasingly violent because that frustrated him. Some of his victims said their attacker was trying to use the violence to arouse himself, but it didn't work. They were all raped with a foreign object."

A memory clicked into place. "Jesus. Yes. That night I was with him . . . I was sure he was on something because there was no way a man his age should be able to keep going the way he did. Probably Climaxxis or Khumitrol." Memories of what Littlewood had done to him that night, over and over, battered at his consciousness, trying to pummel their way inside. He forced them out like he had hundreds of times since it had happened. "I thought that also explained some of his aggression, since it's a known side effect, especially if you get it on the streets. That's what my rich clients used to do, to keep it out of the national medical records database."

Xolani looked appalled. "If the violence was always sexual for him, and then he couldn't do that anymore . . . God, it must have infuriated him when he ran out of pills. Of course he escalated."

Zach smiled weakly. "Yes, but my point is, if he thinks Rhys is infected with Alpha, even though asymptomatic, he's not going to be able to be very violent with him. Littlewood can't rape him, and he can't abuse him."

Xolani didn't look thrilled by that revelation. "Which begs the question of what he *can* do. If Rhys fits Littlewood's victim profile, he's going to find a way. Or he's going to take it out on others until he can get his hands on Rhys somehow."

Nico's gut lurched so suddenly he thought he might puke. "Oh *fuck*." He saw the realization strike the rest of them at almost the same instant, a wave of horror rippling across their faces. "That's why he wants the Alpha strain. In his mind, arousal and the ability to inflict pain and damage are all joined. If the Alpha strain can give him the latter, it can give him the former, right?"

"You think he believes it will give him back his virility?" Zach's skepticism was almost desperate. "It can't do that. Right?"

"I doubt it," Xolani said bleakly. "And if he's as psychotic as you say, that's just going to piss him off even more, if he gets his hands on Alpha and it doesn't work. And he'll be a hell of a lot more capable of dealing out carnage when it does."

"But Rhys *isn't* infected with Alpha." Darius gave Zach a pointed look. "Right?"

"Right." Zach drew his knees up to his chest, as though he were cold despite the heat of the evening. "I falsified that to make the bait irresistible."

"Does Rhys know this?" Xolani asked.

Zach shook his head. "After a point he said he didn't want

to know any more about what Nico and I had planned. He wasn't sure he could lie convincingly enough to pull it off."

Darius made a snorting sound that might have been a laugh. "Guess that's true. If you're right, this fucker Littlewood might just be in for a surprise."

△△△

As PROMISED, a guard was waiting for Rhys outside his cell that evening to lead him to Littlewood's quarters. He was accompanied by Dr. Thanh, who was coolly polite as she asked, "Did you produce the sample we requested, Mr. Cooper?"

Rhys's face flamed. "Um, no, not yet. I, um, I couldn't . . ." He looked down at the floor, unwilling to meet her eyes in case she saw the lie there. His embarrassment at talking about it was genuine enough, but he'd peeked inside that footlocker in his cell and slammed the lid shut, refusing to open it again.

Obviously someone had put some thought into how best to enable him to donate the sample they required. A few of the items in the trunk were familiar enough—he'd become well acquainted with plugs of every variety during his early months with the Jugs. Even now, when Darius was back from patrol and on base at Fort Vancouver, he liked to fuck Rhys several times during the night and plug him up in the morning. He'd make Rhys go through his day that way, carrying multiple loads of Darius's spunk inside him.

But that was where his familiarity with the aids they had provided ended. That pump-like thing that sort of looked like a mouth? He wasn't keen on messing with it, even if it hadn't been modified with tubing to be some sort of collector.

Another one looked like an altogether different orifice, one he had no actual familiarity with, given the sum of his sexual experience was with men. Rhys could guess at its purpose, but he didn't want anything to do with it.

In the end, he hadn't been able to make himself use any of them. Performance and willingness issues aside, it was probably better that he not give them anything they wanted too quickly or easily.

Dr. Thanh's mouth pressed into a tense line. "As you mentioned, Mr. Cooper, time is something of an issue here. The sooner you can give us what we need, the sooner we can all have our freedom."

Did she really believe that? Because Rhys didn't see how someone like Littlewood just let everyone return to their lives after this was all over and he had what he wanted.

"I'll do what I can," he muttered and hurried past her in the direction the guard indicated.

Littlewood's quarters were far more comfortable than the cell they had put Rhys in. It was a lavish apartment suite on the opposite side of the compound from where Rhys was housed. The food spread out on the table was simple—smoked meat of some kind, and stewed and preserved vegetables. It was the same sort of fare they had been given when they were staying in quarantine outside the Clean Zone. Rhys suspected the Clean Zone was provisioning this operation out of their common stores, even if the general population didn't know it. He'd certainly seen nothing resembling a garden on the premises.

"Thank you for joining me, Rhys." Littlewood's smile was charming, and it left Rhys feeling like he needed to shower a sheen of oil off his skin. "Please, sit down. It's not much, but we've all managed to learn how to make do since the pandemic, haven't we?"

"Yes, sir." How he managed to twist his mouth up into a smile, Rhys had no idea. He sat at the table and began picking at the plate Littlewood set in front of him.

"Call me Stephen," the secretary entreated. He leaned back in his chair, plucking lazy bites off his own plate. "Tell me more about your time with the Juggernauts. We normal people know so little about them. I imagine they've become quite uncivilized, living as they do."

"I suppose that depends on how you think they live . . . Stephen," Rhys said tightly.

"As I understand it, they forced you to service them sexually several times a day. What else should I call them, if not uncivilized? Perhaps even *savage*." Littlewood tutted. "And they kept you with them, even though it was no longer necessary to save your life. Tell me, do they all still force themselves upon you or has one of them claimed you?"

I'm sorry, Darius. If salacious details were what would keep Littlewood in a chatty mood, then that's what Rhys would give him.

He bowed his head because he couldn't quite manage to force a blush. "The leader of the squad that found me at the monastery. I belong to him."

Even knowing he was deliberately saying it to misrepresent the situation for Littlewood didn't stop the small thrill that zinged through Rhys at the words. Yes. He belonged to Darius. And that didn't seem like a shameful thing anymore.

When Rhys looked up, Littlewood's eyes gleamed, and he actually licked his lips. "Does he hurt you?"

"Yes." Rhys glanced away again. He didn't want to see

Littlewood getting some warped pleasure from this. None-theless, he still caught the motion of the secretary's hand dropping off the table and down into his lap.

"Is it distressing you to talk about it?" The man's voice was breathless, almost dreamy.

"*Yes.*" No lie there, either. It was bothering the fuck out of him to act like these things, which were special between him and Darius, were something perverted and wrong in the way Littlewood wanted them to be.

Littlewood rose from his chair, rounding the table to approach Rhys. Under his lashes, Rhys snuck a glance at the placket of his trousers, which boasted perhaps a little bulge, though nothing remarkable. Littlewood rubbed the heel of his palm against it like he was trying to coax it into something more.

"I'll be honest with you, Rhys," Littlewood said huskily. "It's been a very, *very* long time since I've felt the things I've felt when you tell me about what they've done to you."

"I-I don't know what you mean." Rhys's voice shook with the shudder that ran through him when Littlewood's other hand landed on his shoulder.

"You don't need to know what I mean. You just need to do what I say, the way you did what the Juggernaut who claimed you commanded. Forget about him. You'll obey me now."

"Obey?" Rhys blinked at him in disbelief. He made it sound so beneficent, as if he were doing Rhys a favor. Did this twisted fuck honestly believe he was a step up from Darius?

"I want you to strip."

"*What?*" Rhys sprang to his feet and whirled to face Littlewood.

"Do it now, Rhys. I want to see the body they used over

and over." When Rhys stood there staring at him, a dangerous look narrowed Littlewood's eyes. "*Don't* make me get my cane."

Cane.

Rhys swallowed against his rising gorge.

Oh fuck.

Of everything he and Darius had done together, every torment Darius had devised that somehow in Rhys's strangely wired senses had become pleasure, using a cane was the one thing Darius would never, ever do. They'd never talked about it, but Darius couldn't have missed, on those first couple of nights they were together, the hideous purple-black stripes—both fresh and fading—on Rhys's backside and thighs. Xolani certainly hadn't when she'd seen Rhys shower that first day at the monastery. She'd known them exactly for what they were. Father Maurice had always favored his cane . . .

"I can see that thought terrifies you. Good. You need to understand that I control things here. This whole facility is under my discretional authority." Littlewood's lips turned up in a tight smile. "Congress doesn't want to know what goes on here, as long as they have hope that someday they'll get what they want from it. They don't care what we have to do to get it. The guards answer to me. You have nowhere to go and no choice but to do as you're told. Now strip."

Rhys's hands went to the buttons of his shirt automatically, but a hot twinge between his shoulders made him pause. *Oh . . .* He'd forgotten about that.

He bowed his head to hide his smile and quickly opened his shirt. He didn't bother to suppress the shudder of revulsion when Littlewood's hand ventured down his unmarked torso.

"You look so clean," Littlewood murmured. "Not polluted

by their hands. Not some disgusting receptacle for them to pump their filth into. A sweet, innocent boy made into such a hideous whore through no fault of his own. How you must have suffered as they degraded you. Turn around."

Gladly, Rhys thought viciously. He pulled his shoulders tight until he felt the scabs on his back crack open, and spun on his heel.

Littlewood's gasp was almost masked by his stumbling retreat, the crash as he tripped over his own furniture and tumbled to the floor. Rhys whirled back around, sneering down at him as he jerked his shirt back over the oozing welts Darius had left on him the night before Rhys had let himself be taken.

"Like what you see *now*, you *sick fuck*?" Rhys spat.

Littlewood managed to get to his feet, but he cowered against the far wall, cringing, and Rhys advanced on him. Rhys got up close, right in his face. His hand shot down and gripped the flaccid lump in Littlewood's trousers, giving it a brutal twist.

"You were so busy trying to work yourself up over what Darius and the Jugs had done to me that you never asked me one very important question. Want to know what that question is?"

Littlewood gibbered incoherently, his face ashen, and Rhys gave his 'nads another cruel yank. "*Ask me!*"

"*What?*" Littlewood wailed.

"You never asked whether I *liked* it." Rhys licked his lips ostentatiously. "I *loved* it. Begged him for it. Couldn't get enough of it. You want a victim? *Fuck you*. I'm not a victim, and I never will be. Not for some pathetic old bastard like you who can't even get it up." He released Littlewood's junk and made a show of wiping his hand on his shirt. "You all thought I was safe, but you fucked up. Now you better hope your researchers come up with a vaccine fucking *immediately*, or in a few weeks, that pitiful slug you were trying to get to rise to the occasion is going to rot right the fuck off."

He backed away from Littlewood, and with one last scornful look, left him whimpering as Rhys shut the door and left the secretary's quarters.

14

FALLOUT

Rhys had only been back to his own cell for twenty minutes or so when Dr. Thanh and Logan came pounding on his door, dressed in full hermetic suits.

"Why didn't you tell us you were wounded? Do you know what you've done?" she demanded. She sounded shaken. *Good.*

"By the time I found out I was infected with Alpha, you and your guards had already been around me." Rhys shrugged. "But here. I'm sure you want this."

He crossed to the sink basin, which still had the mouth-like suction toy/device/thing with all its attached tubing in it, draining dry. He picked a lidded specimen cup full of milky fluid off the edge, tossing it to her. "Might want to hurry with that."

She rushed from the room, leaving Logan behind. Rhys leaned against the wall, his arms folded across his chest, and stared into the masked face. He smiled sardonically. "Bit late for the suit, isn't it?"

He supposed it said something about him that Rhys

couldn't bring himself to be horrified by the fact that he'd infected all the people here. He hadn't known he was positive for Alpha, and they had abducted him, and with their complicity they had put a stamp of approval on Littlewood's activities. They probably didn't actually deserve what they'd gotten, but right now, with his skin still crawling from the brush of Littlewood's hands, it felt like they did.

Or maybe he was just too fucking tired to care.

"I guess it is." With the sound of seals releasing, Logan took off the hood and met Rhys's eyes. He looked old, and tired, and weighed down with a tremendous burden. "You realize if she can't deactivate the virus and synthesize a vaccine, we're all dead. Even if she can, it might be too late."

"Did I ask you to kidnap me and bring me here?" Rhys demanded. "This is your doing. How many years has this been going on? How many people have you kidnapped for your research? How many people have you put in Littlewood's hands, knowing what he does to them?"

"How did you . . .?" Logan's eyes widened. "You're a plant."

"Do you really think the Jugs would trust anyone from the Clean Zone enough to leave me unsupervised, unless it was deliberate? They're coming for me. They'll be here within days."

"How do you know so much about our operations?" Logan made himself comfortable on the edge of the bunk.

Rhys waved off the question. He wouldn't blow Zach's cover. "Doesn't matter. The people you've taken, the ones suspected of having been sexually involved with Jugs . . . How many actually have been?"

"None. We've been seeking a source for the Alpha strain

for years to no avail."

"Why kidnap them? Why not try to get volunteers? Hell, why not ask the Jugs?"

"Volunteers? From among people who have spent potentially *years* in seclusion, then gone through quarantine, and finally found a home inside the Clean Zone? Do you think after all that, they would volunteer to leave their homes to go someplace where people might be working with live samples of the Bane virus and be experimented on?" Logan gave the question a skeptical twist. "Littlewood has convinced congress that our work here has to be classified, that there would be a public panic if the population knew we were trying to obtain Bane samples. In addition, pressing subjects into service in the lab provides him with a convenient cover for his *extracurricular* projects."

"His victims, you mean." Rhys sneered at him. "You're as bad as he is. 'Subjects.' 'Projects.' They're fucking *people*."

Something flickered in Logan's eyes. "You're not the first to make that point. I admit I've had to cultivate a certain detachment about it all."

"Where are they now? The *subjects*. Did they even survive? Or did Littlewood get his hands on them?"

"Not all of them were abused, no. Littlewood only took an interest in a particular few. As for the others, the people we strongly suspected of having been exposed to Alpha, we *had* to get them away from the Clean Zone so there was no danger they would infect anyone else. Once they were here, it made sense to find a use for them. We don't have the ability to do computer modeling of the potential test results anymore. Live trials are our only sure way to get the data we need."

Logan cleared his throat. "We do what we can with

animals who can contract the virus, of course. But there have been times when we've needed to observe the progress of the virus in a living human, particularly when we thought we might have something to counteract it. For the people who weren't needed, we've given them housing nearby. We provide them with rations, help them support themselves. Some of them have made homes with the personnel who work here in the lab. They can't go back to the Clean Zone, even though it turned out they weren't infected with Alpha after all."

"Why? Because they might tell people about your operations?"

Logan nodded slowly. "That's part of it, yes."

"Uh-huh. And how many of them did Littlewood get his hands on?"

Logan's eyes slid away from his. "Too many."

"Why didn't you do anything to stop him?"

"You have to understand my position here, Rhys." The look on Logan's face was wearily earnest. "I have no power or control. And I think Littlewood keeps me alive for petty revenge. I once was party to manipulating him, and I think he relishes his authority over me."

"Who *are* you?"

"I should be dead," he said, not answering the question. "I was sentenced to die for my role in implementing Project Juggernaut, but I struck a deal. I knew congress would assemble a department to work on preventing another outbreak of the pandemic, and I agreed to work with them, tell them everything I knew. Back then, of course, we had no idea that Thanh was still alive. I'm a soldier, not a scientist, but I was all they had. They couldn't discard such a potential resource." Logan sighed, plucking the sheet at the edge of the bunk. "So they kept me imprisoned to consult with the scientists they were able to assemble. Eventually Thanh came along, and that was when the decision was made to set up a lab outside the Clean Zone so that we could obtain live samples of the virus and work with them without endangering the bulk of the population."

"I'm a soldier, not a scientist." Rhys's eyes widened as something fell into place. "You're General McClosky."

The old man nodded. "I am."

Rhys snorted. "Wow, do I know some people who would *love* to see you dead."

McClosky nodded with a rueful smile. "Yes, I hardly blame them. And if what you said about the Juggernaut troops coming after you is true, they'll get their chance soon enough. I guess it's long past due."

"Am I supposed to feel sorry for you?"

"No." McClosky rose, wandering toward the door with bowed shoulders. "It'll be a relief, actually. I've evaded justice for long enough. And if your Jugs don't get to me, well, I suppose the wounds you kept hidden from us will do the trick with a much more poetic flare, don't you?"

"WHAT THE FUCK HAVE YOU DONE?" Schuyler demanded when Rhys insisted on seeing her again the next day. Apparently the research facility personnel had decided that quarantining him was futile at this point, since they didn't protest taking him out of his cell, despite the new discovery of his open wounds. "I've been hearing panicked voices all over the place out there."

Rhys rubbed the back of his neck. "I, um . . . Remember how I told you they said I was infected with Alpha? I didn't remember at the time that I had some healing welts on my back."

The color fled from her face. "Oh fuck." She sank down on the edge of her cot. "How many people are out there?"

"I'm not sure." Rhys shrugged. "Two dozen, maybe? A couple virologists. Lab techs. Guards. *Littlewood*."

"The secretary of the DPRP is here?"

There didn't seem to be any sense covering up his secret agenda now, even if they were being monitored, so Rhys gave her a brief rundown of what Zach had told him about Littlewood and the DPRP's sinister agenda. Then he told her what had happened that night in Littlewood's quarters.

He thought he might have seen some respect in her eyes when he finished.

"You know what he could have done to you if you weren't infected with Alpha, right?"

Rhys nodded, looking anywhere but at her frank stare. "Yeah, I knew."

"And Darius *agreed* to this?"

"He, um, wasn't exactly thrilled with it, but it was my choice."

She rolled her eyes. "Of course it was."

"Oh Jesus! What did I do now?" Rhys snapped, suddenly beyond his tolerance for her disdain.

"When you're with someone, you make choices like that *together*. It's called being partners. If Emmy ever pulled something like that, or Ka—" She threw up her hands in disgust. "Maybe you could try taking what he feels into account for once instead if it always being about you."

"Oh, fuck off." Rhys glared at her. "Just because he didn't like it doesn't mean we didn't decide together. Hell, Joe and Toby and Xolani all weighed in too. I didn't do it behind their backs."

They fell into a sullen silence. Some portion of him wanted to storm out and leave her to stew in solitude, since she was obviously always going to think the worst of him, but his reluctance to be alone overruled it. She was a part of his life among the Jugs, even if she was a contentious one. He needed that connection right now, needed to remember that Darius was coming for him and that he wouldn't be alone here when these people began to die.

"I don't see why you insist on thinking I don't care about him," Rhys said, deflating after a moment. He poked at a threadbare spot of fabric threatening to become a hole near the knee of his fatigues. "I mean, I know in the beginning it . . . took me a while to accept the way my life had changed, the things I thought I needed to do to survive. But since I settled in, have I ever given anyone any reason to think I wasn't committed to staying with Darius?"

"Have you ever given anyone a reason to think you *were*?" Schuyler shot back. "Look, I know my way around undemonstrative people. Delta Company is full of them. But I see you and Darius, in the canteen at Fort Vancouver or wherever, and he can't keep his eyes off you. He can't keep his *hands* off you. But you won't make eye contact with *anyone*, like you're embarrassed to be there, and while you'll let him touch you, you never reach out to him."

Rhys shrugged, resisting the urge to squirm. "I'm just not comfortable doing that."

"Doing what? Showing someone you care about them?"

The hole in his fatigues got bigger, and Rhys focused on widening it even more.

"Cooper, do you have any idea what Darius was like before we found you?"

That got his attention. He stopped picking at his pants and finally met her eyes. "I know what he was like when I met him."

"That's a start. He's different now, right?"

Rhys nodded. The Darius he knew now would not have been as cold and unfeeling as the Darius he had first known. It might have made a difference in the way Rhys had handled things back then.

But the way Rhys had handled things back then had been part of the catalyst for Darius to change, hadn't it? Darius hadn't felt right about what he'd done to Rhys in the name of keeping him alive, so he'd softened, started finally listening to Rhys and figuring out what Rhys needed to make everything bearable.

It had taken time, but they'd finally begun to understand each other.

Schuyler let him mull on that for a while. "Darius had seen too much, done too much. Every time his squad had to put down an infected survivor, he was the one who pulled the trigger because he wouldn't make any of his people do it. He had to stop feeling or it was going to drive him to eat a bullet. Some of us wondered if he was shutting down, but then you gave him something to care about again."

Rhys returned to worrying the hole at his knee. "I know."

Schuyler made a frustrated sound. "Look, it's simple. Do you love him, even a little? And if you do, would it kill you to act like it?"

"It's not that easy." He needed to be done with this conversation. Now.

"Yeah, it really is."

"It's *not!*" Rhys shot to his feet, stalking as far away as the four walls of the cell would allow. "I won't make him any promises I can't keep."

Schuyler hissed a curse. "You little fucker. You *are* planning to leave him."

"No!" He whirled on her. "But it's not like I have a choice."

"You don't have a choice about whether or not you're going to have a future with him?"

"*What* future?" Rhys's voice rose so high and loud it cracked, and he pulled it back down. "God, it's all people talk about lately. Where we're going to go after Lewis-McChord and then after that, whether the Jugs will ever have a place to settle down. What's going to happen with the Clean Zone in five, ten, twenty years if they don't get their act together. But you of all people should know there's *no such thing* as a future."

"Me of all people?" She scoffed. "Why would I know that?"

Rhys lifted his chin. "Because you can't have children."

Schuyler's face flushed with fury. "Did Kaleo tell you about that?"

"He told me things weren't easy for some of the Jug women, that you were all the strongest of the Jugs because of it." He shifted his weight from one leg to the other, her stillness making him nervous. "After seeing what Emmy had to do, having an abortion so her baby wouldn't be born with the Rot after Jacob infected her, it wasn't hard to figure out what Kaleo meant or who he was talking about."

"And you think that means I don't have a future?" Her upper lip curled into a sneer. "You've been listening to too much of Xolani's fatalistic bullshit. Fuck you, Cooper. You don't know shit."

"I'm just saying, more than most people, *you* should get it. There's no sense on counting on a tomorrow that won't be there. There's only the moments you're here until you *aren't* anymore." Rhys began pacing, no longer concerned with her anger in his desperate need to make her *understand*. His words came tumbling out in an uncontrolled torrent. "I was nine years old when I went into a bunker. I came out three years later and everyone was just gone. The whole world, *gone*. I watched everyone I knew drop off, one after the other until there was only me and Jacob. A dozen people entered that monastery, and seven years later, only two were left."

He swung his hands, whirling on her violently. "One after another. Year after year. All gone. I put a bullet in the head of the only person who cared about me when my mom was sick and Jacob was making my life hell. I saw a colony of twenty-some people kill themselves for no reason. I saw Kaleo a-and one second he was walking through the woods to check on something he'd picked up on his scanner and the next he was on the ground with half his head missing. Gone. Gone. *Gone*."

Fuck. His eyes were burning now. Rhys wiped them angrily with his sleeve. "But now I have Darius and Xolani and Joe and the rest of the Jugs, right? And I'm *happy*. I am! Stupid as it is, I really am." He met her stare squarely, willing her to see the truth he was trying to speak. "Only, I'm not one of you, and I never will be. I'm too weak. Too fragile. Xolani says my heart might be damaged from years of starvation. It might be tomorrow or next week or next month, but sooner or later, *I'm* gonna be the one who's gone. And I accept that. I'm ready for it. But why would I tell Darius I love him and promise him a future there's no way I can deliver?"

He held her gaze as her face grew a little pale, her freckles darker than usual. "Shit, Cooper." She shook her head, muttering in disgust. "All right. I get it. You've been dealt a rotten hand and seen things no kid should see at way too young an age. But you don't stop living just so no one notices when you die. You live even *more*, live *harder*, live like you've got nothing to lose." She snorted, flopping back against the wall along her bunk. "Hell, for all Xolani's cynicism, even she does that. Pack a hundred days' worth of living into every day you've got, so when that moment comes and your number's up, you didn't miss out on anything."

Rhys swallowed against the thickness in his throat. He wanted to believe her. Wanted to let go and just exist without the constant awareness of his own doom hanging over him. Wanted to enjoy life and enjoy being with Darius without holding back, without wondering if losing him would eventually fill Darius with the same aching emptiness Rhys had felt after each consecutive loss.

Maybe he could. But how did he learn to stop looking past tomorrow in anything but vague, hypothetical terms?

"I've got to go," he muttered, hunched over as though he could hold the contents of his chest inside. He couldn't seem to uncurl and straighten up to meet her eyes.

"Sure." He couldn't quite read her tone. It wasn't the resigned disgust he was used to, at least. That was something. "I'll give it another week, and if no one shows up, we're breaking out of here."

Rhys nodded quickly and rapped on the door, waiting for

the guard to respond. Unable to resist, he asked over his shoulder, "Did Kaleo decide *with* you, when he made the choice to go after Jacob?"

The guard opened the door just then, so he almost missed her answer when she whispered, "No."

Dr. Thanh was waiting for him when he returned to his cell.

"We need another sample," she announced without preamble. He couldn't see her very well through her hermetic suit, but something about her presence screamed exhaustion. He doubted she'd slept in the last couple of days.

"The three I've given you already haven't been enough?"

"No."

Something about the way she said it made him freeze where he stood. "Have the samples I've given you even made it to the lab?" he asked, swallowing thickly. "Or have they been rerouted to people who might want to infect themselves with Alpha to protect against Beta? Perhaps just *one* certain someone?"

"*Please.*" The whisper hissed from the speaker of her hood, a broken, desperate sound. "None of us here have a choice. He's promised the guards he'll infect them and give them immunity if he can just get infected with Alpha first, and they're desperate enough to believe him. They'll kill us if we don't cooperate."

Rhys bowed his head, understanding for the first time Zach's need to pray. It certainly felt like he could use some guidance here. "I'm sorry. But no. No more. Not if it means *he* becomes a Jug." He looked up, staring squarely into her mask. "You know how dangerous he'll be if that happens. I won't give him the Alpha strain."

"You're *killing* us!" she said urgently.

"How many people has *he* raped and killed?" Was this what Darius had felt when Rhys had first met him? Or when he had made the call that someone had to be put down? Numb to the prospect of another lost life? Unmoved? Did he just shut down because it was the only way to stay sane? "You people abducted me knowing I was infected with Alpha. And yeah, I set myself up to be taken so I could stop you, but I didn't make you do it. I'm sorry if that means more people have to die, but he *has* to be stopped."

"What about our families? Do you understand that my children will never see me again?"

There was despair in her tone now. Rhys brushed past her and lay on his bunk, curling into a fetal ball with his back to her. "He did this to you. I didn't."

The sound through her mask of her weeping was haunting. He'd be hearing it in his nightmares for years to come. Once he got past this strange feeling of not giving a damn.

This wasn't anything like what he'd imagined when he'd agreed to Zach's plan. And why had Zach asked him to do this at all if he knew Rhys was infected with Alpha?

Had Zach *hoped* for this?

"Just the tubing on the collector. Please?" She spoke so softly that Rhys almost didn't hear it. "I don't need much, and I won't let him know I have it. Discard the rest of the sample if you want, but let me have the tubing?"

He rolled slowly, blinking at her, then nodded once. "Come back in an hour."

15

GRACE

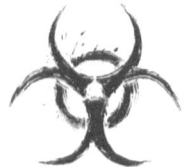

They found Joe on the shores of the Great Salt Lake just before sunset on the fourth day of their pursuit. Darius greeted him with a tight smile, looking him up and down to assess his condition. He looked like he'd been waiting there for a while, at least long enough to have bathed and rested.

"You send Toby and Titus to get reinforcements from Seattle?" he asked immediately. He nodded in approval when Darius confirmed.

"I followed the trajectory of the personnel carrier until I got to the lake," Joe went on, "but I figured that by the time I skirted around it, I'd have lost track of their route. Do we have any idea where they went?"

Xolani nodded at Nico, who was helping a pitiful-looking Zach off his bike. "He does. Says he got the location from the nav system of their skim-craft."

Joe narrowed his eyes at Nico. "Looks familiar. Do we know him?"

Nico's lips quirked into a slight grin. "I've been hearing

that a lot lately. I used to be with Sierra Company. I'm a friend of Kaleo's."

"Right." Joe nodded, and there was an edge of exhaustion that could be heard in his voice, despite the fact that he wasn't very verbose. Darius suspected he hadn't been resting here by the lake long enough to make up for the labor of chasing after a lightcar.

Xolani shoved his rucksack at him, which Zach had been carrying since he hadn't had one of his own. "Eat. You didn't take any supplies with you."

Joe dropped to the ground and began tearing into his pack, diving voraciously into his rations. "Didn't have time. Snared a rabbit a couple days ago, so it hasn't been that bad."

Darius worked with Xolani and Nico to set up camp. Zach was too destroyed to pitch in, but he hadn't uttered a single complaint. It reminded Darius of the way Rhys had been when he'd first begun traveling with them, especially on the harrowing pursuit of Jacob Houtman. Despite the conversation they'd all overheard, when Nico had refused to touch Zach, now he hovered over him, laying out his bedroll, fetching him rations, rubbing his legs when they cramped up.

They were all too tired and concerned for much chitchat, though Nico made the attempt.

"Will Kaleo be coming back with Toby and Titus?" he asked innocently. "I was surprised to see Schuyler was here without him."

Darius exchanged looks with Xolani and Joe, then sighed. "Kaleo's dead. Killed in action a couple years ago." He pointed to Zach. "By his brother, matter of fact."

Zach's head shot up. "What?"

They ended up telling the entire story, all the bits Rhys

had omitted when he'd told Zach the short version of his experiences with Jacob Houtman and his father. How Houtman had become infected with Alpha and then abducted and infected three civilians with Beta, including Rhys's only surviving friend from his adolescence to torment Rhys when Houtman's attempts to turn the Jugs against Rhys had failed.

"I'm sorry," Zach whispered when they finished. Darius snorted softly when Nico drew Zach protectively against him.

Yeah, that resolve wasn't going to last long.

"Wasn't your fault," Joe muttered.

"No, but considering the history, I've certainly given you no reason to think any better of me or my family." He sighed. "I'm sorry I tried to talk Rhys into keeping our plan from you. I was afraid what might happen if you knew—"

Xolani sniggered, and Darius shook his head, chuckling softly. "You really think Rhys would keep something like that from us?"

"I realize that now," Zach murmured. "You're doing all this despite having no reason to trust us. I understand."

"How generous of you," Xolani said flatly. "You spent six years waiting for an opportunity to fall into your laps so you could stop Littlewood rather than making the opportunity yourselves. If Rhys hadn't come along and given you an opening, you'd still be sitting around playing espionage in the DPRP while Littlewood continued to do his thing."

"Hey, now—" Nico started to argue, but Zach cut him off.

"You're right," he conceded. He drew his calf out of Nico's grasp, hugging his knee to his chest. "I know we should have done something sooner, but I don't know what we could have done. Or maybe it's just self-interest that kept me from acting. Maybe I'm making excuses." He met Nico's eyes with a bleak smile. "I kept hoping we'd find a way that wouldn't exacerbate bad relations between the Clean Zone and the Jugs."

Nico pulled his hands into his lap as if only now realizing how thoughtlessly he'd been touching Zach just moments before. Darius rolled his eyes and turned away. Until Rhys was safe, he was having a hard enough time not beating down one or both of them. He didn't have any sympathy to spare for the pair's star-crossed-lovers routine.

Zach apparently didn't have anything else to say as he pushed himself to his feet with a barely suppressed whimper and wandered down the street.

Nico began scrutinizing their surroundings. "This whole area's been cleared of revs, right?"

Before Darius could confirm that Delta Company had patrolled Utah and Nevada years ago, Nico jumped up and chased after Zach anyway.

Xolani snorted when they were gone. "It's worse than watching you and Rhys angst over each other, back in the day." She curled up on her side on her bedroll, turning her back to everyone. After a moment, Darius and Joe did the same.

NICO'S FOOTFALLS announced his approach before he spoke.

"You shouldn't wander off by yourself," he chided. Zach ignored him, idly inspecting the exterior of an abandoned lakefront house that must have been quite lovely back before the pandemic.

"How are you feeling?" Nico tried again.

"Like I've taken a beating on every major muscle group for

fourteen hours a day." He'd meant to come off as flippant, but it emerged as exhausted. "I'm fine, Nico. Go get some sleep."

"You think I'd be able to sleep with you out here alone?"

His eyes burned, but he refused to turn to face Nico. "I've been alone for ten years. It's familiar. And better than being surrounded by people who don't trust me . . . or who resent me."

"You never made new friends in the Clean Zone besides Morris?" There was a plaintive note in Nico's voice, begging Zach to say that his life in the Clean Zone wasn't as lonely and melancholy as Zach always made it sound.

Until Nico had returned six years ago, Zach hadn't had a chance to tell him about how most of his uninfected friends had abandoned him because they had feared Zach's relationship with Nico would result in him passing the Beta strain to them all. By the time Nico knew just how alone Zach had been during those years, it had been too late. Zach's isolation and unwillingness to trust anyone again had taken on a life of its own.

"I have acquaintances who come to my weekly Bible study groups. Quite a few, actually. We had to find a bigger venue. Some of them went on to start their own ministries, though. They've even made handwritten copies of passages from my annotated Bible for their congregations." He smiled wanly. "So when I'm not spying on the DPRP, I've become a one-man seminary."

Nico swallowed audibly, his voice thick with pride and affection. "Who better?"

"I even almost had a relationship once. She was lovely. Sassy. Funny. She understood about you. I spent a while trying to convince myself it wouldn't really be adultery, and she spent a while trying to convince herself that she was okay with the fact that I'd never be able to give her my whole heart." Zach shrugged, reaching down to strip the seeds off a long stalk of grass. "Neither of us could quite manage it."

"When was that?"

"Just before you came back from Texas." He felt Nico behind him, not quite close enough to touch, and it hurt. He'd needed the help Nico had been giving him to keep up with the Jugs, and the comfort and assistance at the end of the day, but it didn't mean that so-close-but-not-quite contact wasn't its own brand of agony. "Fortuitous timing, I suppose."

He finally turned and made himself look at Nico. He could barely see the man he'd met all those years ago. Back then, just a few months after the first wave of the pandemic, Nico hadn't quite lost all the dazzle and polish that had made him an escort who commanded top dollar from powerful and famous people. He'd had a certain cockiness, a flare that had drawn Zach like a flame draws a moth. Zach's life until then had been all about black and white, austerity and moral absolutes.

Nico had changed everything.

It was hard to see that sparkling rentboy under the grizzled man who stood before him. Zach didn't know exactly where in the ruins of Colorado Springs's uninhabited areas Nico had made his home when he hadn't been combing the desert trying to locate the DPRP's secret lab, but wherever it was, it was rough. Nico's face was densely bearded, his hair a long, thick black mane. His clothing was threadbare in places and fraying in others, and his face was deeply lined at the corners of his eyes and mouth from too much sun exposure.

He wasn't the same man Zach had committed his heart to

ten years ago, and yet he was. Those fathomless brown eyes were still unspeakably gentle when they settled on Zach, and still as full of yearning. Sometimes he wondered if, after this many years, he and Nico really still loved each other and not just the *idea* of each other. But it didn't matter any more than it had mattered that they had fallen almost before they even got their first full glimpse of each other. Here at the end of the world, the rules about how to wisely conduct relationships, like taking it slow and waiting for the perfect, compatible partner, didn't apply.

Nico was standing closer than he usually did. If nothing else, the last few days had broken down that barrier. Zach smiled sadly. He'd beg if he had to. There was just no point to pride.

"Will you hold me? You've been touching me for days. It doesn't matter. Please?"

Nico stood frozen for far too long, long enough for Zach's heart to sink and anger to start simmering in his gut at his own idiocy for even asking. But then Nico's arms were around him, Nico's body pressed up against his, and nothing else mattered. They were both sweaty and dirty from days of travel, and neither of them smelled clean, but Zach didn't *care*. He wrapped his arms around Nico and clung to him as though his very salvation depended on it.

Nico's grasp was no less desperate. He held Zach until he couldn't breathe for being squeezed so tightly, until they were both shaking with the emotion of it.

"I've missed you so fucking much," Nico whispered brokenly, and Zach turned his face, seeking the full lips under the bushy beard. His poor, touch-starved Nico, who craved contact the way other people craved food. Living in isolation except for the few times a year when Zach slipped out of the Clean Zone on a hunting party to meet with him and confer on what Littlewood and the DPRP were up to. How had Nico endured it? How had he had the resolve to keep himself from touching Zach until now?

Nico's lips parted, pulling Zach's seeking tongue into his mouth, and then he had Zach pinned against the wall of the house and he was all over him. Hands and teeth and tongue everywhere, on each salty inch of stubbled skin. He grabbed Zach's backside roughly and ground his hips against Zach, the pressure both a relief and a torment against the restrained bulge in Zach's trousers.

"God, Nico. Yes . . ." Zach sobbed between kisses, seeking more. Nico's trembling hands tore at their flies, his callused fist clasping both of them together as he thrust. Zach buried his hands in the tangled waves of Nico's thick hair to get more traction so he could push back. "I love you, Nico. God, I love you. Please. More."

Nico stopped thrusting long enough to shove Zach's pants down his hips, and Zach practically tripped trying to kick his boots off so he could step out of them completely. He ripped his shirt over his head and threw it aside, then jerked anxiously at Nico's shirt too, unable to stand the separation any longer. And afraid, if truth be told, that Nico might change his mind and put that horrible, soul-killing distance between them again.

He didn't, though. Instead, he seized Zach's ass and hauled him up until his feet left the ground. Zach wrapped his legs around Nico obligingly, and Nico slammed him against the wall again. It was rough against Zach's back, but he didn't care. What he cared about was Nico's thickly matted chest grating against his own sparsely furred one, about the sweat slicking their skin, making them glide together.

Nico spat on his fingers and reached behind and underneath, and Zach groaned at the burn as a single digit forced its way into him. Ten years had passed since Nico had used his fingers to spread and open Zach. Not his cock, of course. Never that, not while Zach refused to accept the Alpha strain. But once upon a time, Zach had become intimately familiar with the pleasures of having that tight muscle pried open, having fingertips against his prostate, catapulting things that already felt amazing into a whole new stratosphere of pleasure.

It ached now, but Zach welcomed it. He reached down to continue what Nico had started earlier, gripping their cocks so they could slide against each other, pumping and groaning. Another finger relentlessly invaded Zach's ass, and he answered the pain with a cautious bite at Nico's lips. Nico growled in response, knocking their teeth together for an uncomfortable instant as he sought another savage kiss, which he pulled back from quickly when it started spiraling out of control.

Zach was careening toward the edge, knowing that beyond the precipice waited a heedless plunge into bliss. He sprinted for it, fucking himself on Nico's fingers while his hand pumped them both. His head thudded against the house behind him, and he cried out, so close to that peak it was almost unbearably good, the release hovering just out of reach, taunting him.

It was the threatening presence of a third finger, rough and dry and pushing against his rim, that put him over. Nico's mouth latched on to Zach's throat as he cried out, biting and sucking firmly while Zach spilled over his fist, his seed slicking both their cocks and his muscles clamping around Nico's fingers. Zach's climax seemed to break down what little restraint Nico had left. He rutted against Zach with single-minded ferocity, groaning and panting as he chased his own release.

It was beautiful when it happened—the sound he made, the way he shuddered in Zach's arms and went slack. Zach hung on to him with arms and legs, unwilling to let go as Nico held him against the weather-beaten wall and caught his breath.

He felt the conflict and reluctance seep back into his body, making him tense in Zach's arms, making him try to draw away.

"No." Zach held on tighter. "No. No more."

"Zach—"

"I said *no*." Zach lifted his face away from Nico's shoulder and glared at him. "If you're going to leave me again, you're going to have to sneak away and run off like a coward, because I'm not letting you do it this time."

"I can't risk—"

"*I can.* It's *my* life. *My* risk." He unwrapped himself from around Nico, lowering his weight to the ground, but he didn't let go, not even to fix their clothing. Semen was drying on his right hand, and his ass ached from the intrusion of Nico's fingers, but he held on. "Can you look me in the eye and tell me it's been worth it, being apart? Because the last twenty minutes have meant more to me than the last decade."

"I've caused so many deaths, *cariño*. I know I was used, and it wasn't my fault, but I *did*. If I can save just one person, just *you* . . . I couldn't live with myself if I was the cause of your death. I couldn't."

Zach shook his head adamantly. "There are no guarantees,

Nico. None. Yes, there could be an accident and I could get infected. I could also die of any number of other mishaps, whether you're with me or not. If it's going to happen, I'd rather be with you."

Nico closed his eyes, his face anguished. "Do you have any idea what it would do to me if you died and I was the reason?"

"So you'd be okay if you *weren't* the reason?"

"No, of course not, but—"

"If I died of the Rot tomorrow, I'd do so content, knowing I'd spent tonight where I belong, *with you*." He clasped Nico's face between his hands, compelling his gaze. "No guarantees. I won't accept the Alpha strain because that's not the Lord's plan for me. But what we have, Nico, it's *grace*. It's a gift from God. I won't let you reject it."

A tear tracked down Nico's dusty cheek. "I don't have your faith in God."

"Then have faith in *me*."

"I do." Nico collapsed against him, trembling, and buried his wet face against Zach's throat. "I'm so afraid."

"Don't be." That grace he'd spoken of, the surety of God's benevolent will and purpose, filled Zach. He felt incandescent with it, radiating certitude for the first time in years. "This is right. You know it is. It always has been."

Nico didn't try to argue again, and Zach knew he'd finally gotten through. Finally, Nico drew back and sucked in a shuddering breath. He met Zach's eyes, calmness smoothing his beloved features. "No guarantees."

"Just every day we have available to us, together. Where we're meant to be."

The smallest hint of reluctance shadowed Nico's eyes, but he nodded. "Every day."

16

UNRAVELING

Every bone and muscle in Rhys's body ached when he awoke, lying on his bunk where they had dumped him, semiconscious, the previous night. It had been midafternoon the day before—he thought—when the guards had come for him and hauled him into a lab. Dr. Thanh hadn't been there, just more guards, one of whom had ordered Rhys stripped, put in restraints, and hooked up to a saline IV. A collection device had been wrapped around his penis, and then . . .

Rhys winced and shuddered at the way he'd screamed and seized when the electrified prod was jammed behind his balls, forcing convulsions that had pumped semen into the collector without any regard for Rhys.

At least it had been clinical rather than sexual, thank God. Littlewood's absence was telling. If he'd been there, Rhys had no doubt the prod would have gone somewhere a lot worse. But Littlewood was too afraid of Rhys to show up and take any pleasure in watching him be forced to produce semen to inoculate Littlewood himself.

They had repeated the procedure every couple of hours until late into the night when they returned him to his cell. Now it hurt to move. The muscles of his lower back, abdomen, and thighs had all spasmed and locked with each forced ejaculation. Rhys lay there curled into a ball and didn't dare try to stretch. He was too intent on his misery and on wondering at what point it would be too late to save the people here, if Dr. Thanh could come up with a way. He could take some small consolation from the idea that Littlewood was hiding in his quarters, frantically using Rhys's semen in an effort to live.

Would it be enough for Littlewood to succeed? Would he become a Jug, or would he die the way he deserved to?

Rhys wasn't sure how long he lay there, but eventually his door crashed open. Terrified that the guards had returned to take him back to the lab, he struggled to sit up, but it was just Dr. Thanh.

She looked . . . absolutely *livid*.

"What the hell do you think you're playing at?" she snarled, slamming the door behind her.

"What do you mean?" he croaked. His mouth was dry, despite the IV fluids they had given him, his eyes parched and gritty. He staggered to the basin and drank from the tap, scooping the water to his mouth with his hand.

"There's not a trace of Bane in your sample, Alpha or otherwise!" She stormed irately from one end of the cell to the other. "Was this a *joke*? Do you have any idea the panic you've provoked here? We were all convinced we were dying!"

He gawked at her, and then a startled laugh burbled out of him. Fuck, it hurt, but he couldn't stop. The pain of each spasm only made him laugh harder, tears running down his face as he collapsed to the floor.

"Wait. Wait. *Wait.*" He flapped a hand helplessly at her. "So Littlewood's been shooting himself up with my spunk for *nothing?*" He dissolved into hysterical peals of laughter again, almost sobbing with the pain of his abused abdominal muscles but utterly beyond controlling it. "Oh Jesus. That's almost worth every bit of it."

When he calmed enough to wipe his eyes and look up at her, the hilarity of that image had caught on, and she was leaning against the wall, trying to contain her own merriment. Their gazes locked, and they lost it again.

"I swear, I didn't know," he vowed when they had finally gotten control of themselves. "I'm sorry. But remember, when I got here I was surprised you thought I had Alpha."

"Whoever you were working with in the Clean Zone was serious enough about disrupting Littlewood's plans that they falsified your records to make you irresistible," she surmised, and Rhys nodded. He felt something lift off his chest at the realization that Zach hadn't lied to him, after all. He'd *asked* to be kept in the dark about Zach's master plan, so he couldn't be caught out in a lie.

Thanh turned that over for a moment. "This is both bad and good news. On one hand, we're not dying. On the other, neither is Littlewood, and now you have nothing protecting you from him. And I am back to having no Alpha to use for a vaccine. We don't dare approach your Jug comrade for it."

"Could you get it from her, anyway?" Rhys asked, his brow furrowing. "I mean, safely."

She frowned. "The two things needed to trigger the mutation from Alpha to Beta are air and the clotting agents of an open wound. With a vacuum tube and sufficient anticoagulants—and a tremendous amount of caution—we might be able to extract Alpha from a blood sample without it mutating."

"But then Littlewood really would have his hands on Alpha. Unless—" Rhys blinked, his head coming up. "Unless he's too distracted to know what you're doing."

"What are you proposing?"

"Does he know yet? That I'm not infected?"

Thanh shook her head. "He had no idea I'd obtained a sample from you to work with."

"Fine. Then let him keep thinking that he's dying. I'll talk to Schuyler, see if she'll *volunteer* to let you take a blood sample. You have the anticog—antiagu—"

"Anticoagulants."

"Those. If she agrees, can you do this safely?"

"I can. I made sure we were stocked in case this opportunity ever arose."

Rhys licked his lips. "I can't promise she'll do it; she hates civvies and I can't really blame her. But if she does, I'll keep Littlewood's attention on me while you work." He groaned, rubbing his forehead. "Just promise me you'll give me something for my muscles. I don't know how many more jolts of that prod I can take."

"You won't have to. I told him if he kept it up, sooner or later he was going to stop your heart." Thanh smiled grimly. "Make him think he's won your voluntary cooperation somehow. Keep providing him with what he wants. I'll do my part. I'd just better hurry, so we can let everyone know they're not going to die of the Rot. People will start preemptively killing themselves before long."

She had her hand on the doorknob, about to excuse herself, when Rhys stopped her. "If you hear anyone talking about doing that, go ahead and let them know. That part, I mean. The part where I didn't infect anyone. Don't say anything about having a live Alpha sample. If Littlewood finds out it was all a hoax, he'll take it out on me, which will keep his attention off the lab, too."

She winced at that but nodded, then hurried off while Rhys asked the guard to take him to Schuyler.

RHYS HAD JUST RETURNED to his cell after convincing Schuyler to cooperate with Dr. Thanh, when Littlewood arrived. The man looked like he'd aged twenty years and hadn't slept in a month. The expression in his eyes was now less cruel and more desperate, and it burned with a deep, *deep* spite for Rhys.

"Thanh tells me I'm in danger of killing you if I force any more deposits from you," he announced, giving Rhys a venomous look. "I'd be more than happy with that risk, except it wouldn't accomplish my ends. Therefore, I have an ultimatum for you."

Rhys smiled tauntingly. He knew this conversation would end with Littlewood "gaining" the upper hand somehow, but he couldn't make it too easy on the bastard. "What can you do to me? You can't force me, and I'm sure as hell not going to give it up on my own."

"Oh, I won't do anything to *you*." Littlewood smiled, and Rhys went utterly cold at the gleam of pleasure in his eyes. "But I have the personnel carrier that brought you here standing by. You'll give me what I require, or I'll return to the Clean Zone, taking the Rot with me."

Rhys forgot he was supposed to be playing a role. He stared at Littlewood in horror. "There are thousands of people there! You're willing to kill them *all*?"

Littlewood shrugged indolently. "Why should I care? Oh, I may lose one or two potentially amusing toys, but I won't be around to enjoy them anyway, will I? Unless, of course, you cooperate."

The only thing that kept Rhys from complete desperation was recalling that this was all an act. Littlewood couldn't hurt anyone. But, oh, his casual willingness to do so was terrifying all on its own.

"Fine," he whispered, hanging his head. "I'll give you what you want."

"I thought you'd see reason." Now Littlewood looked smugly benevolent. "And when I have the Alpha strain, Rhys, you will become my very special plaything. Whatever you may have enjoyed with your brute of a Juggernaut, I can assure you, you'll find no such pleasure at my hands. Think on that while you work to make me a god among men. Gods are notoriously capricious, and someday you'll understand what that means."

Rhys sank, trembling and aching, onto his cot long after Littlewood was gone, knowing that no matter what he'd ever thought of Father Maurice and Jacob, he had now seen true evil.

CROSSING the Nevada desert during a late-spring heat wave

was second only to crossing the Nevada desert during the height of summer on the list of experiences Nico'd rather not have. After an assessment of their location, destination, and the availability of water along the way, the other Jugs had decided to travel at night and in the early morning hours before the afternoon heat set in. With the region cleared of revenants, they could be looser with their operational protocols, which made visibility and potential encounters with other predators the biggest hazards they faced.

The desert and subsequent abandoned towns made an eerily beautiful tableau in the moonlight. The houses seemed even more haunted, the landscape cold and pale and barren, like the surface of another planet entirely. Nico hardly noticed since he'd walked this desert more than once, sometimes for months on end, seeking the secret DPRP research facility, but Zach kept remarking upon it. Zach, who had spent the last ten years of his life fenced into a repurposed suburb surrounded by trenches full of razor wire. Despite his exhaustion and the constant travel, he was radiant in his newfound freedom.

How had Nico never noticed how miserable Zach had been with his life in the Clean Zone?

Did you not notice? Or were you so determined that Zach be safe there that you never stopped to consider it?

Whatever the answer, he was now swayed by Zach's certitude that their choice to be together was the right one. Being with Zach felt as natural as it ever had, even if he was just lifting Zach off his bike when they made camp in the late morning, forcing some rations on him, and then holding him when he passed out and slept like the dead. Usually, after he woke, Zach would slip away somewhere secluded and wait for

Nico to join him, and they'd make love as the sun set, before it was time to travel again.

It was so perfect it left Nico vaguely uneasy. Surely it couldn't be so simple.

"Stop it," Zach chided, reaching for his clothes in the dusky red-gold light. They were both sweaty and sticky and probably wouldn't come across another body of water suitable for bathing until sometime tomorrow, but they didn't care. It was amazing just how much they were willing to compromise on hygiene when the alternative was a whole day of not touching.

Nico smiled and rolled onto his side, their blanket soft atop the dry, already-scorched grass. "Stop what?"

"Stop worrying about things that are in God's hands." Zach buttoned his sweat- and dust-stained shirt and bent to kiss Nico. He was losing weight on their lean rations and incessant travel—they all were—and Nico suspected they would need to stop and hunt pretty soon, despite the delay it would cause. Maybe he'd see if he could find game while they marched tonight.

"How do you know that's what I was worrying about?" He slipped a hand under Zach's shirt, sliding it around his waist to tug him off-balance and send him toppling to the ground on top of Nico. Zach grunted in surprise, then smiled brilliantly, kissing him.

"Because I know you." He didn't seem in any hurry to rise, and Nico wasn't in any hurry to go, either, but Darius might very well decide to leave without them if they didn't rejoin the party.

Regretfully, Nico eased Zach off him with another kiss and started gathering up his own clothing, shaking it to make sure no scorpions or other desert wildlife had wiggled their way in while he'd been preoccupied with Zach. While Nico dressed, Zach reclined on the blanket and chattered idly.

"Did you hear what Joe was saying about this place?" He gestured around at the compound they had camped on. The estate had obviously belonged to someone wealthy. Rusty iron fences cordoned off a huge tract of land that had the sort of lawn that didn't grow naturally in this region. A dry swimming pool was in the backyard, and beyond a stand of trees, there was a tennis court and even a putting green and driving range. The derelict house itself was enormous and must have been very ostentatious before age and neglect had set in.

Nico shook his head. He'd been aware of Joe, Darius, and Xolani talking about the place, but his attention had been on making Zach comfortable after the way he'd pushed himself to keep pace with the Jugs again. "What was he saying?"

"He thinks it's been inhabited since the pandemic. Not recently, of course, but maybe early on, after the first wave, someone had hidden out here for a few years." Zach looked at the mansion with an assessing eye. "He warned me about booby traps. Said he almost tripped one near the front door. I wonder why they left."

"Maybe they went to the Clean Zone." Nico fastened his trousers and sat to tug on his boots. "One of the Delta Company squadrons cleared this region, didn't they? Or was it Bravo? They might have recovered the survivors."

Zach nodded and turned a slow circle, squinting at the trees. "I think there may be game in the greenbelt there. I saw something moving."

"I'll go check it out. Will you tell them to wait for me?"

He jerked his head in the direction of camp, where they'd left Darius, Xolani, and Joe still sleeping an hour earlier.

"Finally learn to field dress a kill?" Zach teased.

Nico snorted. "I've had more practice at it these last few years than you have." He stood and grabbed Zach's ass, hauling him in for a kiss that left Nico aching. "I'll be back in a few."

Nico shouldered his rucksack and fastened the harness across his chest before picking up his assault rifle. It wasn't the best option for hunting, but it was all he had. Keeping a firm grip on his weapon, he slowly approached the tree line.

The shadows were deeper in the greenbelt, almost full dark. He let his eyes adjust, scanning the sod around the base of the trees carefully, looking for tracks. Zach might have seen a coyote or wolf or cougar just as easily as anything more suitable for eating, and the last thing Nico needed was to be pounced by an angry predator.

He heard a rustle ahead and flipped off the safety on his rifle. There it was; he could just see it moving through the trees, too tall and massive to be canine or feline. An elk? Nico moved cautiously, stepping lightly to avoid startling it. Hopefully his body odor wouldn't waft in that direction before he could get a clear shot.

He sensed Zach approaching behind him almost subliminally. He moved differently than the Jugs; his entire presence felt different. Maybe it was Nico's heightened senses that picked up on the subtleties. Nico didn't speak or acknowledge him. Zach knew how to hunt. He'd remain quiet and still when necessary, and having him here would mean they'd get the animal dressed and ready for transport that much quicker.

Another step forward, then another. The elk lifted its

antlered head, sniffing the air. Nico almost had a clear shot. One more step forward . . .

He heard the whistle of something flying through the trees almost before his foot had snagged on something that shouldn't be there. He dropped his weapon and spun, shoving Zach back so hard that he slammed against a tree trunk. Heat sliced through Nico's arm as he did so, and then there was a small, sharpened wooden bolt sticking out of either side of his forearm.

A trip wire. Connected to some fucking booby trap from some goddamned survivalist wannabe who didn't want anything sneaking up on his hideout. Nico focused on that because the rest was too horrific to contemplate.

Blood was seeping out around the edges of the bolt, dripping off the end. And two small, deadly drops had splattered onto Zach's cheek.

"Oh no." He heard the crack in his own voice, the way it rose in pitch, almost like a child's plaintive plea, like he'd regressed to the age of magical thinking where if he wished really hard, he could make it not be true. "Oh God. Zach. *No*."

He watched the realization spread across Zach's face. Fear and consternation and then resignation. Even acceptance. He blinked slowly, then nodded once. He almost smiled.

"It's okay, Nico. It's okay. Let's get you to Xolani."

He reached for Nico with gentle, reassuring hands, and *fuck him* for being so fucking calm. Like the world wasn't fucking crashing down around their ears.

"*No!*" Nico roared, thrashing. Jerking away from Zach's reach. The pain in his impaled arm was both incredible and insignificant as he wrapped his hands around a sturdy sapling and ripped it out of the ground by its roots. He threw it against another tree and rushed after it, pummeling the tree until the thick trunk began to splinter and crack. "*No!*"

"Nico, stop! Stop!" First it was Zach's voice, full of loving entreaty, but then Darius, Xolani, and Joe were there and they were restraining him. The red haze faded from his vision. All around him, a half-dozen trees showed damage from a rampage he didn't remember.

He dropped to the ground, sobbing until it felt like he'd puke. When he finally stopped, he was back where they had camped during the day with no memory of how he'd come to be there. His head was in Zach's lap, and Zach was crooning soothing nonsense to him. The stake had been removed from his throbbing arm, and a blood-tinged bandage was wrapped tightly around it. The position of the moon suggested that a good portion of the night was already gone.

His head ached, and his diaphragm was sore from the wracking sobs that hadn't let him catch his breath while he was in his fugue.

He felt Zach's lips against his temple, and a tear landed on his skin. "It's okay, my love. This is God's plan for us. We just need to have faith."

Nico wanted to argue, wanted to rail at Zach, because fuck him and fuck his God, if this was the sort of bullshit plan in store for them. But his voice seemed to be broken, his throat so raw he could swear he tasted blood. Jesus, what had he done?

He wanted to jerk away from Zach and lash out in anger at him for convincing Nico that they could be together without this exact thing happening. But he couldn't. Because now the clock was ticking, and every minute he spent pushing Zach away in anger was a minute they would never recapture.

On the other side of the campfire, Joe sat staring into the flames. The look on his face was one Nico had never seen before, full of haunted recollections. Past him, Darius prowled the perimeter of their campsite. He had to be dying to get on the road, but his impatience was tempered. He wasn't saying a word to hurry them along.

No, that was Xolani, whose husky voice was gentle with sympathy. She patted Zach's shoulder and reached down to help Nico to his feet. "We have to go. We need to get to water before we camp again or we're going to have trouble. And the sooner we get to Rhys, the sooner we see if we can come up with an antiserum before it's too late."

Nico let her pull him up, never taking his gaze off Zach. Zach's eyes were red rimmed, but they were placid. That same serene glow he'd had since the night on the shores of the Great Salt Lake was firmly in place.

He put his fingers on Nico's lips before Nico could say anything. "Not one word about infecting me with the Alpha strain. I won't do it, and I won't waste the time we have arguing about it. Understand?"

"Please," Nico whispered desperately, and even that much speaking made his throat burn.

Zach merely shook his head and kissed him softly on the lips. "This is the right course. I know it. Just take the time we have left for the blessing it is."

He kissed Nico again, slowly, lingering. His hands were gentle on the sides of Nico's face, cradling him. And then he stepped away with a beatific smile and helped Joe bury the campfire.

17

INFERNO

"**I** did it," Thanh reported to Rhys, Schuyler, and McClosky in a clandestine meeting in Schuyler's cell. Thanh and McClosky were in hermetic suits, as it hadn't been safe to be near Schuyler without them for the past few days.

Rhys thought it said something about Schuyler that, as much as she resented civvies—and absolutely despised McClosky—she had still warned them against being there unprotected. She had intended to break Rhys and herself out of the research facility days ago, but she had decided to wait until the only danger of infecting someone came from the possibility of them shooting her, in which case it would be the person's own fault. She'd asked Rhys to obtain plastic bags in which they could triple-wrap the bloodstained cloths she'd been using. When the meeting was over, Rhys would walk the rags to the incinerator himself.

"You rendered the virus inactive?" McClosky asked eagerly, and Thanh nodded.

"We can let people know they're not infected now. I

disposed of the remaining live virus from the sample Schuyler donated, so Littlewood can't get hold of it." Her voice sounded grimly satisfied. "As soon as I get back to the lab, I'll work on finding a stable medium for the inactive virus, and then it will be ready for testing."

Schuyler scowled. "That's all well and good for you people, but what's Littlewood going to do to Rhys once he knows he's been had?"

Rhys grimaced. "Whatever he thinks he's going to do, he'd better bring reinforcements because I'm not going to make it easy on him." Schuyler gave him a dubious look, and Rhys narrowed his eyes at her. "I can take care of myself. I've been training with Titus and Xolani for two years. Unless he knocks me out or has his guards restrain me, he's going to have to work for it."

"In which case, he might not bother with you at all," McClosky observed. "Stephen likes helpless victims, not those who put up a fight."

Rhys nodded, conceding the point. He still cringed at the way Littlewood had tried to gentle him into compliance before springing his trap.

That just seemed to make Schuyler angrier. "You want to tell me why the fuck you never put a bullet between his eyes?" She looked back and forth between McClosky and Thanh. "You knew what he was doing. You were out here away from the Clean Zone where no one could say otherwise if you reported that he had an unfortunate accident."

McClosky cleared his throat. "Rhys asked me much the same when he first got here. I will only say that I felt we had no choice, and that the alternatives were worse."

Schuyler leveled a threatening finger at him. She leaned

forward, dropping her voice to an almost-calm murmur. "When this is over, I'm going to deal with you personally. I don't give a rat's ass what your bullshit rationalizations are."

He took his time responding, his voice as soft as hers. "Fair enough."

They all stood there, caught up in the tense silence, until Schuyler broke it by waving them away. "Get the fuck out of here. Make your vaccine before I decide none of this is worth it and tear this place apart just for the satisfaction of it."

Thanh and McClosky rose in unison. He shuffled toward the door, while she turned toward Rhys. "When you're done here, I'm going to have the guard bring you to the lab. If I can spin down an antiserum from some of your blood, it would be a good thing to have in case— Well, nothing is sure in the testing phase. It might make a difference."

Rhys froze, staring at her. "You're going to test it on a living person?"

"Eventually. If the tests on the blood samples and lab animals are promising." Thanh met his eyes squarely. "I promise you, we have a volunteer who knows the risk and is willing to accept it."

"Who?"

"Me." McClosky turned from the door. "I figure if someone should put themselves in danger of dying to test it, it should be me."

Schuyler gave him a scathing look. "And you conveniently get to be the first person to have access to the vaccine if it works."

"I could tell you that's not why I volunteered, but you're more than entitled to whatever you wish to believe."

McClosky bowed his head and ducked out of the room. After a moment's hesitation, Thanh followed.

"You think he's not sincere?" Rhys asked cautiously.

"I don't give a shit if he is or not." Schuyler flung herself onto her bunk. "That man is responsible for billions of deaths. If he feels bad about it, I don't care. The fact that he's escaped justice this long tells me he's not willing to accept the consequences of what he did."

"Maybe he's just practical enough to realize his death won't actually help undo anything and that there's a better use for him."

She grunted. "Whatever. Go. Get out of here. I'm not in the mood to deal with anyone else right now."

She turned her back to him as Rhys knocked on the door to summon the guard. "Tell that to Hope," he thought he heard Schuyler murmur as it closed behind him.

⋀ ⋀ ⋀

"IF THIS IS GOING to work, it needs to work soon," Thanh muttered, looking into the lab from the window in the exam room where she'd taken Rhys's blood. She was pulling on her hermetic suit—mandatory for anyone working in the lab— and getting ready to go do whatever she would need to do with his blood to make the antiserum.

"Why's that?" He cocked his head curiously. "You're all out of the woods since I don't actually have Alpha. False alarm, right?"

Her mouth twisted. "You mean until your Jug friends get here? And don't tell me Schuyler is planning on letting us keep her locked up indefinitely. She's either staying put to give you time to do what you need to do or waiting for reinforcements, or both."

"Well, just surrender calmly and hand us over when Darius gets here, and no one needs to bleed or be exposed to anyone's blood." He said it to be flippant, but he met her eyes squarely, hoping she'd take the advice.

"You forget that the guards don't answer to me. That's the problem." She halted with her hood in her hands, then set it on the examination table and sighed. "You have to understand about Littlewood. He's psychotic, but he's always been very controlled. He's a cold, calculating predator, not some rabid dog attacking indiscriminately. He knows how to bide his time, how to hide in plain sight, and how to cover his tracks."

Rhys shuddered. "I noticed."

"But he's *losing it*." The intensity in her voice made Rhys do a double take. "You've given him a scare, and you've done something he never expected. You've made him feel powerless."

"He doesn't seem all that powerless to me." Rhys still went cold when he thought of how easily Littlewood had threatened to kill thousands of people in the Clean Zone just to have leverage over Rhys. Even if Rhys knew he wasn't actually capable of carrying through on the threat, *Littlewood* hadn't known it. And he hadn't been bluffing.

Rhys had continued to indulge Littlewood's false under-standing of the situation to buy Thanh more time to work on her vaccine. After two days of masturbating every four hours, any amusement he'd enjoyed at Littlewood's expense had defi-nitely faded. His wrist was sore and his dick was chafed, with a raw band where the mouth of the suction collector *thing* wrapped around the shaft. His balls ached. Coming was more painful than pleasurable. Even his best memories of things he and Darius had done together were losing their ability to arouse him, and he wondered if he'd ever be able to enjoy a good handjob again. But as long as Littlewood was hiding away, trying to infect himself with Alpha, Thanh was free to operate as she needed to.

Thanh shook her head in disagreement. "Maybe you'd have to have known him before, but he's desperate, and that makes him not only dangerous but unpredictable. We can't count on his self-restraint anymore."

"If he comes after me, I *will* kill him," Rhys said with a steely look. Thanh's eyes widened. "You think I won't?"

"You don't seem the type."

"I've spent the past two years living with people who killed any of their comrades who started talking about using the Alpha strain to mistreat uninfected people. They wouldn't have dicked around with Littlewood; they would have put a bullet between his eyes and moved on." Rhys rolled down his sleeve with jerky pulls. "*No one* is more aware of how dangerous the Alpha strain is than the Jugs. And a lot of them may hate civvies the way Schuyler does, because the civvies completely shit on them, but it doesn't mean they're going to act on it."

After a moment, Thanh nodded and fastened her hood to her suit. "Do what you need to do. If I ever make it back to the Clean Zone, I'll vouch that it was necessary." She paused with her hand on the door. "It may be a bit before the guard returns to take you back to your cell. Go ahead and rest. At least Littlewood can't push you for another semen sample while you're out of your cell."

Oh, thank God. After she was gone, Rhys realized just

how tired he was. The constant stress of the last week, and the past two days in particular, playing his high-stakes game, was beginning to wear on him. Fuck it. He hopped off the examination table and crossed over to the control panel, turning down the lights until the cubicle was dark except for the illumination coming through the window into the lab across the room from him. He glanced at the smaller window in the door on his left to find the hallway bright but quiet. Then he curled up on the table, wrapped his arms around himself to ward off the slight chill of the climate-control system, and closed his eyes.

△ △ △

SOMETHING JERKED HIM AWAKE, a crash Rhys wasn't certain had been in his dream or real. How long had he been asleep? From the grit in his eyes, the stiffness of his muscles, and the pressure in his bladder, it felt like hours.

He heard another crash, and then a shout. Furious and masculine and coming from the lab. Rhys scrambled off the table to peer through the window into the lab. Littlewood was storming around, flinging trays of instruments out of his path and leaving the orderly space in shambles. He was screaming at Dr. Thanh.

"*Where is he?*" he demanded. At first Rhys wondered how Littlewood had missed him. He would have walked right past the door to the room Rhys had been lying in to get to the lab. Littlewood must not have seen into the darkened cubicle from the brightly lit corridor and lab.

Even though Dr. Thanh was suited, Rhys thought he could

see tension and fear in her posture. "If the Juggernaut troops are approaching, the best thing we can do is stand down and hand Rhys and Schuyler over peacefully," he heard her say. "Anything else would be suicide."

Darius!

Despite the anxiety of the moment, Rhys couldn't contain the thrill of knowing Darius was coming for him. He'd never doubted it, of course, but he hadn't realized it would be so soon. He'd half expected Schuyler to break them out of here and they'd meet the other Jugs on the road somewhere nearby before returning to end operations at the research facility permanently.

"I had the guards tase that Juggernaut bitch and chain her up. She's not going anywhere. Now they're arming up and heading for the rooftops. The Juggernauts will be dead the moment they get within firing range." Littlewood stalked closer to her. "We're not done here until I've gotten the Alpha strain."

Thanh's posture went rigid. "Were they in suits?" she demanded. "The guards who tased her. Were they in suits? Because if they weren't, you've just risked their lives. You've got to get them in here. I'll have an antiserum soon, and I even have a possible vaccine. It's untested, but we have to hope for the best."

"We're all dying anyway!" Littlewood roared, sweeping his arm along a workbench. Instruments, beakers, and other equipment crashed to the floor in a shower of shattering glass.

"No, we *aren't!*" Thanh shot back, and there was a taunting note of satisfaction in her tone. "You've been chasing after the Alpha strain for days when Rhys never had it to begin with.

This was all a setup by one of your DPRP personnel in the Clean Zone to stop you from hurting more people."

Littlewood stared at her in disbelief, and then Rhys saw his arm move. Saw him catch the heavy microscope by one of its arms and fling it at her as he screamed in rage. Saw the way it toppled end over end through the air until it connected with the side of her hooded head. Even through the thick glass separating him from the lab, he heard the sickening sound of it cracking against her skull.

Thanh dropped like a puppet whose strings had been cut, and Littlewood . . . Littlewood just stared down at her, his head tilted inquisitively, as if puzzled by her sudden motionlessness.

Rhys moved before he realized he'd even intended to, slamming out of the examination cubicle into the corridor, and then through the vestibule to the lab, which Littlewood had left carelessly open at both ends.

"Dr. Thanh!" he called, rushing toward her still body. Even from a few feet away, he could see the blood staining the inside of her mask. Littlewood snatched at him, but Rhys shoved him aside, kneeling to carefully remove Thanh's hood.

There was swelling at her temple and blood matting her hair. This wasn't good. He needed to get her to Xolani, and he needed to do it now.

"Are you happy now?" he snarled, springing to his feet and advancing on Littlewood, who began backing away with fear in his eyes. Yes, he was *afraid* of Rhys, and that gave Rhys far more pleasure than it should have. He actually felt the first small stirring of arousal tugging at his balls, but overriding all that was fury. "You may have just killed the only chance there was to create a vaccine for the plague."

Despite the terror shadowing his hollowed eyes, Rhys's words made Littlewood smile. "Why should I care?"

Rhys went wide, circled around Littlewood, getting between the secretary and the door. Littlewood pivoted to keep facing Rhys, walking backward to maintain a distance between them, but now his course took him deeper into the lab and farther away from escape.

"I'm going to beat the shit out of you," Rhys promised. "I might not get my jollies from it the way you do from hurting people, but I'll still enjoy it. And then I'm going to let the Jugs have you. Because they know just what to do with people who mishandle the Alpha strain, and because I want you to *really* see what it means to be a Jug before you die."

He leaped for Littlewood, and Littlewood flung himself backward, tripping over Thanh's body. He tried to scramble upright again, but Rhys already had him by the collar, yanking him into Rhys's oncoming fist to add more momentum to the blow.

Littlewood's nose shattered with a spray of snot and blood, followed by a burbling cry of pain. Rhys's knuckles burned, but he hauled back his fist for another punch. Littlewood's eye slammed shut and began to swell. Blood began trickling from his split lips with the next one.

It was euphoric. Rhys felt like he could have gone on forever, pummeling the man's face to a pulp, and he enjoyed every moment of it. It didn't matter that Littlewood was an old man nearly three times Rhys's age and unable to defend himself. Rhys was going to inflict upon him every moment of suffering Littlewood had inflicted upon others . . . in triplicate.

Only a flash of yellow in his peripheral vision stopped him long enough to notice what was happening around them.

Thanh's suited arm dropped away, leaving something glittering sticking out of Littlewood's quadriceps.

A hypodermic syringe.

Rhys released Littlewood and let him fall where he lay, whimpering and staring at the needle in his leg. Beyond him, Thanh's bloody face was contorted into a gruesome grin, her death mask.

"Guess he won't be infecting himself with Alpha now," she gasped, and then her eyes went empty, gazing sightlessly at Rhys.

All desire to hurt Littlewood fled. His attention was transfixed by that syringe. The experimental vaccine Thanh had concocted. Maybe the only dose of vaccine anyone would ever be able to generate, and she'd used it to put a permanent end to Littlewood's ambitions of acquiring the Alpha strain.

Rhys gently passed a bloody-knuckled hand over her eyes to shut them.

"You're not worth killing," he spat at Littlewood, his eyes burning. Thanh would never be going back to her life in the Clean Zone, to the husband and children she'd been taken from. "I think I like the idea of you living for years, facing justice, knowing that even if you were to go free, it'd be impossible for you to ever become a Jug."

Littlewood slumped to the floor and closed his eyes. Whether he was unconscious or he'd simply given up, Rhys didn't know. And he didn't really care.

Darius was out there, and Rhys was going to find him and make sure no one took a shot at him.

He went to Schuyler's cell first, which was unguarded, but he didn't have the keys. Looking at the monitors in the security station down the hallway, he could see that inside the situation was just as Littlewood had said it'd be. She'd been tased again and was lying unconscious on her bunk with shackles on her wrists and ankles. One suited guard was in there with her, equally unconscious—or perhaps dead. Given the fact that the guard's comrades had left him lying there, Rhys was betting on the second option.

Schuyler hadn't gone down without a fight.

Littlewood had said the guards were taking up posts on the roof, to fire at Darius and the others as they approached. Rhys focused on finding a way up. Except for his one trip to Littlewood's quarters, Rhys's familiarity with the facility was limited to the cells and the lab. The rest of the place may have been a labyrinth, and he wasted precious minutes trying to find the access ladder to a hatch on the roof.

McClosky had beaten him to the guards. "They're Juggernauts, you idiots!" he shouted. "Put those guns down and surrender. They don't want to hurt you; they just want their people."

"We don't take our orders from you!" one of the guards snapped back. He'd taken off the hood of his suit and was wiping his face, which was streaming with sweat. Other guards had done likewise. It was sweltering on the roof, the sun beating down on them mercilessly. Wearing those suits under it must be like wearing a portable oven.

"No, you take your orders from Secretary Littlewood, who just murdered Dr. Thanh," Rhys called out from the doorway. McClosky whirled, staring at Rhys in horror. "I subdued him, but he's going back to the Clean Zone and he's going to face justice, and I'll testify that any of you aiding him by carrying out his orders acted as accomplices."

They stared at him in disbelief, but Rhys didn't have the patience or the breath to argue with them in this heat. He rushed to the edge of the roof, looking out over the surrounding grounds of the compound. Which were empty.

"Where are they?" he demanded of McClosky.

"They ducked for cover beyond those warehouses over there when the idiots took the first shots at them." McClosky pointed to the east. "Now they're probably just waiting for nightfall so they can get to us unseen." He turned back to the guards. "Come on, people. Some of you have families just outside the compound here. Are you really going to risk getting infected and never seeing them again?"

Rhys could see the guards weakening, giving in, but something was scratching at the edge of his senses trying to get his attention. He went still and closed his eyes, trying to focus on it.

There it was. His eyes flew open. "Do you smell smoke?"

Panic rippled through the guards. "They're trying to burn us out!"

"Not them!" McClosky snapped. He pointed toward the open access door leading back down into the research facility. "It's coming from inside. We've got to go! We'll be trapped up here!"

Faced with the prospect of being burned alive, the Jugs beyond the warehouses were suddenly the least of the guards' concerns. They scrambled for the access door, rushing down the ladder with Rhys and McClosky on their heels.

The corridors were cloudy with smoke. Clearly someone

had disabled the fire-suppression system. "Littlewood!" McClosky hissed.

"I've got to get Schuyler out of here!" Rhys yelled, crouching low. Already his eyes were streaming and his lungs burning.

"The records! Thanh's research and notes!" McClosky argued.

"Salvage what you can!" Rhys gave him a gentle shove. Thanh wouldn't want her research lost, not when she had just had a breakthrough and possibly created a working vaccine. "Give me your keys. I'll help once I know Schuyler is out!"

McClosky nodded, coughing, and shoved his keys at Rhys before rushing off for the lab.

Half blinded by smoke, Rhys fumbled through the corridors toward the cells, but Schuyler's was already open. The shackles were in fragments on the floor, and it looked like she'd torn through the door. Hopefully she'd already headed out to safety. Rhys changed direction, blindly trying to find his way back to the lab through the thickening smoke. He and McClosky wouldn't have much time to get anything out.

Suddenly someone grabbed him from behind, and Rhys spun, fists flashing out to ward off any threat. They were caught in a huge, dark hand, and he was jerked against a solid body to stare disbelievingly at a very familiar face.

Despite the smoke making tears flood from their eyes, Darius spared him a beaming smile. "Come on, boy! We're getting you out of here!"

"The research! The vaccine!" Rhys dissolved into a fit of coughing, trying to tug Darius toward the lab.

Someone came up beside him, hacking loudly. Xolani had a semiconscious McClosky hanging off her. "The fucker set fire to the labs and records room first!" she shouted over the roar of the inferno, the effort making her double over with more spasms. The air was scorching. Rhys could feel it singeing his lungs. "It's all gone!"

"We have to go! *Now!*" Darius barked. He hauled Rhys across his shoulders in a fireman's carry and began sprinting down the corridor. Behind him, Xolani did the same with McClosky.

"Schuyler!" Rhys tried to protest, but it came out as a strangled gasp. Whether they heard him or not, they didn't stop. Not until they had burst out into the fresh air, their course taking them well out of range of the burning building.

Finally Darius stopped to ease Rhys down off his shoulders. As soon as he was on his feet, Rhys flung himself at Darius, wrapping both arms around him and clinging without concern for who might see him acting so unreservedly. Darius returned the crushing embrace just as ferociously, his lips pressing against Rhys's temple.

"You okay, boy?" he asked, his voice thick with more than smoke.

Rhys nodded against Darius's shoulder. "I'm fine. No one hurt me. I didn't give him the chance, I swear."

Darius's arms tightened in response, but he said nothing.

"I love you," Rhys whispered against his ear. Darius turned, his lips mashing against Rhys's. They both tasted like smoke, and not the pleasant campfire kind. This was foul and pungent, full of chemical residue, but it didn't matter. He kissed Darius back with everything he had, until another spasm made his lungs jerk and he pulled away, trying to expel the foul fumes he'd inhaled.

"Did Schuyler make it out?" he asked weakly when the fit

had passed. He spat gray-black phlegm onto the ground and wiped his mouth.

"She got out, and in better shape than you did," Darius reassured him. "She got Littlewood out too."

Rhys's head shot up. "*Where?*"

18

JUSTICE

Beyond the warehouses and the fence surrounding the compound was a small cluster of housing for the people who had worked at—or been abducted to—the research facility. The residents had gathered by the fence to stare, and the guards and technicians with families were calling out reassurances from where Joe was holding them at gunpoint twenty yards away.

Nico and Zach kept themselves away from everyone. Nico's arm was healing, but it had only been three days since he'd been impaled. It wasn't safe to let him near uninfected people. And Zach, of course, would never be safe to be around again . . . Nico envied Darius the security of Cooper's immunity.

Schuyler had joined him and Zach, which meant she was quarantining herself for some reason, and she'd dragged Littlewood with her. And Xolani had deposited McClosky with them, as well. Apparently neither of them gave a fuck if those two men became infected.

Darius kept his arm around Cooper as they shuffled over to join their small group. Nico couldn't look at them for too long. It hurt too much. Instead, he focused on McClosky, whose presence shouldn't have been possible. He was supposed to have been executed ten years ago.

Nico wished he could feel something about seeing the man who had once been his friend and mentor, before he'd become the person Nico despised most in the world. Even Littlewood didn't compare. But all he felt was empty. Maybe it was because McClosky was already dead to him. Or maybe Nico had just lost his capacity to feel anything, ever again.

He listened with half an ear as Cooper gave a rundown of events in the lab. ". . . Thanh injected him with the vaccine before she died. If it works, he'll never be able to contract Alpha." Cooper smiled tightly as he finished his report. "But all Thanh's research is gone. All the equipment."

Nico swallowed hard and met Xolani's eyes. "No anti-serum?" he asked hopelessly. Oh, there was his emotion. More of it than he could ever possibly cope with. It felt like he was shattering all over again.

"I'm sorry," she murmured. Cooper's eyes widened and he looked at them each in turn. His gaze fixed on Nico's bandaged arm before flicking to Zach. Nico turned away from the dawning understanding in Cooper's expression, the echo of Nico's own pain and impending loss.

"*Zach*," the kid whispered, his smoke-roughened voice a broken croak.

"It's okay, Rhys." Zach smiled that saintly smile and slipped his fingers between Nico's, squeezing tightly.

Nico pulled away. What was happening to and with Zach wasn't for Littlewood and McClosky to see. When he dared look at anyone again, sure enough, there was just the smallest gleam of cruel pleasure on Littlewood's face. He was enjoying Nico's pain. Even twelve years later, Nico recognized that expression.

A hole blossomed between Littlewood's brows before Nico even realized his sidearm was somehow in his grip. Blood and brains and bone chips splattered McClosky, who jumped at the explosion, his astonished gaze flying to Nico. In the distance, the other guards and the civilians on the other side of the fence cried out. Only the Jugs were unfazed.

In fact, Schuyler stepped up to McClosky, holding out her hand for Nico's gun. "Nico's got the right idea. I don't trust the Clean Zone to hold these guys accountable for what they've done," she said flatly. Nico laid the piece across her palm.

With Littlewood's blood running down his face in rivulets, McClosky blinked at her slowly, then nodded once and closed his eyes. "I understand."

Nico turned away before McClosky's body hit the ground, but the shot rang in his ears.

IT TOOK some doing to convince the guards and civvies that they weren't going to be summarily executed. As much as Darius understood and even approved of their actions, Nico's and Schuyler's preemptive justice made for a hell of a headache. He, Xolani, Joe, and Rhys spent the rest of the afternoon and evening explaining to the remaining personnel and their families that those who had worked for Littlewood would be taken back to the Clean Zone and remanded to whatever justice their complicity deserved. If they had just been following orders, or had no knowledge of what Littlewood was doing and no way to blow the whistle if they did, well, that was between them and the Clean Zone criminal justice system.

As for the people who had been abducted, they had the choice of returning to the Clean Zone or traveling to the northwest to join the new settlement the Jugs intended to establish. The more Darius thought about it, the more he realized they really should have set up a second settlement years ago. Sending everyone to the Clean Zone was a case of putting all their eggs in one basket. All it would take was a single case of Beta or Gamma slipping past quarantine—like the one Littlewood had threatened to set loose, according to Rhys—and every survivor they'd managed to round up in the past decade would be dead, except for maybe a handful who might possibly be immune like Rhys.

The northwest was also much more suitable for setting up a largely agrarian settlement, which this would have to be. The only thing that had enabled the Clean Zone to get off the ground was a heavy reliance on pre-pandemic stores, all of which had been used or were now long past their shelf life. The only thing Colorado Springs had going for it as a location for a settlement was its proximity to Cheyenne Mountain, where the earliest survivors had hoped they'd find shelter. Otherwise, it was too hot in the summer, and too arid and rocky for anything more than subsistence farming.

Hopefully the other companies of Jugs would see it that way too. If not, maybe they would come up with alternative locations that would work as well.

An unsurprising number of the abducted people had been in favor of going to the new settlement. That said a lot about what they had been through and how little they trusted the Clean Zone to protect them.

When that was all settled, Darius could finally turn his attention to Rhys, who waited for him in the Jugs' small camp. There was something different about his boy since they'd recovered him. He'd always been quiet, but now there was a gravity to him, a deeper maturity than he'd possessed even a week ago. Whatever he'd seen and done—and he swore to Darius that those experiences had nothing to do with Little-wood—it had put a coat of varnish on him, making him harder and more impervious, but also somehow more open.

He startled when Darius sat down beside him on the bedroll, having nodded off in front of the fire. "I'm tired," he sighed, leaning against Darius in a way he rarely had before. He still smelled like burning plastic and insulation; they both did. The Jugs had requested access to one of the residences and the running water therein, but they'd been too weary to take advantage of it before it was time to bunk down. Tomorrow would be soon enough for a shower.

Darius drew him close, letting him lie with his head in Darius's lap. "Then get some sleep. Nothin' we need to say tonight that we can't talk about tomorrow."

"Lie down with me." Rhys sat up and waited for Darius to take off his boots and stretch out before he was pressed close again, clinging to Darius like a limpet. "Thank you for coming for me."

"You knew I would." He could get used to this new side of Rhys, who was no longer self-conscious in his displays of affection. "Seemed like you were handling things okay, by the look of Littlewood's face when we got him out."

"I should have bound him before I went up to the roof. It's

my fault he was running loose, torching the place. He did it just for spite." Rhys shuddered in his arms. "As much as I enjoyed the idea of him going through life knowing he'd failed, I'm glad he's dead. He was *evil*."

"Guess you made the right call, then, decidin' you were gonna go in and stop him." He pressed a kiss to the top of Rhys's head, ignoring the smokiness. "Good thing we listened to you. You made us proud."

Rhys tucked his face into Darius's shoulder. "Darius . . . you know I'm not going anywhere, right? Not if I can help it. You know I'm not just with you while I'm waiting for some other opportunity to come along?"

"Yeah, I know." Rhys's anxious tone made Darius frown and lift his head. "Doesn't mean I'd blame you if you did find a chance for a better life."

"I don't want a better life. I want the life I have. *We* have." His hazel eyes were golden in the firelight when he met Darius's gaze. "I'm with you because it's where I want to be. Where I'm happy. Please don't ever suggest I should be somewhere else again."

"It's a deal. You'll be my boy for always." He brushed his lips across Rhys's, lightly once, then again, slower and deeper. He stopped only when Rhys made a pained sound. "Okay?"

Rhys gave a self-effacing chuckle and nodded, settling back in against Darius. He could feel the pressure of Rhys's dick against his thigh, but Rhys made no move to carry things further. "I'm okay. Just spent way too much time the past few days with my hand on my cock." He laughed at Darius's confused stare. "Nothing bad, I promise. It just might be a couple days until I'm really in the mood for more than this."

"All right." Baffled, Darius lay back, watching the stars in the clear sky above as he waited for his own arousal to subside.

He was almost asleep when Rhys spoke again. "Darius?"

"Yeah?"

"Do you think we could go away again? Like we did before, just the two of us?"

He kissed the top of Rhys's head again. "Anything you want. We'll go as soon as things are dealt with here."

ΛΛΛ

The rest of the camp was asleep and Xolani's bedroll empty when Rhys slid away from Darius and pulled on his boots. There was really no need to post a guard, which meant something else had Xolani awake in the middle of the night.

He found her looking over the still-glowing ruins of the research complex, her arms wrapped around herself. The bodies of Littlewood and McClosky, which they'd thrown onto the burning rubble, were no longer visible, obscured by collapsed walls.

"You okay?" he asked softly, knowing she wouldn't have missed hearing his approach.

"Just stuck wondering 'What if?'" She shook her head in disgust. "I want to resurrect that fucker Littlewood and kill him again. All that research and the equipment we needed —gone."

"They should have approached the Jugs years ago," Rhys said bitterly. "They had the ability to isolate the Alpha strain from a blood sample. They said it was because you wouldn't have trusted them."

Xolani flicked a small shrug. "They had a point."

"Yeah, but I think they would have made the attempt, if not for Littlewood."

"You're probably right." She shook her head. "Such a fucking waste. Anyway, what has you awake now after the day you've had?"

The day he'd had. Rhys thought he'd be seeing Dr. Thanh's grisly, bloodied face in his dreams for months, even with her triumphant last act. He'd keep remembering how lost in rage he'd gotten, how much he'd enjoyed beating Littlewood to a pulp—and how careless he'd been about leaving him there unrestrained.

He shook himself when he realized he was getting distracted. "I keep thinking about how we can use an antiserum from my blood to help people who have been recently exposed to the virus."

"It's a rare situation, Rhys. The chances of someone who has been *that* recently exposed having timely access to any antiserum we might make from your blood are astronomically small. We'd have to be there on the spot during what would be a *very* small window of opportunity. Twenty-four to seventy-two hours, tops. It's not likely to ever come up."

"I could have helped Zach, if I'd been with you."

"Maybe. If we'd had the right equipment, we could have spun down your blood and derived the antiserum. *Maybe.*" She gave him a sympathetic smile. "I know you regret not being able to help your friend, but he seems okay with his choice."

Rhys swallowed against the knot in his throat. "I know he is. I'll miss him, but . . . this isn't about him."

"Then what's it about?"

"You could be there on the spot, with the antiserum available, if the person who's been exposed to Beta were a Jug's newborn baby, couldn't you?"

Xolani froze and turned slowly, staring at him with wide eyes.

"*Couldn't you?*" he insisted. "We could help Jugs like Schuyler and Jamie, right?"

Xolani's eyes were glassy in the moonlight, and she was staring at him as though she'd never seen him before. Her words came slowly, thick with emotion, after a shuddering breath. "If we can manufacture the antiserum, then yes. We could save their newborns, if they chose to have them."

"Then the Jugs wouldn't die out. I mean, there wouldn't be any more Alpha-infected Jugs, but—"

"I know what you mean." Collecting herself, she spun away from Rhys and began pacing, gesticulating rapidly as she spoke. "Of course, if Alpha is transmissible in breast milk, we'd have to find a way to engage wet nurses from the civilian population, or keep dosing the babies with antiserum until they're weaned. We *really* don't want toddlers infected with Alpha running around. That could be tricky, though; I have no idea how we could convince anyone to do it. Maybe if we could make them immune, but with the lab and the research and Dr. Thanh gone—" Her shoulders slumped. "Goat's milk might work if we can't find wet nurses, but not every human infant can thrive on it. Cow's milk is definitely not a good option. Hmm. I don't know if it's feasible. Certainly not with the bad blood between the Jugs and the civilians."

"Oh." Rhys sighed. "I guess it was just a thought."

Her voice stopped him as he turned to go back to Darius and his bedroll. "It was a good thought, Rhys. Especially considering how Schuyler's treated you."

"That's not why I did it. She's got her reasons for the way she feels about me. I'm not trying to win her over." He spoke over his shoulder, his head bowed. "Don't tell her about it if it's not going to work out, okay? I wouldn't want to get her hopes up."

He shuffled away, leaving Xolani pacing by the ruins. He was almost out of earshot when she called after him, "Rhys?"

"Yeah?" He glanced back at her, waiting as she shuffled her weight awkwardly from one foot to another.

"I've never been prouder of the fact that I argued to save your life that day at the monastery than I am right now. You've grown into an incredible man. I'm glad I got to see it happen." She cleared her throat and looked away. "Now go. Get some sleep, kid."

ZACH WAS awake and sitting by the fire when Rhys returned to camp. Rhys glanced at the bedroll where he had been curled up with the new Jug, Nico. He lay there sleeping with a strained frown on his face, as if troubled by terrible dreams, and Zach was watching him with concern.

"You can't sleep either?" Rhys asked, dropping to sit beside him, cross-legged.

Zach nodded slowly, shifting his troubled stare away from Nico. He offered Rhys a wan smile. "Right now I'm trying to hold desperately to my belief in God's benevolent will. To remember that He has a purpose and a plan for everything that has happened. Some moments are easier than others. When I told Nico I didn't care if I got infected tomorrow, I didn't mean it almost literally. I knew an accident might happen, I just— I thought we'd have more time."

"I wish I could have been with you in time to do something." Despite Xolani's reassurance, he couldn't help but feel like he'd failed his friend. He had, locked within his blood cells, the ability to stop the progress of Bane, but it wasn't going to do Zach a damn bit of good now.

He said nothing else about it. Dwelling on it would only make things harder for them to face.

"So, when you mentioned someone called Nico, you didn't tell me he was a Jug. Or that the two of you—"

"We weren't. Well, sort of. Not really." Zach chuckled and gave Nico another glance, filled with so much unrestrained adoration that it made Rhys's chest ache. "He's the reason why I ultimately parted ways with my father and brother, you know."

"Really?" Rhys stared at him, wide-eyed.

"Oh yes." Zach huffed and shook his head. "My father had so little charity left in his soul that he would have begrudged an injured man the use of our garden shed for shelter in the middle of an ice storm. I had to pull a gun to get him to stop threatening Nico. That's when I realized that, for the sake of my own soul, I needed to abandon the safety of numbers and strike out with a complete stranger."

"And you two have been apart all this time?"

"Since the military government surrendered, yes." Zach bowed his head and murmured. "I wish I had the faith to say definitively that what we've done here today, what ended up coming from it, was worth it, but I'm not that self-sacrificing, I guess."

Rhys's eyes began to burn, the pain worse still for the

smoke and heat that had seared them earlier. "I don't want to see another friend die because of the Rot, Zach," he whispered, trying not to let his voice crack.

"You won't need to do what you did for your friend, Gabe."

How could Zach be so calm about it? But then, Gabe had been too, hadn't he, right up until the very end? He'd been sure of the choice that had resulted in his death.

"God willing, even Nico won't. I wouldn't put him through that. Xolani's a physician. I've seen doctors help people die when there was nothing else to be done. She'll know what to do. Until then, all I need is to make the most of these final few weeks."

Rhys wiped his face. "If you think that'll make it easier on Nico, you're out of your fucking mind," he said roughly.

"Could *anything* make this easier on Nico?" Zach asked simply. He met Rhys's gaze, and something bleak flickered beneath that beatific serenity.

"No, I guess not," Rhys muttered. He recognized the anger tightening his chest. He'd felt it that day he put a bullet into Gabe's brain too. There was a near-irresistible urge to rail at the Fates and curse the world in general for being such a fucking heartless place.

"I'll do what I can, of course," Zach continued, his eyes wandering back toward Nico. "Give him as many happy memories as we can make to cherish when I'm gone. I don't think I want to be anywhere near the Clean Zone. I want to go somewhere beautiful and idyllic, and somewhere Nico will never have cause to return to again."

Rhys smiled sadly. "I'll talk to Joe. I bet he'll have ideas. He . . . understands these things."

"Lake Tahoe," came the gruff voice from the other side of the fire. "We're not that far southeast of Reno. Not much farther past that, up into the mountains, you got Lake Tahoe. Been there once. It's pretty."

"Thank you, Joe," Zach answered sweetly and returned to staring at the fire. After a while, Rhys left him there and retreated to Darius's warm body and solid arms.

19

IDYLL

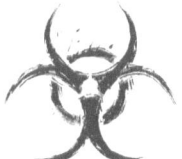

In a hangar, they found not only the transport skimmer that had brought Rhys and Schuyler to the research facility but a carefully charged and maintained cache of spare fuel cells.

Zach listened as Joe checked the craft over and reported to Darius. "Everything is sound. It's in good condition," he attested. "Fuel enough for me to take you all up to Tahoe, then come back and transport the civvies who want to return to Colorado Springs. After that, I'll head north, see if I can intercept Titus and Toby. We'll report in to Luis and then start scouting locations for the new settlement near Portland with the civvies who don't want to go to the Clean Zone."

"I'll go with you as far as Colorado Springs." That offer came from Schuyler. "My people have probably intercepted the civilian escorts from the other companies by now and told them to redirect. They'll be returning to the lake, looking for me. And if anyone in the Clean Zone wants someone who can testify to what went on here, well, if they ask nicely and pull their heads out of their asses long enough to listen, maybe I'll bother telling them."

Xolani added, "Let Perimeter Security know to spread the word that if anyone wants to leave the Clean Zone to help establish the new settlement, they're welcome. No one has to live under the Genetic Diversity Mandate if they don't want to."

Darius nodded his approval. "If we don't have enough fuel to transport them in the lightcar, we'll send escort parties down from Lewis-McChord to guide them until it gets too late in the year to risk the mountain passes."

It was only a matter of hours after that until they were deposited on the shores of Lake Tahoe, well away from the city itself with its empty, haunted hotels and casinos. The mountains around them were lush and the air almost cool at this altitude. Everything smelled of pine and cedar and rich, decaying undergrowth. The lake was the most enchanting shade of blue Zach had ever seen, like a sapphire beneath the sky. The shores were mostly rocky shallows that quickly gave way to dense forests, but there were some sandy beaches, and they made camp on one of those.

"This is perfect," Zach murmured and slipped his hand into Nico's. He appeared as though he wanted to protest, but he mustered a smile and squeezed back.

Zach could feel close to God here, he thought, staring up at the crystalline sky. If he had to choose a place to die, this was a good one. He could pray and feel like none of the artifice and interference of humanity kept him from being heard. Unconcerned with revenants this far from the city, they spread themselves out on the soft, damp earth at the tree line, almost far enough apart to be three separate camps. That way,

Zach and Nico wouldn't have to go far for the privacy they desired.

Thank you, Lord, for providing such a beautiful place for me to spend my final weeks.

Darius and Xolani went hunting and returned with an enormous buck that would easily keep them fed for days. Rhys got a strange look on his face when he saw it.

"Do you remember when Gina killed the moose?" he asked as they all worked on carving and spitting strips of the venison. "She was fighting a group of revenants that were after her calf," he explained for Nico and Zach's benefit. It was the first time Zach had ever heard him speak about his early days with the Jugs beyond what he'd been required to do to survive. It didn't seem like an entirely unhappy memory. "She was doing all right trampling them on her own, and Darius and the rest of the squad were just trying to clean up the ones who were left. But she didn't know we were actually trying to save her, so she charged. The way Toby yelled when she turned on us! I'd never seen anything so huge. I thought we'd never be able to eat it all, but of course it was a whole squadron of Jugs . . ."

He broke off then with a quiet laugh and returned to working with the bloody meat. His cheeks were a hot pink, though.

Darius smiled knowingly. "You're thinkin' 'bout the pool table in the clubhouse that same night, aren't you, boy?"

Rhys ducked his head but nodded. "That was the night you started trying to find ways to make it all easier for me." He slid Darius a sideways glance. "I never thanked you for that."

Darius shrugged, but Zach thought he looked pleased.

After dinner, they bathed in the frigid waters of the lake, and as the sun set, Zach lay in Nico's arms and listened to the almost violent sounds of Darius and Rhys's lovemaking that carried down the shore.

"Jugs are all like this," Nico murmured, nibbling on the shell of Zach's ear. "Comes from the communal living. Completely shameless."

"So in other words, you fit right in?" Zach teased, rolling to trail his hand down Nico's body to the hard cock nudging his hip.

Nico gasped and pushed into his hand. "Philosophically, at least." He bit his lip and let his head fall back, the front of his throat bobbing. "I spent a lot of nights fantasizing about you being the one to make the noises I was hearing."

"I wish I had been." Their chatter broke off for a long while because Nico's lips were just too tempting. Zach kissed him until they were both breathless and aching for more, until the rhythm of Nico's hips in time to Zach's stroking had grown almost desperately urgent. Zach gentled his pace, brushing whisper-soft kisses along Nico's throat under the line of his beard. "I want you to do something for me."

"Hmm?"

Oh, that distracted sound was good. It told Zach that Nico was nearly out of his head with desire, far past the point of thinking too hard. He'd been afraid that the specter of Zach's infection might have made it difficult for them to give themselves to the pleasure of being together here.

Zach reached for his pack and the small jar of sunflower seed oil Rhys had given him, and pressed it into Nico's slack palm. "I want you to have me."

Nico's eyes flew open, and Zach saw the conversation they

could have had flitter across his face. Xolani had confirmed that by this point, Zach's immune system was making antibodies to the Alpha strain of the virus. There was no possibility of simultaneous exposure. Now they could indulge in the one pleasure Zach's refusal to accept the Alpha strain had always denied them.

Grief shadowed Nico's beloved face for a moment, but then his expression smoothed as he pushed it aside and closed his hand on the proffered jar of oil. "I want that," he rasped, kissing Zach hard. "I want that more than anything."

Zach smiled and rolled onto his back, pulling his knees to his chest. It was a wanton, lurid position to assume, as shameless as Nico had accused the Jugs of being, but he felt nothing even close to shame as he spread himself open and offered all his most private places up to Nico. God's blessing was on their union, he'd always believed that, from the first time they'd pleasured each other. There was nothing to be shy or ashamed about.

He closed his eyes, and Nico explored his crevice with gentle fingertips, then opened them again when Nico paused to dig in his pants for his pocketknife. He carefully pared his fingernails before resuming his caresses. Zach gave himself over to the sensation of those featherlight touches brushing past the ring of his anus, making him tingle with pleasure and anticipation.

He'd had Nico's fingers inside him before, but there was a rare gentleness here tonight between them, a sense of reverence, of worship. Nico knelt between Zach's splayed legs and placed slow, sucking kisses up the underside of his shaft while he coated his fingers with oil. And then there was the counterintuitive pleasure of being stretched and filled. Slowly, so slowly, awkward and not quite comfortable until something changed and made it feel very, very right. Nico lapped the dribbling beads of fluid from the tip of Zach's cock, then drew it in and sucked it down to his throat as the pumping of his fingers intensified.

"Oh God, Nico! Yes!" Zach panted and wriggled, seeking more pressure from Nico's fingers. It felt too easy, now, not enough to fill him the way he wanted to be filled. More would ache, he knew that, he'd felt that, but it didn't matter because he *needed* more, needed that ache, needed to be stretched until he was sure he couldn't bear it, that it would tear him in two.

He released the back of his knees, letting his legs hook over Nico's shoulders as he reached down and held Nico's head still while he pumped into Nico's mouth. A groan vibrated against the head of his cock, a growly sound that meant Nico liked what he was doing. Impaled on Nico's fingers, he thrust into the heat and suction of Nico's mouth, moaning, crying out for more without the slightest concern if his voice carried down the lake the way Rhys's had.

He whimpered when Nico drew away, sliding his full lips off Zach's cock with a teasing swirl of his tongue, and easing his fingers out of Zach.

"No . . ." he pleaded, unbearably empty, and his skin cold everywhere that Nico no longer touched him.

"I've got you, *cariño*," Nico whispered. "Just give me a minute."

Zach twisted to see past his hovering legs to watch Nico fill his palm with oil and slick it along his shaft with a shaking hand. It was messy and drizzly, running down Nico's scrotum and dripping onto his thighs, but Nico didn't seem to care. He poured more oil into his palm and coated the fingers of his other hand again. It ran in sloppy rivulets down Zach's crevice, but then Nico pressed against his rim with three slick fingers and the heedless urgency was snuffed in an instant.

Zach went very, very still, breathless, his eyes locking with Nico's as those fingers slowly progressed, first stretching and then burning almost beyond what Zach thought he could bear. He felt the prickling sweat of effort pop up out of his pores even though he was just lying there, trembling, waiting for the sting to ease.

"All right?" Nico whispered. Zach licked his lips and nodded, never breaking eye contact. He was panting too fast, too shallowly to answer with words. After a long moment, the burn eased and his muscles unlocked. He sighed in relief and nodded again.

"I want to make this so good for you," Nico said, pressing a kiss to the inside of Zach's knee as he guided it over his shoulder, leaving oil on his skin. He cautiously drew his fingers out of Zach and raised the opposite knee over his other shoulder with that hand, while he positioned the blunt head of his cock against Zach's entrance with the other.

"It could never be anything else," Zach murmured, then closed his eyes and gasped when the pressure blossomed, sharp and eye watering. He went rigid again, his hands on Nico's thighs as if he'd push him away.

Nico caressed Zach's calf with his lips. "Relax. Push back against me. Go toward it. Don't try to get away from it."

The encouragement went counter to everything Zach's senses were telling him, and with anyone but Nico, he couldn't have obeyed. But it *was* Nico, and underneath the fear of more pain than he could possibly bear was the triumphant knowledge that he had *Nico* inside him, joined to him like they were one flesh. That massive, intruding presence was the man he'd loved for over a decade, the man he'd spent so many years away from. They were together now, in every possible sense, and so Zach drew a deep breath and used his legs on Nico's shoulders and his hands on Nico's thighs as leverage to pull himself *toward* Nico.

The fiery ache eased, something popped through his resisting muscles, and they groaned in unison as Nico slid deeper inside.

Oh, and it was *good*. The burn was hardly even a memory now. Everything was full in a way that should have felt wrong but instead was so very *right*. Especially when the electric pleasure of Nico brushing against Zach's prostate began. He worked into Zach in small thrusts and nudges, and Zach thrust back, hurrying him along, *needing* Nico as deep as he could possibly go.

Zach was beyond controlling his own body, beyond doing anything but reacting. He reached for the blanket by his head with both hands because it felt right to have his hands up there, to have his upper body as splayed and open and helpless as the rest of him. Nico thrust a little harder, a little deeper as he made love to Zach's calf with his lips and tongue. A small smile touched his mouth as he took in Zach's position.

"You want me to hold you down, *cariño*? Cover you and pin you to this blanket and just cut loose?"

Zach's cock, which had softened while he was adjusting, gave a fierce jerk and tightened, leaking against his stomach. "Yes!" he gasped, then he cried out as Nico pushed into him with even more force.

Nico's hands were slippery with oil as they traveled up Zach's torso. His fingers combed through Zach's armpit hair, wrapped around Zach's arms, and slid all the way up to his wrists. The position stretched Nico out, brought him forward until he hovered over Zach, nearly folding Zach in half. It wasn't an easy position for Zach's hips and knees, but it lifted his ass and opened him to Nico even more shamelessly and more vulnerably than before, and that was *perfect*. Nico's hands locked around Zach's wrists like bands as he hauled his hips back and began to drive in deeper. "Like that?"

"Yes!" Nico's cock drove the shout from him, a breathless exclamation of pleasure as much as the confirmation Nico sought.

Nico grinned, the smile fierce under the thick growth of his beard, and pistoned his hips faster, harder, pushing more helpless cries from Zach's throat. He buried his face in Zach's armpit and began licking and sucking the sensitive skin there until Zach's entire body was alive with sensation and taut with pleasure. Nico's rough stomach rubbed against Zach's cock with each thrust, and it wasn't until that became too much that he realized he'd climaxed and hadn't even noticed.

Nico must have, though, because he slowed down. He released his grip on Zach's wrists and laced their fingers, joining them there as intimately as the rest of their bodies were intertwined. He kissed Zach, their tongues tangling and thrusting, as he rocked gently against Zach.

"Too sensitive?" Nico asked when he came up for air. "Need me to stop?"

"No!" Zach shook his head emphatically. He didn't want this ever to end. And judging from the ache in his balls and deep in the pit of his gut, and the fact that he was still hard, his body wasn't through yet. "Keep going. I want you to come inside me."

Nico blinked, then nodded. "Tell me if it becomes too much," he warned, but that was the end of his restraint. He locked Zach's wrists down against the blanket once more, plundering Zach's mouth with lips and teeth as his hips pumped relentlessly. The hollows of his pelvis clapped against Zach's sweat-dampened flanks, adding to the cacophony of moans and wails and grunts. And God, yes, Zach was going to come again, and this time there was no way he could miss it happening. It was building at the base of his spine like a super-storm rolling in, threatening to unleash all its fury and leave utter devastation behind.

"That's it," Nico hissed, pushing his weight up off Zach. He reared back, grabbed Zach's hips, and began jerking him to meet each thrust. His eyes were screwed shut with pleasure or concentration, but then he slit them open. "Touch yourself, Zach. Do it. Let me watch you."

Oh, those were familiar words. Nico's favorite pastime, Zach had once called it. The first time had been in a car in the middle of nowhere, while Nico was disoriented with a head injury. He loved watching Zach masturbate, and Zach had long ago learned to let go of any self-consciousness he might have had about it.

He reached down, wrapped a sweaty hand around himself, and began jerking in time with Nico's thrusts, which were pounding into him like a pile driver.

One of them was yelling, and he was pretty sure it was him. Especially when Nico's hips slammed against him, and Nico went still, shuddering powerfully. Nico's cock twitched and pumped inside him, and Zach added a twisting motion when his hand encircled the crown of his own cock, piling on just enough friction to loose the torrent of pleasure building up between his balls and spine. It ripped through him, almost painful in its intensity. It zinged up his backbone and left him tingling, nerveless, while lashing hot streams of seed all the way up to his chest. He yanked his hand away from his own cock because, in an instant, even the lightest touch was *too much*. Nico's softening shaft inside him started to feel uncomfortable.

"Enough!" he gasped, squirming, and Nico eased out and dropped to the blanket at his side, seemingly as boneless as Zach. His anus was wet and burned a little, but Zach didn't have the energy to do anything about it.

He felt euphoric. Exhausted, but over the moon. Would it be inappropriate to thank God for letting him have that experience before he died? Didn't matter. Zach closed his eyes and thought a short, grateful prayer anyway.

"Thank God," they heard Xolani call out irritably. "Maybe now I can get some sleep. Tomorrow I'm making camp somewhere else, and the four of you are on your own. Jesus. Should have told Joe to bring Titus back this way if he finds him."

Hot embarrassment flooded Zach's cheeks, but Nico caught his eyes, merriment sparkling in his gaze, and the next thing Zach knew, they were both laughing uncontrollably.

⩕ ⩕ ⩕

THOUGH RHYS SPOKE of him and Darius taking some time to go on another walkabout together, Zach noticed that they never specified when. He kept waiting for Rhys to come and let him know he was leaving, but instead Rhys stuck close to camp. When Zach and Nico weren't slipping off into the woods to make love—which they did far more often than was probably dignified—they spent their days by the lake, talking and warding off the heat by skinny-dipping. Darius, Xolani, and Nico took all the guns one day and walked around the lake to the city, where they liberated several decks of cards from the casinos and fishing equipment from one of the houseboats. After that, evenings by the fire were spent playing poker and gin, and the venison in their diet was mixed up with fish, fresh out of the water.

It was the perfect, peaceful retreat Zach had hoped it would be, except—

"Why haven't you and Darius left yet?" he demanded of Rhys as they were lying in the sun on the edge of the lake.

"I'm in no hurry," Rhys said vaguely, and Zach lifted his head.

"Rhys, you don't want to be here to watch me die."

Rhys sighed and rolled over, cradling his head in his arms with his face turned toward Zach. "No, I really don't. But—" he shrugged "—I don't want to leave and come back to find you're gone, either. Besides, it might be better for Nico if we hang around."

"You'll take him to Seattle with you after, won't you?" Zach pleaded. "I don't think he ever had all that many friends in Sierra Company, I'd hate to think of him trying to go back and fit in again."

"We won't even let him try." Rhys gave a halfhearted smile and closed his eyes. Which, Zach decided, probably meant he'd had enough of facing the reality that he was going to lose someone else he cared about in another week or two.

Three weeks was about how long it took Beta symptoms to manifest. It could be up to six, but as much as Zach wanted every last moment with Nico that he could get, he was afraid that if the process drew out too long, it would be worse for everyone.

"Have you thought about how you want to handle things?" Xolani asked when Zach approached her in the third week about his options.

As if he'd thought of anything but.

"I considered going for a swim." He smiled slightly, only half joking. "When the lethargy starts to set in, I could just swim out and wait to go catatonic. The hypothermia would probably help. But then, I suppose Nico might like to be able to burn my remains."

Xolani gave him a firm look that in no way diminished her hard-bitten kindness. She reminded him of Chantal, the doctor he'd worked with when he'd first come to the Clean Zone. Minus the backstabbing, of course. "This isn't about what Nico wants. This is *your* death. We need to honor your choices."

Zach sighed. "What I *choose* is to take as much pain from this process as I can for Nico. I don't want anything violent or bloody. No bullets or slit wrists. Do you have a 50 cc syringe? Back before the overthrow, the doctor I worked with preferred an air embolism to the brain when euthanizing the patient was necessary."

"I can do that." She blew out a slow breath. "I could also suffocate you after you go catatonic."

It was so mundane, discussing how he wanted to die the way he might once have discussed what refreshments his father wanted in the green room when he'd done the pundit-vid circuit leading up to his run for office. No life-and-death decisions here, though, because death was already a foregone conclusion. Now everything was just a matter of preference.

"That might be better," he said, swallowing thickly. "Then Nico won't have to watch me stroke out. Thank you."

He passed that third week, and into the fourth, with an odd sense of detachment. Not from Nico; there was nothing detached about their increasingly desperate lovemaking. And not from Rhys, either. He clung to the friendship they'd formed, and thanked God that he'd had the chance to perhaps undo some of the pain his father and brother had caused Rhys.

But outside those two crucial connections, Zach unplugged from everything else. Hunger didn't matter. If he wanted to stay at the edge of the lake and watch the sunset instead of eat dinner, it was all the same. He had nothing to fear in starving. He could swim longer, past the point where the cold water made him ache and shiver, because what did it matter if he froze? He could perch on the most precarious ledges when he and Nico went for a walk, because the worst that could happen was that he might fall and break his neck. It was bizarre and liberating, and he both missed the presence of fear of his own mortality and reveled in his freedom from it.

The rash began so subtly that Zach cursed himself when he finally noticed it. He might have lost some critical detail of his final hours, missed some opportunity to assure Nico of his love, or *something*, because he hadn't been paying attention, had been unaware that the end was finally here. Suddenly, there wasn't enough time to say everything he needed to say and do everything he needed to do, to make sure there wasn't a doubt in Nico's mind that every breath in Zach's lungs belonged to him.

Should he have accepted the Alpha strain? How could he have cheated them of the life they should have had together?

Lord, please, place Your hand on my heart and give me the peace of knowing that I've done Your will!

Nico, who had been napping beside him in the afternoon heat, woke with a start, his eyes flying to Zach's face. Zach didn't know what his expression conveyed, but it was enough. He saw the tragedy of loss begin to fill Nico's eyes and grief contort his features.

"No!" Zach placed a hand over Nico's mouth before he could say anything. "No. Just make love to me and hold me until I'm resting, then get Xolani. She'll know what to do."

Tears spilled from Nico's eyes, but he nodded and took Zach in his arms.

20

PRIME

Rhys felt the first frisson of unease as the quiet from Zach and Nico's end of camp stretched through the whole afternoon and into the evening. Occasionally, he heard murmurs—and even moans—but they didn't respond to calls to come eat supper or join the rest of them for cards or conversation at the fire that night after the sun sank.

The next morning, he awoke at dawn to Nico sobbing. It roused them all. Rhys quickly dressed and joined Xolani by the fire, where she waited with her med kit in her hands, watching Nico approach from down along the lakeshore. His face was drawn and wet with tears.

"I think he's catatonic now," he said without preamble when he reached Xolani, swaying on his feet. "Or mostly so. He reacts when I try to wake him, but—"

His voice cracked, and Rhys's own eyes overflowed.

"I'm going to go say good-bye," he murmured and squeezed Nico's shoulder once, a pathetic gesture of reassurance, as he passed.

Zach lay naked on his bedroll, and he smelled like sex and looked like he was just sleeping off a long night of passion. But Rhys could see the angry rash across his chest and creeping up his neck and jaw. Patches of it were appearing on his belly and arms, and, Rhys assumed, other parts hidden by the blanket. Within a couple of hours, that rash would start to darken into bruise-like lesions.

He knelt and took Zach's hand, making no effort not to cry. For so long he'd refused to let anyone see his tears. They were a weakness Father Maurice and Jacob had taken far too much enjoyment in exploiting. But he let them spill for Zach, as he had for Gabe, two years ago.

If anyone had told him two months ago that he'd feel this sort of pain at the prospect of losing *Jacob's brother*, of all people, he would never have believed it.

"Thanks for being my friend," he whispered, unable to think of anything more profound to say.

Zach stirred but didn't respond.

After a while, Xolani joined him, with Nico behind her. By then the sun was up over the trees to the east and nearly blinding them. Xolani knelt beside Rhys, her face carefully neutral.

"When did the rash appear?" she asked over her shoulder.

"Um, yesterday afternoon, I guess?" Nico said hollowly. "Zach noticed it before I did. He knew what it meant so we . . . just *waited*."

Xolani muttered under her breath, "This isn't right. He should be showing lesions by now. And he's not catatonic, he's just asleep."

"What does that mean?" Nico demanded, his eyes snapping behind the sheen of tears. "Zach said you knew what to do!"

"I *do*, but—"

"Then *do* it!" Nico's voice broke, and he dropped to his knees, tears spilling down his face. His shoulders jerked with the force of his sobs. "Please. I can't— Don't drag this out. He wouldn't want that."

Rhys looked up as Darius appeared behind Nico, reaching down to grip his shoulder firmly. "Steady, son. We've got you. What's the problem here, Xolani?"

"I've *seen* this rash before." She tugged hard at her braid. "I don't know where, but— *Shit*."

"Are you saying he might not have the Rot?" Rhys asked plaintively.

"I can't— I don't—" She gave Nico a helpless look. "I don't want to give anyone false hope or disrespect Zach's final wishes, but I'm not comfortable going through with this until we know for sure that this is what we think it is."

"What else could it be?" Nico moaned, shaking his head in bewilderment.

"I'm not—" Her head shot up, and she stared at Nico with her mouth agape. "You were never in Russia!"

It came out almost as an accusation, and Nico jumped as though she'd charged him with doing something horrific. "No, I wasn't. I wasn't deployed with the 1st Juggernaut Battalion. I was a civilian. You know that."

"Yeah, I know, and I'm a fucking idiot for not realizing this before." Xolani sprang to her feet, kicking up sand as she paced. "It was always speculated that something environmental *in Russia*, where Alpha was first deployed, triggered the lethal mutation."

Rhys nodded in tandem with Nico; Xolani had told Rhys this the first day they met, when she explained the virus to him.

"I think I vaguely remember McClosky mentioning that," Nico said.

Xolani's own nod was jerky and distracted. "But *you* were never there. You carry a version of Bane that was never exposed to whatever turned the Beta strain into the Rot and enabled the Gamma mutation that made the revenants." She swept a hand out, gesturing to Zach. "If I'm right, this is *Beta*. I mean, the *real* Beta, what Beta was *supposed* to be. Call it, I don't know, Beta-Prime, or something. A nonlethal rash and a couple months of debilitating exhaustion and malaise."

"He's not dying?" Oh, the hope on Nico's face made Rhys begin to cry all over again. He squeezed Zach's slightly feverish hand, letting himself begin to hope as well.

Xolani shook her head, her expression conflicted. "I don't know. It's too soon to say. God, Nico, I'm sorry. I know this must be hell for you. I could be wrong, but—" Her shoulders slumped helplessly. "I think we should wait. But I also think you should be prepared. In case I *am* wrong."

"If you're wrong, we'll have gone against Zach's express wishes," he murmured. Some of the hopeful joy had faded from his features, and he just seemed resigned. "What about if you're right?"

"I've never actually dealt with this particular strain. I saw pictures—or computer models of it, rather—at the briefing they gave the medics after we were infected with Alpha." She returned to Zach's side, reaching down to lay a hand on his brow. "He's going to feel like hell for a while, and we'll have to be careful to keep him fed and well hydrated, but unless something unforeseen happens, he'll live. *If* I'm right. *Which I may not be*," she tacked on emphatically. "Please. You need to understand that."

Another tear tracked down Nico's salt-crusted cheeks and disappeared into his beard. "How long until we know for certain?"

"Another day or two, maybe?" Xolani shrugged. "If we don't see any lesions by then, and if he can still be roused, we can proceed as though we are actually dealing with Beta-Prime. At least until we find out otherwise. We can't ask him, so it's up to you," she said gently. "Do you think he would prefer to err on the side of hope or the side of not drawing this out any longer than necessary?"

Nico lifted Zach's hand and pressed a tender kiss to it. "Hope. Always hope." He swallowed, never taking his eyes off Zach's face. "Two days. We'll give it two days."

◭ ◭ ◭

Rhys, Nico, and Xolani all sat vigil beside Zach throughout the day, while Darius hunted and tended to camp. Toward the evening, Zach stirred. His eyes had sunken into exhausted hollows by then, but they opened, and he blinked groggily at the three of them. "Waz goin' on?"

Xolani laughed, looking younger and less burdened than Rhys had ever seen her except when she was high in the canteen at Fort Vancouver. This was what they'd been waiting for. If Zach truly were succumbing to the Rot, he wouldn't rouse once he'd slipped away.

"I'll let you explain," she said to Nico, patting his shoulder as she jumped to her feet and rushed off to report to Darius and no doubt start laying plans to get what they'd require for Zach's convalescence.

Smiling so hard his cheeks ached and wanting nothing more than to fling himself on Darius and celebrate, Rhys followed her. A moment later, even down the lakeshore near the fire, they heard Zach voice rise in slurred protest.

"*We lost* ten years *to this?*"

⚑ ⚑ ⚑

With nothing to do but keep Nico entertained between Zach's brief spurts of semiconsciousness, Darius decided to use the downtime for an excursion with Rhys. In a week or two, they would meet up with Nico, Xolani, and Zach at a nearby lodge, since Nico announced he wanted a proper bed for Zach to rest in while he was ill, and a roof overhead in case the weather turned wet. Xolani and Nico carried Zach one way along the lake, while Darius and Rhys departed to hike the old Tahoe Rim Trail in the other direction.

Darius was still adjusting to the new Rhys who had emerged from that research facility in Nevada. It was difficult to put his finger on exactly what the difference was. Rhys was both quieter and more talkative at times, and the sort of things he spoke of when he did talk kept tripping up Darius.

"The new Clean Zone, er, settlement," he said as they hiked, "do you think they'll be as strict about keeping people out? I mean, the whole area's been patrolled for revs already and the survivors we bring are all quarantined for up to six months before we take them, so maybe they can have different policies, right?"

"Maybe." Darius glanced over his shoulder at Rhys's thoughtful face. "Why, you think it matters?"

Rhys swallowed audibly. "Just, maybe if they're not so—what was that word Xolani used?—*xenophobic*, maybe they won't mind Jugs settling near them. Maybe there won't be an exile."

"We still got a lot of work ahead of us before we can think about where we're gonna settle." He had to force himself to acknowledge that point, because Rhys's chatter was so hopeful.

"I know, but—" Rhys stopped hiking, peering out through an opening in the trees. They were quite a ways above the lake and not far from the edge of the rock cliffs overlooking it. Beyond and below the trees was an enormous stretch of sapphire water. "If it turns out that some of the Jugs can start families, Xolani says they're going to need wet nurses. Maybe if the Jugs have a better relationship with the new Clean Zone, it might work."

Darius smiled, giving in to the urge to pin Rhys against a tree and kiss him stupid. "That's a good thought," he said when they were done and Rhys was slumped against the tree trunk, looking dazed. "We can hope."

That was the difference, he decided as they started hiking again. The things Rhys talked about now were forward-looking and optimistic, anticipating what might happen months or even years down the line. Imagining ways life could be better for people—Jugs and civvies both. He'd never spoken that way before.

The quality of his silence was different, as well. Darius had always assumed his quietness was defensive, an ingrained habit from trying to stay off Houtman's radar. Now it was thoughtful, as if he was lost in building the future scenarios he eventually gave voice to. And there was something deliberate about it. Like Rhys was *making* himself take the time to consider all these things. Some sort of exercise, like toning a long-disused muscle.

They made camp that night when the trail took them back down near the water's edge, along a sandy strip of beach where they might as well have been the only two people in the world. Darius watched Rhys as he stared out over the water, wondering what was going through the boy's head.

Sex was different now, too. If Rhys hadn't assured him that Littlewood had never laid a finger on him, Darius might have thought he was processing something that had happened back there. Rhys was both more forward and more inclined toward gentleness, as if he didn't feel the same need for violent and painful sex he had before. Which, honestly, suited Darius just fine. He couldn't quite say it, but he wanted to coddle Rhys awhile longer. There was no question that sooner or later, their penchant for roughness would reassert itself, but this tender interlude was nice.

As if attuned to Darius's thoughts, Rhys began talking as they prepared the day's catch for dinner.

"I'm having a hard time getting Littlewood out of my head," he confessed, laying another trout filet skin-side down on a flat rock near the edge of the fire. "He was—" Rhys shook himself sharply. "He was warped."

"How so?" It was the first time Rhys had opened up about what had happened while he was inside that facility. Darius sort of wished Xolani was around. Of any of them, she knew best how to play counselor. But he wasn't about to shut Rhys down if he was finally talking.

"From the reports he'd read, he'd gotten this idea that—"

Rhys drew in a deep breath and blew it out with a shudder "—that you all had treated me the way *he* would have if he'd been a Jug. That was what he imagined: having your strength and using it that way." Rhys smiled slightly and turned his eyes toward Darius. "But it wasn't true."

Darius shrugged, knowing the tension in his gut came from uncomfortable memories he'd never quite reconciled with. "I remember some moments I'm not quite proud of," he muttered.

"I know." Rhys's voice was understanding. It wasn't that Darius hadn't *forgiven* himself, as such, for the things he'd done back when he'd thought they were necessary to help Rhys survive. But the memories would never sit well with him. Whatever the circumstances had dictated at the time, he'd crossed lines he'd always sworn he would never cross. "But I said I wanted to live, and you did what you had to do to make sure that happened. It's not the same."

"Turns out it wasn't necessary." Fuck. There was the part that kept grating on him. In the end, crossing those lines had been *futile* because of Rhys's immunity. His life had never been in danger to begin with.

"That doesn't change what we believed at the time." Rhys used a stick to push the hot rock with its steaming trout filets away from the fire. "For Littlewood, imagining what happened back then was all about imagining you doing things to degrade me. It was never like that, no matter what we did."

He crawled across the sand to Darius, pushing him onto his back and kissing him slowly. "I'm not ashamed. I never will be again. Not of any of it."

The trout was cold by the time they broke apart.

THEY'D BEEN HIKING for the better part of a week when Rhys asked out of nowhere, "Do you remember what we talked about when we were at the Garden of the Gods? About you marking me?"

Darius froze in the act of throwing another stick on the campfire. The sun hadn't set, but Rhys had wanted to make camp early, while it was still warm enough to enjoy lounging on the sand.

"I remember," he answered slowly. "Why?"

"You said if I ever wanted your marks on me for my own sake, that I should ask." Rhys pushed himself up, drawing his legs to his chest so that he was no longer stretched out in full, nude glory on the beach. There was something shy and maybe a little nervous about that posture. "I'm asking."

Darius's heart began to pound a little faster. He wiped bits of bark and lichen off his hands and stood, crossing the strand to crouch next to Rhys. "Tell me why."

Those mossy-brown green-gold eyes were soft and calm, and Darius stared into them, trying to get a feel for how deep this went for Rhys. "Because I'm proud of who I am and who *we* are and what we do together. I told Littlewood I belonged to you, and he thought I meant it in a terrible way, but for me, it was a good thing. I have a *life* and a *home*, with someone who will always love me and won't ever make me feel ashamed or wrong. And I don't care who knows it or what they think about it."

Darius groaned softly and kissed him. No wonder this boy had thrown him off his stride from the beginning. He reached into all the soft, vulnerable places Darius had always tried to keep protected, and planted himself there, like roots burrowing deep into sheltered, shaded soil. Darius'd been a hard-assed bastard toward Rhys in those early weeks because he'd sensed, even then, that Rhys was dangerous to him.

He could never regret letting him inside, though.

"We'll do it after the sun goes down," he promised.

He wasn't sure why he needed darkness, but he did. There was something primal in the thought of making his mark on Rhys in the glow of the fire and the moon. Almost ritualistic. It just felt right.

He didn't fuck Rhys, though Rhys's naked body on the warm sand was more than willing. That would wait until after, until he could do it seeing his mark on that fair skin. Instead, he went hunting and fed them a solid dinner, then told Rhys to wash off in the lake as the sun set.

They didn't speak after that. Again, it felt like a ritual, something reverent and prayerful in their silent preparations. Not cluttering up the space between them with words. When it was fully dark, Darius pulled his hunting knife out of its sheath on his belt and laid it with its blade in the coals at the edge of the fire.

Rhys's eyes widened, his face going a little whiter. But his gaze was steady as he watched Darius strip, then took off his own pants. They would both be nude in the heat of the fire and the sweltering summer night for this, their skin shining with sweat.

Without being told, Rhys spread out one of the blankets from their bedroll beside the fire and lay facedown on it. Darius knelt beside him, resting a palm in the middle of Rhys's long, pale back. He quivered beneath Darius's touch, but he didn't flinch.

"You're sure?" Darius asked. Just that one question. Nothing more.

"Yes." Rhys's response was quiet but emphatic. Darius didn't ask again.

Rhys's skin was smooth and freckled, peeling at the tops of the shoulders from a sunburn that never seemed to settle into a tan, despite weeks on the lake. It was a lean, strong back. Lines of beautiful muscle undulated beneath Darius's caress in the flickering firelight.

Darius pressed his lips to the knob of Rhys's spine, just below the long hair Rhys'd refused to trim in defiance of ghosts from his past. He kissed his way from one bony ridge to the next, stroking Rhys's ribs and hips with his hands. Rhys moaned and ground his pelvis against the blanket, prompting Darius to reach around and grasp the swollen dick trapped underneath Rhys.

"Fuck. Darius, *yes*," Rhys panted, pushing his ass up to give Darius's hand more room to stroke. It offered another opportunity too delicious to pass up, and he licked his way down Rhys's shamelessly proffered crack. With his free hand, he spread Rhys's buttocks. He circled that sensitive, puckered ring with his tongue, drilling and twisting and wriggling to get inside.

"Taste so good," he muttered, his moist breath rebounding against his face off Rhys's sweat- and spit-slick skin. "Love eatin' your ass. Love you movin' like that, makin' those sounds . . ."

He nibbled and licked and devoured Rhys's asshole until Rhys's dick was rigid in Darius's hand, until he was crying out on the verge of release. That was when Darius eased off. He wanted Rhys feeling good, flying high on pleasure. He drew his hand away and kissed along the line of Rhys's spine, sucking up a dark mark on the side of his neck.

"Lay down, boy," he whispered, and kissed Rhys's ear.

Rhys settled back onto the blanket with a shudder, growing very still and quiet except for the short, sharp pants of breath Darius could make out under the crackling of the fire.

The blade of his knife glowed red when he pulled it out of the coals, and he knew he'd have to work quickly. Rhys twitched when Darius brought it near his skin, going tense. Biting his lip and narrowing his eyes, he made sure his hand was steady and laid the sharp edge against the flat plane of Rhys's shoulder.

Rhys's shriek rang out through the trees on the first stroke, a diagonal slash inward. The scream erased the sizzling sound the knife made as it passed along Rhys's skin. The scent of cauterized flesh filled the air, and Darius tightened his lips and made a second slash, starting at the bottom end of the first and moving horizontally outward. Rhys's cry was softer for the second cut, as if it didn't register quite so badly in the wake of the first one.

One more. Darius rotated the blade so that the flat of it would sear a broader line. Rhys screamed anew, a longer, broken, wailing sound, because this stroke was slower. Again, the line was on the diagonal, connecting the first and second lines on the right side and closing the symbol he'd drawn.

He tossed the knife aside as Rhys whimpered and sobbed. His entire body quaked in shock and pain. Darius caressed his hair and arms soothingly, placing reverent kisses on his unmarked shoulder.

"You're okay, boy. I got you. I'll always have you," he vowed, and the words made Rhys weep harder, his tears even more unrestrained than after a whipping. They were cathartic tears, Darius knew, cleansing and liberating for a man who'd shut down all feeling for years to protect himself. But they still made his heart ache—in understanding that Rhys needed this, in grief that Rhys found it necessary, and in pride, both at Rhys's strength and resilience and at the fact that he, of all people, was the one Rhys trusted.

He whispered all that and more against Rhys's skin, pledging his adoration and devotion. Letting Rhys fill his heart and soul, a beacon of joy and hope in a cruel, hard world.

It took longer for Rhys's tears to subside and for him to transform all that emotion to passion. Darius hadn't been sure it would happen tonight, but it did. Rhys craned his neck to try to kiss Darius without rolling onto his back. It was sloppy and awkward, and filled with heedless, unrestrained need.

"Up," Darius murmured, lifting Rhys and turning him without making any contact between his back and the blanket, so that he was upright and facing Darius. He grabbed the lube and knelt on the blanket, pulling Rhys astride him.

Rhys didn't need to be told what to do. His eyes were feverish and intent as he coated Darius's dick and rose up, holding it still while he sank down and impaled himself. He was tight, the pain of what he'd endured still riding him and making him tense, but the expression on his tear-stained face was sublime.

Rhys was high, euphoric, glowing with it as he started to ride Darius. There wasn't much strength in his trembling thighs, though, so Darius gripped his hips and worked Rhys up and down his cock like a glove. Sweat poured off them both, making their skin slide as their hands tried to find purchase. Their kisses were messy and wet. Rhys's cries were as much pain as pleasure, but he never asked to stop and Darius knew better than to doubt that his boy knew exactly what he wanted.

It didn't take long. With his senses overloaded, Rhys came quickly and quietly. Not a huge explosion of rapture, but a shudder and a pulse, rippling around Darius's dick and spurting onto his belly. No, the explosion was Darius's, only a moment later, as he slammed Rhys down onto his cock and ground up into him, shooting into his guts, breeding him, marking him as thoroughly inside as he was now marked outside. Rhys's tight smile when he felt Darius come was fierce and triumphant.

"Okay?" Darius asked when he could breathe again. By then, Rhys had melted against him, all the strength draining out of his body. He was so slack Darius feared he might have passed out, but he nodded slowly.

"Mm'kay," he mumbled. He was boneless as Darius maneuvered him back onto the blanket on his stomach. They were really too close to the fire to rest comfortably, so Darius pushed himself to his feet. He took another blanket from their bedrolls and spread it out farther away, then carefully lifted a semiconscious Rhys and carried him to it.

He expected Rhys to be asleep before he finished tending the fire and cleaning up anything they might have left lying around that could attract unwanted wildlife. But Rhys's eyes were slit open as Darius checked his guns and laid them out within easy reach, then began oiling and whetting the carbon-blackened blade of his knife.

"What is it?" Rhys asked, his voice a rusty croak after all the screaming he'd done. Darius didn't need him to clarify what he was asking. Instead, Darius leaned over and drew the same figure on the ground that he'd seared into Rhys's shoulder. Rhys would recognize it and understand what it meant. Some of their people etched or drew it on their equipment, especially in recent years as the Jugs started to feel their identity as being separate from the rest of humanity.

Rhys's lips curved when he saw it. Then his eyes fluttered shut and he was gone.

Darius smiled and admired his handiwork, now indelibly carved into Rhys's flesh. Three lines, each touching the other, the one on the right thicker than the other two.

Not a triangle.

The letter *delta*.

21

IMMUNITY

"Xolani?" Zach called softly. Nico was out hunting, as now that Zach was starting to get more energy to eat, Nico was determined to stuff him silly and help him regain the weight he'd lost in the last couple of months. Rhys and Darius were down at the beach. Their honeymoon or whatever had clearly done them a world of good, and since they'd returned, they'd been absolutely soppy over each other.

Even walking the ten or so yards between the room he and Nico had claimed at the ritzy old lodge they'd ensconced themselves in and the door to Xolani's room had Zach's legs trembling. Which was progress. A week or two ago he'd needed help just sitting up to use a bedpan. He could easily see why the people who had developed the Bane virus had been confident of Beta-Prime's ability to bring a nation to its knees. The virus had been designed to spread through the population like wildfire before anyone even suspected it was there. Infrastructure would have collapsed once it manifested in the general populace; the economy would have tanked for lack of productivity and consumption. In the weeks or months until the virus had run its course, even a country as large as Russia would have been ripe for the picking, but only for a nation with troops who were immune to it, like the Jugs.

Xolani sat cross-legged on her bed, absorbed in writing in a notebook. She looked up when Zach approached, scowling. "What the fuck are you doing out of bed? Why didn't you just call for me?"

"I did." Zach smiled, but he was starting to regret his choice already. Xolani put her notebook aside and rose, wedging herself under Zach's shoulder to take his weight and guide him back to his room.

"You're lucky I don't just toss you over my shoulder," she muttered, but she didn't seem truly cranky. Just her usual irascible self. Zach had gotten used to the abrasiveness, and he understood why Rhys was so fond of her. There truly was no better ally.

"Sorry," he murmured. "I just really wanted a chance to talk to you without Nico hovering nearby."

"Yeah? What about?" She swept his blankets back, waited for Zach to climb obediently into bed, and then covered him up again. Even though the summer heat was oppressive, Zach needed the layers. He always felt chilled without them.

Zach had to fight the impulse to drop back to sleep immediately. He'd been sleeping easily twenty-two hours a day for the first couple weeks of the virus, and then a good sixteen to twenty hours since. It was tapering off, though. He could stay awake for longer stretches now.

"I want you to try to infect me with Beta. *Your* Beta."

She gave him a long, searching look, but he could tell she caught his meaning immediately.

She'd already considered this, hadn't she? Of course she would have been contemplating the possibilities during those weeks when he was too sick to think at all.

"Nico would kill me, even if it works the way we think it will," she said. But it wasn't a refusal.

Zach nodded. "I know. But we have to know if having Beta-Prime makes me immune. If it *does*—"

"Then we finally have a way to inoculate people," she finished for him. "Crude, but effective, as the saying goes. Providing Nico is willing to donate samples of his blood. It's his version of Alpha that we need to make it work."

"Exactly." Zach sank into the mattress. Even that much conversation left him feeling drained.

"And if it doesn't work?" she asked cautiously.

"Then I'll die of the Rot, after all. But at least we'll know. And if it *does* . . ."

If it did, whole new worlds of possibility would open up for them all.

It would change the quarantine process. Now, instead of isolating new survivors until they were sure they weren't a danger, they could infect newly recovered civilians with Beta-Prime before integrating them with the civilian population.

Then the Jugs could freely mingle with the civilians too. Those who hadn't had the flexibility to find long-term companionship among the mostly male Jug population could marry civilians and have children without infecting their partners. The ones who had menstrual cycles wouldn't need to isolate themselves from contact with uninfected people. Coupled with Rhys's idea of using an antiserum derived from his blood on infants born to Jugs, they could keep those children safe until they were old enough to survive being infected by Beta-Prime themselves.

If they could inoculate everyone until the revenants were exterminated and the last of the 1st Juggernaut Battalion died, the threat of another outbreak would finally be a thing of the past.

He knew Xolani was aware of all the ramifications and no doubt worked through all the possibilities and permutations herself. But she must not have been willing to ask Zach to submit himself as a test subject, so he'd had to take the first step and volunteer.

"You're sure you don't want to clear it with Nico?" she asked, unsnapping the sheath on her belt and drawing out a knife.

"He'd never let me if I did, and you and I both know we *have* to do this." God's hand was at work here, Zach knew it. Everything made sense now—why it had never been right for him to let himself be infected by Alpha, why he'd *had* to break down the barriers keeping him apart from Nico, regardless of the danger. This was God's plan, to use him and Nico to protect the surviving population. It just required one last act of faith.

Xolani nodded and drew the blade across the back of her forearm.

⚠ ⚠ ⚠

"I'm going to fucking kill you!" Nico snarled, nose to nose with Xolani. Her scarred face pulled up into a smile.

"Yeah, good luck with that." Nico barely had time to

register her moving before she had him in a wristlock, pinned face-first against the hotel wall.

"I get that you're pissed," she said from behind him, keeping his hand just high enough between his shoulder blades to ache and ensure she had his attention without dislocating his arm. "But it was Zach's choice."

Fuck this. He might be out of practice, but that didn't mean he was helpless. Nico's hand went through the half-rotten plasterboard of the wall as he shoved back, thrusting her off-balance and twisting out of her grasp, using his momentum to turn and grab the hand she had locked around his wrist. Xolani drove an underhand jab into his ribs before he managed to flip her to the floor, though she bounced right back to her feet as if she were on springs. She ducked his roundhouse kick, but he managed to catch another blow to her jaw, staggering her.

Nico charged furiously after her, rage making him more aggressive than strategic. Which he paid for when she swept his legs out from under him and had him on his back, a knee pressing against his larynx, before he even realized what was happening.

"Feel better now?" she asked calmly, her brows climbing high. Grudgingly, he nodded, and she rose, offering him a hand up. "That was fun. We should spar again sometime."

"You shouldn't have done that without talking to me," he insisted once he was on his feet.

"It wasn't your call. You may be a Jug, but that doesn't mean you own Zach. Unless you're thinking of going the way of Charlie Company. Are you?" He bristled at the suggestion, and she gave a brusque nod. "Good. I'd hate to kill you. But if you're not, better ask Darius how well it works out, trying to tell your civilian partner what to do."

Nico swallowed hard, turning away from her so she wouldn't see the way his eyes were burning with tears. "I don't want to control him, but damn it, I already came so close to losing him."

"If it's any comfort, I wouldn't have agreed to it if I didn't think there was a significant chance of it working." She squeezed his shoulder in a sympathetic grip. "I'm not interested in wasting lives needlessly, and Zach's a good man. The two of you have been through enough. But this was a completely plausible hypothesis, and unfortunately, we have no other way of testing it." She rubbed her ribs where he'd hit her. "I mean, sure, we could get back to the Clean Zone so Zach could access the equipment he used in testing Rhys. He could have tested his antibodies, exposed a sample of his blood to a sample of my blood and watched what happened, but in the end, it still would have come down to this. A live, human trial. And since he is the only person *anywhere* to have been infected by Beta-Prime, he's the *only* possible test subject. And he thinks it's worth it."

He wanted to hate her for that pragmatism. He'd been away from the Jugs for too long. This was what they did. They weighed the costs and benefits with cold reason because they didn't have the luxury of sentimentality. Everything they did was about survival. For a while, he'd been able to look at the world that way himself, but it had been some time since he'd been a part of their uniquely fraternal culture.

"So what happens now?" Nico asked after a moment, sinking into a chair across from Xolani's bed.

"Well, hopefully Joe will be back with that skim-craft

soon, if he's still got fuel for it." Xolani sat on the edge of the bed, facing him directly. "It will be months until we can get Zach anywhere with lab equipment, otherwise. He can't make the journey on his own power and probably won't be able to before it's too late in the year to pass over the mountains."

He pressed his hands to his knees to stop their anxious bouncing. "Okay. Let's say we get him to a lab. What then?"

"We'll watch his blood, see if the antibodies he's got from his Beta-Prime exposure are combating the lethal Beta exposure. Then, we wait until it's certain he hasn't been infected with the Rot, just to make sure our live trial confirms what the microscopes are telling us. Which, as I said, I think there's a really good chance that will be the case." Xolani pursed her lips, considering. "We'll give it, say, four to six weeks before we call it conclusive. That's when things will get really interesting."

Something about her smile made Nico sit up straighter. It wasn't a pleasant expression, but it sure looked like she was enjoying herself.

"Interesting *how?*"

"Leverage." Her smile broadened. "We may just have the means to make the Clean Zone enact some badly needed reforms."

"ARE you really going to keep giving me the silent treatment?" Zach asked softly as Nico sullenly puttered around the room, making sure everything was secured before he settled into the armchair to sleep. He hadn't shared the bed with Zach since Zach had confessed what he had done.

"Are you really going to act like I don't have every right to be pissed off at you?" Nico shot back. It was the longest sentence he'd uttered to Zach in days.

"No, you definitely have every right to be angry." Zach plucked at the covers, feeling his eyes growing heavy. The damned malaise wasn't going to allow him much time to hash this out with Nico, and this was a conversation they desperately needed to have. "But that doesn't mean that I did the wrong thing."

Nico's eyes narrowed. "I'm less upset by what you did than the fact that you did it totally unilaterally. After everything we've been through, you just decided by yourself—"

"Like *you* decided by yourself to leave me behind?" Zach shot back. "*You* decided that your desire to protect me overrode any right I might have to choose to take the risks involved in being with you." *There. Good.* The irritation was giving him a little more energy to have the discussion they needed to have. He'd pay for it later, but at least he wasn't trying to make his case while half-asleep. "I'll grant your anger is understandable, Nico, but I won't tolerate you rapping *me* across the knuckles for being autocratic."

Nico's mouth fell open for a moment before he sneered. "Right, okay. So, you insist your choice wasn't wrong, and I'm apparently a hypocrite for being upset that you didn't even consult me. So much for me having every right to be angry."

"You're not angry because I chose the wrong thing, because you *know* that what I did was right. You're not even angry because I chose it without asking you first, because you *also* know you couldn't have forced yourself to agree to it even though it was necessary. If I wanted to do the right thing I *had* to leave you out of the decision-making process." Zach closed his eyes a moment, the burst of energy fleeing as quickly as it had come. "You're angry because you're scared. And that's valid. We just had a near miss and now this. But just . . . put it in the right place, would you? Because I'm tired enough without worrying whether we'll be able to get past this and forgive each other when I come out on the other side of this thing."

Nico didn't answer. He crossed to the window and stared out through the dusty, cobweb-laden panes at the twilit sky outside. His shoulders drooped, and Zach desperately wanted to go to him and hold him and assure him everything would be fine. But weariness was weighing him down, sucking him into the mattress until he couldn't move.

He didn't mean to fall asleep, but when he opened his eyes again, the room was dark except for the moonlight filtering in through the dirty windows. Nico's face was before him as he knelt beside the bed and stared at Zach in the darkness.

"Never again," Nico whispered, and his voice was ragged, his eyes too shiny in the bluish half-light of the room. "If you survive this—and I'm trying like hell to share your faith that you will—nothing like this happens again. I don't care how much greater good is at stake. We don't make any more choices that could take us from each other, no matter what. Promise me?"

"Never again," Zach agreed, reaching out to caress the faintly silver-shot curls tumbling around Nico's shoulders and the stubbled chin where he'd finally shaved off his thick beard. "After this is over and I'm in the clear, it's our time to just *be*. I promise."

Nico smiled and captured Zach's hand, pressing a kiss to his fingers. The sense of rightness in that touch, the surety of

God's blessing upon them, made the room feel like daylight was flooding in, enveloping them both in its radiance. He smiled drowsily and tugged at Nico's hand, silently entreating him to join Zach in bed. Never mind that Zach hadn't had the energy for more than a sponge bath for weeks. He needed to be held.

Nico obliged, wrapping Zach up with his arms and legs and holding him as if he'd never let go. "I promise too," he whispered, and Zach drifted off again with that vow filling his heart.

"Wapato Island Refuge?" Darius looked up from the documents Joe had delivered.

Toby nodded eagerly. "That was the indigenous name. We decided to go with that instead of calling it Sauvie Island."

"That was mostly farmland, wasn't it?" Xolani asked as Darius passed her the papers.

"That and wildlife conservation," Toby confirmed. "It's gorgeous. Room enough for a few thousand people and still plenty of space to grow crops and house livestock. It's been fallow for years, so the soil is rich, and there's no need to build any sort of perimeter because there's just one way on and off the island. Could have quarantine or—" he nodded to Zach "—Beta-Prime convalescence housing on the other side of the river before newcomers cross the bridge to join the population."

Darius rubbed his chin, smiling slightly at the excited light in Rhys's eyes as he listened to the conversation. "Is the bridge sound?"

"Seems to be," Joe answered. "If not, we can come up with a ferry system."

"What did the other companies say?" Xolani scanned the pages in her hand, her attention only half on them.

"They're taking it back to their COs, but they were satisfied enough to leave their civvies in Portland after Schuyler's people told them to divert from delivering to the Clean Zone. They figure worse comes to worst, they can always go to the Clean Zone later." Toby shrugged. "Consensus seems to be that the other companies will agree to helping set up the Refuge as a second settlement so long as we get a promise that there won't be another exile. We'll have to work on whether the Jugs will live in the Refuge or just nearby or what, but we won't be pushed out again. We want representation in whatever government is established, and we want to be assured of a home to return to. Everyone up at Lewis-McChord seems to agree."

"That's reasonable," Nico said. He swallowed forcefully, but he made himself continue speaking. "If Zach's in the clear with regard to contagion from the Rot, exile won't be an issue anymore anyway, right?"

Xolani smiled. "Exactly. We just make sure everyone going to the Refuge gets Beta-Prime exposure and goes through convalescence first."

Zach spoke up from where he was huddled in a bundle of blankets beside Nico. "Schuyler should be part of drafting whatever constitution they come up with." He met Nico's eyes. "Wasn't that the plan, during the overthrow? She studied political science. She knows the law."

"She made that point too," Toby said. "I'm not sure how it's going to work, throwing her in with a bunch of civvies, but, you know, the survivors we recover are *different* from the ones who were already entrenched in the Clean Zone before the overthrow. They aren't as afraid of us, especially since so much time has passed since the first wave of the plague."

Xolani drew a deep breath. "I think we should have more than one Jug helping make the constitution. In fact—" her eyes locked on Zach and Nico "—I think whatever interim government or committee gets set up, you two should head it up."

Zach jerked upright, looking more awake than he had for the entire conference they had put together once Toby, Joe, and Titus arrived. "*Us?*"

"You studied political science, too, didn't you?" Rhys pointed out. "You told me your dad made you do it."

"Well, yes, but—"

Toby smirked. "The symbolism is nice and heavy-handed. No one could miss it. Partnership between a civvie and a Jug, running things together. The civvie looking all safe and happy. Nothing to fear."

Darius smiled in satisfaction, pleased with the direction in which his people's minds were working. "That, and Nico's gonna need to stick close to the Refuge to make sure they have enough samples of Beta-Prime to infect new arrivals. And Zach's worked as a medical assistant. He can help nurse the convalescents at first, because we'll be short on medical personnel for a while."

"So this is it, then?" Rhys had stars in his eyes, and Darius started feeling the urge to call the meeting to a close just to get him alone. He ran his hand up the back of Rhys's shirt, carefully thumbing along the outline of the *delta* etched on his shoulder. Rhys shivered. "It's really going to happen?"

"It is." In a rare gesture, Xolani gave him a rough kiss on the temple and rose. "If we have the fuel cells left for it, I want to go back to the Clean Zone. Worst-case scenario, I want to let the people there know they have alternatives, and make it clear that we won't stand for their congress restricting any Clean Zone citizen who wants to relocate from doing so. But I have a better proposal too, if they're willing to listen. Now, if you'll excuse me." She grabbed Titus by the collar and hauled him to his feet. He went willingly enough, looking mildly amused. "*Some* of you may have been fucking nonstop for the past couple months, but I need to get laid. Good night."

EPILOGUE

Beginnings

RHYS STOOD beside Xolani as she faced the Congressional Science Committee through the glass. Sweat trickled down his back, making the brand on his shoulder itch. On Xolani's other side stood Zach, and behind them were Darius, Nico, and Schuyler. Xolani's voice was firm and confident, as if she had no nerves about addressing the committee.

"As you can see from the lab results Mr. Houtman included in the report, there's no question that Beta-Prime infection results in immunity to all other strains of the Bane virus, including the Rot and the Gamma strain." She put a document up on the projection display. "Following the plan I detailed, by quarantining small groups of the population at a time and exposing them to Beta-Prime, you can inoculate your population in phases, without adversely impacting the productivity of the Clean Zone's workforce. And if you do it during the winter months like I suggest on page eighty-seven, you can inoculate larger groups without worrying that there won't be enough personnel for agricultural operations during the growing season."

"Why should we trust you with this?" one congresswoman demanded, her voice amplified by the pickups on either side of the partition that divided them. Zach had made a distressed sound when he'd seen her, and Rhys realized this woman—who was chairperson of the committee—had been a friend of his, the doctor he'd once told Rhys about, Chantal.

Xolani smiled coldly. "Congresswoman, I don't care if you trust me or not. You can take this offer and do what you like with it, and no matter what the outcome, it doesn't affect me. Neither myself, nor Mr. Fernández—whose blood you'll require to infect your people with Beta-Prime—wants to see more lives lost to this virus, so we're making the offer. That's the beginning and the end of it."

One of the congressmen cleared his throat. "You mentioned specific terms attached to this offer?"

"Those begin on page ninety-five," Xolani replied and waited for them to shuffle through their packets. "It's really quite simple. One: the Clean Zone Congress will do nothing to interfere with the establishment of the Wapato Island Refuge or the immigration of any Clean Zone citizens who wish to move there. Two: any and all operations of the Clean Zone Department of Pandemic Research and Prevention involving experimentation on nonconsenting persons will be suspended, and any such future experimentation will be expressly outlawed."

She paused, drawing a slow breath as she deliberately moved her gaze from one person on the committee to the next, until she had stared them all down. "Three: the DPRP and any other agencies acting on behalf of the Clean Zone Congress or its people will cease any and all attempts to acquire Bane Alpha, regardless of its intended use. And four: the Clean Zone will ratify an amendment to their constitution revoking *any* acts of government that either restrict or compel the reproductive choices of Clean Zone citizens, and forbidding in perpetuity the implementation of similar laws infringing upon citizens' sexual and reproductive freedoms."

There was an immediate furor over that. "You can't do that!" someone snapped, while someone else argued, "Our laws are none of your business!" Rhys schooled himself to keep his expression sober; it was actually rather amusing to see them scrambling so defensively.

Xolani had to raise her voice to be heard. "*These conditions are nonnegotiable.* We're offering you the ability to inoculate your population as a gesture of goodwill from the Wapato Island Refuge to the Colorado Springs Clean Zone. The conditions will be implemented in full before Mr. Fernández will donate a single drop of blood on your behalf."

There was a lot more arguing, then, which Xolani ignored. Finally they grew quiet, and the first congresswoman spoke again. "And if we refuse these conditions?"

"Let's be very clear: we *will not* extend this olive branch to a government engaged in flagrant human rights violations." Xolani gave them all another hard stare. "If you refuse, you're on your own against the possibility of another outbreak. Unless you really want to take your chances trying to abduct the new Chairman of the Wapato Island Interim Government." She tipped her head toward Nico. "Personally, I wouldn't recommend it."

She held out her hand, and Rhys handed over her rucksack. As Xolani shouldered the pack, she looked at the Congressional Science Committee evenly through the glass. "To be quite honest, I don't think a single one of us gives a fuck. Send a courier to Portland when you make up your minds, and we'll consider it, providing you've met our conditions."

She strode out then with her head high, and Rhys fell into step beside Darius and followed.

Outside the intake center, their personnel transport waited. A number of Perimeter Security officers and their families were boarding. Among those were Gillett Morris, Zach's old friend, and Corporal Tucker, the man who had been unhappy about being compelled to carry another pregnancy. Other Perimeter Security guards were staying behind, but they were spreading the word through the population that escort parties would be returning in the spring to collect anyone who wished to relocate to Wapato Island. Early rumor had it there was a great deal of interest, especially with the offer of inoculation against the Bane virus as part of the deal.

Rhys's shoulder brushed Darius's as they waited for the civilians to finish boarding. The tall fences and treacherous perimeter trenches of the Clean Zone towered before him. As beautiful as Colorado Springs had been on his first walkabout with Darius, the Clean Zone seemed anything but. Maybe that was to be expected, with the start the Clean Zone had had. Maybe it had been impossible to build a better system on the bones of the old one, especially at a time when so many people had still been so afraid.

But it didn't matter anymore. Rhys had a life and future elsewhere to worry about. So, taking his last look at anything related to the Clean Zone, he turned his back on it and boarded the transport. It was time to go home.

JUGGERNAUT

A STRAIN NOVEL

They helped destroy
the world.
Now they have to survive
the new one.

AMELIA C. GORMLEY

JUGGERNAUT

A STRAIN NOVEL

They helped destroy the world. Now they have to survive the new one.

NICO FERNÁNDEZ has a charmed life. Working as a high-end rentboy for the agency his mother started beats the hell out of being trafficked for slave wages in some corporate brothel. And no one needs to know about his occasional side jobs, seducing political and military dignitaries and "nudging" them with mind-altering agents to swing their votes and opinions to favor his longest-standing client.

Zach Houtman's life *should* be charmed, but isn't. His father, the Reverend Maurice Houtman, has insisted Zach advise him as he pursues his political aspirations, ignoring Zach's calling to minister to the most vulnerable outcasts of society. Politics, however, are gradually turning Zach's father away from Christ and into malicious zealotry, and his campaign is courting violent fundamentalists.

When one of Nico's "special jobs" results in military approval for a weaponized virus that mutates, unleashing a deadly plague to claim billions of lives, Nico and Zach are thrown together. Each burdened by terrible guilt for their unwitting roles in the calamity, they find safety and solace in each other. But the new world is a dangerous, violent place, where the handful of survivors are willing to do anything and kill anyone to get by.

STRAIN

In a world with little hope and no rules,
the only thing they have to lose
is themselves.

AMELIA C. GORMLEY

STRAIN

In a world with little hope and no rules, the only thing they have to lose is themselves.

Rhys Cooper is a dead man. He's spent years hiding from the virus that wiped out most of the human race, but an act of futile heroism has him counting down his remaining days. The timely arrival of superhuman soldiers offers some feeble hope—but only if Rhys can reconcile himself to doing what is necessary to take advantage of it.

Sergeant Darius Murrell has seen too much death and too little tenderness, seeking out survivors only to put the infected out of their misery, or send the uninfected to a safe haven he and his fellow Juggernaut troops can never enjoy. Rhys's situation is different, though. Not only is there an improbable chance that Darius won't have to put a bullet in Rhys's head, but he has somehow managed to get under Darius's skin.

The virus Rhys must infect himself with is sexually transmitted, and optimizing his chance of exposure requires him to submit as often as possible to Darius—and the other soldiers. Though the boundaries of morality have shifted in this harsh new world, what they must do has them asking if their humanity is too high a price to pay for Rhys's survival.

OTHER BOOKS BY AMELIA C. GORMLEY

THE IMPULSE TRILOGY

Inertia

Acceleration

Velocity

SEASONS IN SAUGATUCK

The Field of Someone Else's Dreams

Sea Change

Risk Aware

THE STRAIN TRILOGY

Juggernaut

Strain

Bane

Player vs. Player

(Coming Soon)

ABOUT THE AUTHOR

Amelia C. Gormley published her first short story in the school newspaper in the 4th grade, and since then has suffered the persistent delusion that enabling other people to hear the voices in her head might be a worthwhile endeavor. She's even convinced her hapless spouse that it could be a lucrative one as well, especially when coupled with her real-life interest in angst, kink, feminism, and pretty men.

When her husband and son aren't interacting with the back of her head as she stares at the computer, they rely on her to feed them, maintain their domicile, and keep some semblance of order in their lives (all very, very bad ideas—they really should know better by now.) She can also be found playing video games and ranting on Tumblr, seeing as how she's one of those horrid social justice warriors out to destroy free speech, gaming, geek culture, and everything else that's fun everywhere.

http://ameliacgormley.com
http://ameliacgormley.tumblr.com

facebook.com/ameliacgormley

twitter.com/ACGormley

goodreads.com/ameliacgormley